MYS

FALLEN ANGELS

A MERCY ALLCUTT MYSTERY

FALLEN ANGELS

ALICE DUNCAN

FIVE STAR
A part of Gale, Cengage Learning

GALE
CENGAGE Learning

Detroit • New York • San Francisco • New Haven, Conn • Waterville, Maine • London

GALE
CENGAGE Learning˙

Copyright © 2011 by Alice Duncan.
Five Star Publishing, a part of Gale, Cengage Learning.

LIBRARY OF CONGRESS CATALOGING-IN-PUBLICATION DATA

Duncan, Alice, 1945–
    Fallen angels : a Mercy Allcutt mystery / Alice Duncan. — 1st
ed.
        p. cm.
    ISBN-13: 978-1-59414-959-7 (hardcover)
    ISBN-10: 1-59414-959-3 (hardcover)
    1. Murder—Investigation—Fiction. 2. Los Angeles (Calif.)—
Fiction. I. Title.
PS3554.U463394F35 2011
813'.54—dc22   2011004261

First Edition. First Printing: May 2011.
Published in 2011 in conjunction with Tekno Books and Ed Gorman.

For all my L.A. friends. I miss you guys,
although I fear I don't much miss L.A.

ACKNOWLEDGMENTS

Many, many thanks to Carola Dunn and Deb Brod for their editorial assistance. I need all the help I can get!

CHAPTER ONE

"Is September always this hot in Los Angeles?" I wiped my perspiring brow with a handkerchief hastily snatched from my handbag before I could disgrace my sister and drip on our luncheon table. "Back east, the leaves are starting to change by this time, and the weather's getting brisk."

"In September, it's generally hotter than it is in August, actually," aforementioned sister, Chloe, murmured.

I thought that was kind of depressing but didn't say so. I'd only lived in Los Angeles since late June, and three months isn't really a long enough time by which to judge a city. Besides, there were so many things I loved about my new life away from Boston that I really couldn't complain about anything as trivial as hundred-degree heat in autumn. Well, except that my parents (and Chloe's, too, of course, since we're sisters) had decided to buy a winter home in Pasadena. When I first moved out here to the City of Angels, I'd hoped to keep a couple of thousand miles between our parents and me forever, barring certain holidays and stuff like that. Still, Pasadena is twenty-some miles away from Los Angeles, so Chloe and I shouldn't be bothered inordinately by them. We hoped. Hard.

"Hmm, I guess, all things considered, I can live with the heat. I like everything else about Los Angeles, including the people I've met so far."

"So do I. It's ever so much more fun than Boston."

Los Angeles was that, for certain. *Fun* isn't the first word that springs to mind when one thinks about Boston. Not only was Boston and its upper-crust society dull, but my sister and I had been given ghastly names to go along with them. Chloe was actually Clovilla Alexandria, and I was Mercedes Louise. Is it any wonder that Chloe chose to call herself Chloe and I answer to the name Mercy? I don't think Mercy is as nice as Chloe, but at least it isn't Mercedes. Or Clovilla, for that matter.

Chloe and I, you see, were born into a family of Boston Brahmins and had grown up feeling pretty darned—a slang word I'd never have been allowed to utter in Boston—stifled thereby.

Chloe'd had the good fortune to meet the man who was to become her husband, Harvey Nash, at a big society party in New York City. Although our parents weren't as smitten by Harvey as Chloe was, they didn't kick and scream when Chloe and Harvey decided to marry, probably since Harvey was considered a big cheese by the same New York society that had hosted the party in his honor. Since Harvey owned and worked at his own moving-picture studio in Los Angeles, it was considered natural for her to move there with him after they were wed. Mother didn't like it, but she didn't have much say in the matter. I don't think our father cared a whole lot, to tell the truth.

My own story entailed considerably more drama than Chloe's. I not only decided to move west to live with my sister without the lure of a groom to prompt me, but I did so with the intention of securing employment, which is something no other female in my family has ever done. I prepared myself to do so, moreover, by taking shorthand (Pitman method) and typing at the Young Women's Christian Association. Naturally, I didn't bother to tell Mother and Father what I was doing until I'd graduated from the classes.

However, when I announced my intention to depart Boston

for sunny California, my parents were livid. That is to say my mother was livid. I don't think my father cared any more about my moving than he had about Chloe marrying, although he and several aunts, uncles, and cousins, not to mention my beastly brother, George, lectured me endlessly on my unfilial behavior. But really, Father didn't pay as much attention to his daughters as Mother did, more's the pity. Not that I wanted him to pay *more* attention to us, you understand, but I surely did wish Mother didn't pay as much attention to us as she did.

At any rate, I did all of the above regarding shorthand and typing, and Chloe generously invited me to come west and live with her and Harvey. Harvey was probably richer than my parents, but his money didn't count because it was "new" money. That's according to our mother. Personally, I figure money's money, and I wanted the novel experience of earning some of it on my own. This wasn't so much because I craved money, of which I have plenty even without having to work, thanks to a nice, deceased great-aunt's legacy, but because I wanted experience.

Living as a rich and pampered female person in Boston does not prepare one to face the world of regular people. Trust me on this point, because I've learned from experience. My mother discounts my ambitions, mainly because she thinks regular people are beneath her. I know better. I mean, now that I've started working at a real job and all, I've actually met some of them and, with a few remarkable exceptions, they're quite nice. So, by George, I got myself a job.

It took a few days of searching in the searing heat of a Los Angeles June, but I finally secured a real, honest-to-God job!

Then, for two glorious months, I got to live Mother-free in Los Angeles in a charming, albeit huge, house on Bunker Hill. My mother detested the fact that Los Angeles had usurped the name Bunker Hill from her eastern betters, but that's merely one more thing Mother cared about that I didn't. What's more, I was earning my own keep, more or less, by working as a secretary to Mr. Ernest Templeton, a private investigator. He used to be a policeman, but the corruption of the Los Angeles Police Department got under his skin, and he quit. I know that for a certified fact, and not merely because Ernie told me so. Several other people have told me the same thing, so it must be true.

What's more, I have been personally responsible for solving—well, helping to solve, at any rate—a couple of really puzzling murder mysteries. Both times I've been in a teensy little bit of danger at one point or another, and both times were a tiny bit scary toward the end, but afterward I mainly recalled the thrill of having been part of the solution of some honestly vicious crimes.

When my mother learned about my employment, she was outraged. When she learned exactly what my employment entailed, she would have suffered an apoplectic fit if she were a woman who did such things. Being from Boston, she wasn't. She was as icily stoical as any of our Boston forebears and/or their friends. In short, she despaired of me and called me a disgrace to the family.

I think her attitude is total bunkum. Why should it be considered disgraceful to earn the space one takes up on this green earth rather than expect it as a birthright paid for by others? It isn't, confound it! My mother thinks I've given myself over to the dark side—or to Eugene Debs, who is the personification of it—but I haven't. I just want to earn my way in the world and gather the aforesaid experience, and there's absolutely nothing wrong with that, Mother or no Mother.

And why, you might ask, do I want experience? Very well, I'll tell you: I want to write books. Not frivolous books about rich people who don't care about anything and their parties, a la

F. Scott Fitzgerald, but books with meat to them. Never mind that his books are critically acclaimed and nobody's ever heard of me. I want to write books that don't skirt social issues, but perhaps expose them. Even my mother would have to admit, if she ever admitted anything, that one can't expose social issues, or even write about them with conviction, if one doesn't know what they are. She, therefore, is keen on ignoring them, but not I.

Why, during my very first week on the job, I met a little girl who not only washed car windows on street corners in order to earn coins upon which to subsist, but whose mother worked in a speakeasy and lived with a man who wasn't her husband. Not only that, but she—the girl's mother, not the girl herself—had disappeared, leaving the little girl parentless. I never did learn if the child had a father extant. Since that time I've also met a couple of gangsters; a homicidal maniac and a couple of sister siblings who were *not* nice people; and some phony spiritualists. Talk about experience!

I'd also met, in person, a few Los Angeles cinematic celebrities, including Charlie Chaplin, John Barrymore, and Lillian Gish, but they weren't nearly as interesting as the crooks. Maybe that's because I'd been too tongue-tied to speak to them, but I'm not sure about that.

Anyhow, after my—or Ernie's and my—first case, the one involving the homicidal maniac and a certain elevator shaft, and which also involved a black toy French poodle named Rosie, I bought myself a precious and wee apricot-colored French poodle whom I named Buttercup. She's the joy of my life, although another joy is expected soon, because Chloe and Harvey are going to have a baby. Chloe's going to do the hard work, of course, but Harvey participated in the child's creation. Chloe pretends not to be excited, because that's the current fashion trend in Los Angeles where image is everything, but I know she's excited because she tells me so when we're alone.

On this particular Saturday, a little after noon, Chloe and I were taking luncheon in the tearoom atop the Broadway Department Store on Fourth and Broadway in downtown Los Angeles. My workplace was a very few blocks away, in the Figueroa Building at Seventh and Hill. On the third floor. Chloe and I were in the Broadway because we'd been shopping for baby things. I hadn't realized how much fun shopping for baby things could be until that day.

"I hope you have a girl, Chloe. Just think of how much more fun girl clothes are than boy clothes."

Chloe nibbled on a soda cracker. She was occasionally bothered by sickness in those days and claimed the crackers helped to calm her tummy. "Harvey wants a boy."

"Boys are fine, too, I guess."

"I don't really care whether it's a boy or a girl."

"If you have a boy, please don't name him George." I had meant the comment as a joke, but Chloe looked at me with real disgust.

"I would *never*," she declared, "name a child of mine after my brother." She shuddered, although that might have been because of her tummy troubles.

"I'm glad of that. But I want you to have a girl because girls wear prettier clothes than boys do."

She eyed me with something akin to disfavor. "One would never know it to look at *you*."

Chloe had been after me to modernize my wardrobe ever since I arrived in Los Angeles. And I had done so, up to a point. Heck, I'd even had my hair bobbed and shingled. The latter had almost given our mutual mother a heart attack. This day I told Chloe the same thing I always did when she ridiculed my wardrobe: "I'm a working woman, Chloe. I need to appear professional for my job. I can't wear fancy flapper clothes, because they wouldn't be acceptable or professional for someone in my position."

"It's Saturday," she reminded me. "And Mr. Templeton doesn't expect you to work on Saturdays. Not even half days like most people."

"Well, yes, I know that. Mr. Templeton is a very fair and considerate employer." In actual fact, Ernie didn't have enough business to keep the office open on weekends, but I'd never say that to anyone. "However, my salary doesn't run to fancy clothes, even of the non-flapper variety."

She rolled her eyes. "You don't have to dress like a flapper any more than you have to live on your income."

I sighed. "True. But don't you see? Every time I dip into Great-Aunt Agatha's legacy, I'm defeating my entire purpose for getting a job in the first place."

"All right. I understand. But I still think you could spiff yourself up a little bit. I'm sure Mr. Templeton wouldn't mind." Chloe liked Ernie.

I'm sure Ernie wouldn't have minded, either. Ernie was a very casual individual and totally unlike any other man I'd ever met before. My father is a banker, for Pete's sake, and so is my ghastly brother, and you know how bankers dress and act. "That's true," I admitted.

"Very well. Then I'll help you find some duds that look good *and* that go with your so-called *position.*"

"Oh, all right. If you're not too tired after lunch, maybe I'll go look at a new dress or something. I understand the Broadway sells women's fashions off the rack these days."

"Mrs. Martinez can make you something, although you're right. There might be some nice things off the rack, and it might be fun to look." Mrs. Martinez was the seamstress Chloe patronized and who did a great job keeping my sister clad in the very latest and loveliest of fashions.

This day, for instance, Chloe was clad in a peach-colored drop-waisted day dress in a lightweight seersucker fabric. She wore cream-colored shoes, gloves, and hat and carried a cream handbag, and she looked the epitome of early-autumn elegance without disgracing the family legacy by wearing white after Labor Day. Not that my family had anything to do with Labor Day on a regular basis or anything. As far as most of my family is concerned, Labor Day is a Socialist holiday and a disgrace to the great capitalist culture rampant in the United States. I don't agree with that. And no matter what my mother says of me, I'm *not* a Socialist. I figure one can appreciate those who labor to produce the goods one consumes without turning Socialist or becoming a Communist or an anarchist.

But I digress.

I myself was clad in one of the suits I wore to work. It wasn't fancy, but it was relatively cool, since the sleeves were short and it was made of a crisp piquet rather than the wool our mother deems necessary in order to maintain decorum. Nuts to decorum, I say, when the weather hovered in the nineties. I didn't look as fashionable and cool as Chloe, but I wouldn't have done so even if I'd been dressed by the most skillful modiste in Los Angeles. For one thing, I don't have Chloe's angelic looks, with her blond hair and blue eyes. My eyes are blue, too, but my hair is brown, and there's just no getting away from the fact that Chloe is prettier than I am. Not that I'm ugly or anything, but the truth is the truth, after all. I sighed deeply. The truth might be the truth, but I didn't necessarily have to like it, did I?

No, I did not. However, Chloe's always been my best friend, so I've never envied her beauty. Well, not very much, anyhow.

I said, "We can look around a little after lunch if you're up to it. Don't want to wear you out."

"I'm fine," said Chloe, munching another soda cracker.

"Anyhow, I can always take a nap this afternoon."

"That's so." I planned to write this afternoon. With Buttercup at my feet. I'd just started a story based on some of my experiences—see how important experiences are?—and I could hardly wait to get back to it. It was going to be a murder mystery, by gum! My mother would faint if she knew.

Our pretty little waitress, who also looked cool even though she wore a black dress with a white apron, delivered our lunches—a chicken sandwich for me and clear soup for Chloe, along with more soda crackers—and we dug in. Politely, of course. There's no reason to discard all of one's childhood training merely because one doesn't approve of some of one's parents' precepts, after all.

After a few sips of her soup, Chloe sat back and looked at me. I took another bite of my sandwich and looked back at her. She seemed a trifle troubled about something. After I swallowed, I said, "What's up, Chloe?"

She sipped another spoonful of soup before answering. "Harvey wants us to move."

"Move?" The meaning of her words didn't register at first.

"Yes. The studio is going to be building a huge new site to the west of Los Angeles, and he wants us to move west, too."

"I thought this *was* the west." I laid my sandwich on my plate and sipped some water.

She smiled at me. "Overall, yes, this is the west. But there are lots of places farther west than Los Angeles, you know."

"You mean like the beach?" Chloe and I had been to the beach once before. We'd taken a red car all the way to Santa Monica and made a day of it. It had been fun, although I didn't much appreciate all that sand sneaking into my bathing costume or the rather significant sunburn I'd sustained.

"Not quite as far west as the beach, but maybe Culver City or thereabouts."

"Oh." I wasn't sure where Culver City was, although I expected it was somewhere between Los Angeles and Santa Monica.

"He's thinking of having a house built in some hills over that way. A big house. I think he called the area Beverly Hills."

"I do believe I read something about Beverly Hills in one of Hedda Heartwood's columns." Then I grimaced. Hedda Heartwood had been the premier gossip columnist in Hollywood for a while. I had been seated in the very room, at the very table, at which Hedda Heartwood died, at the very time she was murdered, and I still didn't like to think about it. Fortunately, other gossip-loving columnists have taken her place. Well, not fortunately for her, but . . . Oh, you know what I mean. "I understand a lot of picture people are moving out there. Didn't Cecil B. DeMille just build a huge house in Beverly Hills?"

"Yes, he did, and lots of others are moving there, too. It's a very pretty area, and the houses are amazing. Douglas Fairbanks and Mary Pickford live there, and so do Vilma Bankey and John Barrymore. Not together, of course."

"Of course." As I've mentioned, I'd seen John Barrymore at a party once, and Douglas Fairbanks, too. They were both drinking heavily. And this was supposed to be Prohibition time. Ha! If you have enough money, you can always skirt the law. Just ask Al Capone, or whatever that murdering gangster's name is.

"So you're going to build your own house?"

She heaved a weary sigh. "That's what Harvey wants to do. I don't have the energy for it myself, but I'm sure he'll hire someone to draw up the plans and everything like that. I hope I won't have to be too involved. I just don't feel up to it."

I was sure he would. As I mentioned before, Harvey was rich. "It won't be built until after the baby comes, will it?"

"He might begin making the plans, but no. There's not enough time to hire an architect, have the architect create plans, and build a place in six or seven months. Frankly, I'm not sure I want to move anyway. Harvey says Bunker Hill is going downhill, but I don't see it."

"I don't, either." I thought Harvey and Chloe's neighborhood was swell. Granted, it was on a hill right smack in the middle of Los Angeles, and perhaps film people preferred to live away from it all. But I thought the Nash home was wonderful, and Bunker Hill was a sweet place. Besides, the almost vertical railroad, Angels Flight, which took me from Bunker Hill to downtown every day, was darling.

"You're more than welcome to live with us after we move, Mercy," Chloe said in a hurry.

"Oh, I wouldn't want to impose. You'll have enough to do when the baby comes."

"Don't be silly. I'll hire a maid to take care of the baby when I need to rest."

I knew rich people did that sort of thing all the time, but it seemed kind of cold to me. I'd never tell Chloe that, however. "Besides," I said, "I love my job and wouldn't want to leave it."

Chloe nodded. "I've already thought about that. Beverly Hills is kind of far from here. You'd have to drive."

Which would be a problem, since I didn't know how to drive.

Chloe knew that. "I'll teach you, and you can always get a machine."

True, although not on the salary Ernie paid me.

"I'll have to think about it. I really don't want to quit my job."

"I know." Smirking, Chloe drank some of the seltzer water she'd asked for in deference to her tender-tummy problem. "I'd hate to take you away from Ernie. And vice-versa, of course."

I didn't appreciate that smirk. Chloe thought I was more fond of Ernie than our mother would countenance if she knew about it, which she didn't. Not that there was anything to know about. It was true that I liked Ernie. I even admired him, but I certainly didn't have any romantic designs upon him. The very notion was absurd. However, I knew better than to respond to Chloe's smirk. Denial, in my experience, only firms up the other person's convictions. I think Shakespeare wrote something like that once. In *Hamlet*, if I'm not mistaken.

"It will be exciting to have a new house," I said in order to divest my sister of that blasted expression on her face.

My ploy succeeded. Chloe sighed. "I suppose it will be nice to live in a brand-new house. I just loathe the notion of moving."

I hate to say it, but Chloe was kind of indolent. She didn't resent our upbringing nearly as much as I did, except insofar as it had been too confining for her fun-loving personality. She possessed none of my passion about social issues, for instance, or the fact that thousands of people in our glorious nation lived in poverty and ignorance and near-starvation. I doubt that she gave a rap about the downtrodden worker proletariat, although I'm sure she'd feel sorry for and give money to a beggar should one appear directly before her. Since she confined herself to the wealthiest circles in L.A., I doubt one ever did.

"You'll certainly be able to hire people to do all the packing and moving for you, won't you?"

She sighed again. "I suppose so. I guess I'm just so tired, I can't bear the notion of doing anything at all, much less moving into a new home. And one so far away from so many of my friends. I wonder if Francis will still visit." Francis Easthope was one of Chloe and Harvey's closest chums.

"Oh, I'm sure he will. After all, he has that darling little Bugatti that he loves to drive." I'd never been "with child," as the saying goes, so I couldn't truly appreciate Chloe's condition, but I said, "I understand how the move might be upsetting to you, though," because I figured I should.

At any rate, we finished our luncheon and decided to stop in the ladies' dresses department in the Broadway before we went home. There I delighted my sister by buying two (count 'em) lightweight, pretty dresses that were suitable for the office. Lulu LaBelle, who sat behind the reception desk in the Figueroa Building, would be almost as pleased as Chloe.

Then I spent the remainder of the afternoon writing my detective novel. I'd decided to hold the murder in a grand home at a house party, although I hadn't yet come to the murder part, decided who the corpse would be, or determined who would do the evil deed. But I still enjoyed myself.

Chloe napped. So did Buttercup. On my feet, come to think of it.

On Monday morning, I donned one of my new dresses, pinned my hat to my hair, stuck my gloves in my handbag, picked up said handbag, ate the nice breakfast Mrs. Biddle, Chloe's housekeeper, fixed for me, kissed Buttercup good-bye, left Chloe's house and walked to Angels Flight. There I handed the engineer my nickel, boarded the car, and the rest of the passengers and I zipped to the bottom of the hill. From there I walked to Seventh and Hill and entered the lobby.

I felt mighty jaunty that day, and not merely because I was clad in a pretty new dress of light blue wool jersey with a perky jacket and a dropped waist, but because I positively *loved* my job. I greeted Lulu with a cheery, "Good morning!"

Lulu, who possessed a rather flamboyant sense of style and none of my qualms about proper working attire, sat behind her desk filing her nails and chatting with Mr. Emerald Buck, whom I also greeted cheerily and who worked as the custodian at the Figueroa Building. Mr. Buck was ever so much more competent than our last custodian, who liked to hide in the basement and read when he was supposed to be doing his job. Mr. Buck actually enjoyed keeping the building looking neat and tidy. He dusted all exposed surfaces daily, and even polished the brass plate confirming the building's identity and kept the sidewalk outside the front door swept.

This morning Lulu wore a vibrant purple dress with huge white flowers on it. Her bottle-blond hair was cut into a curly bob, and her lipstick, a glossy red, clashed violently with the purple of her clothing. What's more, she had before her on the receptionist's desk a bottle of nail varnish the same red color as her lipstick. Lulu was nothing if not colorful. In fact, she pretty much personified the nation's notion of the flapper.

" 'Lo, Mercy. Ernie left you a note."

My happy mood slipped a notch. "A note? Ernie? He's already been here?"

"Yup. He left you a note."

This was strange behavior, indeed. My boss, Ernie, never got to work at eight o'clock, when I was expected to show up. He generally ambled in at nine or nine-thirty, carrying a copy of the *Los Angeles Times,* an insouciant grin, and an aura of detachment that had initially been as foreign to me as the weather in my new hometown. Now I liked it. For him. I certainly wasn't ready to adopt a slouch or casual walk. Not that I wanted to do either, mind you. It was up to one of us to add the professional touch to the firm of Ernest Templeton, P.I., and that someone, I'd learned very early in our relationship, sure wasn't going to be Ernie. Besides, I considered my crisp efficiency something of a hallmark.

I took the envelope Lulu flapped at me and voiced my thanks. Then I climbed the stairs up to the third floor, since the exercise was good for me. Besides, ever since a certain episode involving the elevator shaft, I haven't felt particularly comfortable using that mode of transport. Elevators in other buildings didn't bother me, but the one in the Figueroa Building sure did.

After I unlocked the office door, removed my gloves, put them and my hat and handbag in my desk drawer, and sat in my chair, I slit the envelope open—using, by the way, the cunning letter opener I'd bought a day or two prior in Chinatown, which was a short walk from the Figueroa Building. Frowning, I read the note.

Mercy. Gone to Mrs. Chalmers' house. Back some time. Ernie

Hmm. I didn't particularly care for the message, probably because I didn't much care for Mrs. Chalmers.

Mrs. Persephone Chalmers, who possessed a name darned near as horrid as Chloe's or mine, had wafted into Ernie's office a week or so before, exuding an aura of exotic perfume and fragile femininity that bothered me considerably, and not merely because she began practically every sentence with a breathy "Oh." I also didn't like it that Ernie had been taken in by her. I knew, if Ernie didn't, that there was something mighty fishy about *Mrs.* Chalmers. She'd told Ernie she wanted to hire him to find some jewelry that had allegedly been stolen from her home. It seemed to be taking Ernie a mighty long time to deal with what seemed to me to be a fairly minor matter. Of course, it wasn't my jewelry that had been stolen, but still . . .

Not that I knew for a rock-solid certainty that she was a faker—yet—but I considered the possibility quite likely. For one thing, if she were truly a married lady, as implied by that *Missus,* wouldn't she call herself Mrs. George Chalmers, or something like that? Didn't proper married ladies introduce themselves using their husbands' first names? I know my mother always did. She was Mrs. Albert Monteith Allcutt, and nobody had better ever forget it. Mind you, I didn't especially approve of that fashion, since it seemed in my estimation to devalue women, but society as a whole wasn't nearly as forward-thinking as I.

For another thing, she was just too . . . too . . . *wafty.* I mean, she acted as if she were a fairy princess who'd managed to get herself lost from a children's storybook and dumped into the middle of Los Angeles, for crumb's sake.

Oh, very well. The main reason I didn't care for her was that Ernie seemed to be positively smitten with the stupid woman. How could a reasonably intelligent person, which Ernie was, fall for a phony like that?

Stupid question. Men adored women who exuded helplessness. Nuts to them all, the women *and* the men, is what I say.

Not that it mattered. Ernie had gone to her house, and there wasn't a single, solitary thing I could do about it.

Phooey.

CHAPTER TWO

Ernie's defection from the office didn't prevent me from pursuing my honest employment to the best of my ability, however. Unfortunately, there wasn't much of it to do at the time.

I'd tried to drum up business a few weeks earlier by placing an advertisement in the *Los Angeles Times,* but Ernie had been furious with me for doing so. Which made no sense, since the ad had worked. Why, even *Mrs. Persephone Chalmers* had hired him as a result of that ad, darn it.

Hmm. Maybe the ad hadn't been such a great idea, after all.

At any rate, Ernie was out gallivanting with a client, and I was left with nothing to do. Although the advertisement had helped secure a few new paying customers, it hadn't garnered us enough work to keep me busy eight hours a day, five days a week. Therefore, I dusted off my desk and polished the brass plaque declaring my name to be Miss Allcutt, and washed the windows using my very own packet of Bon Ami. I'd bought the Bon Ami because Mrs. Biddle, Chloe's housekeeper, used it at Chloe's house. Then, although they didn't really need it, I straightened and dusted the pictures on the wall—pictures I'd added to the formerly colorless office myself, I might add—and repositioned the rug I'd also bought.

After I'd done all those things, I sat with my folded hands resting upon my desk, wishing I'd brought a book to read. Failing that, I figured it wouldn't hurt to work on my novel, so that's what I was doing when Phil Bigelow, a detective with the

Los Angeles Police Department and Ernie's best friend, pushed open the office door. I looked up and was happy to see a friend.

"Good morning, Phil." He'd told me to call him Phil, so I did. I wasn't taking a liberty.

He removed his hat and smiled at me. " 'Morning, Mercy. Is Ernie here?"

"Why no, he isn't."

Phil frowned, took out his pocket watch and scowled at it, which seemed puzzling behavior on his part, since he and Ernie were great friends. "He told me to meet him here at nine."

I glanced at the clock on my desk—which I'd also purchased in Chinatown, and which looked like a little Chinese pagoda. "It's not quite nine yet." Not quite nine, Ernie was nowhere to be seen, and I had nothing to do. Was this any way to run a business? I'd have rolled my eyes, but I didn't do things like that except in front of Ernie, who didn't count.

"Well, hell. Sorry, Mercy. But this is important. I'll just wait for him then, if that's all right with you."

"Certainly. Have a seat." I gestured to one of the chairs in front of my desk. "Are you and Ernie working on an interesting case together?"

"You know I can't tell you about ongoing police matters," he said sternly, the rat.

Exasperated, I said, "I know that, but . . . but you can tell me about recently closed cases, can't you? Even if they didn't involve Ernie? I'm not asking for state secrets, for pity's sake."

With a grin, Phil said, "All right, then. Over the weekend we nabbed two burglars who'd been working along Sunset, breaking into houses and stealing jewelry and so forth. Last week we picked up a bunco artist who'd been trying to gyp a rich lady out of her inheritance. Evidently, this isn't the first time he'd tried that. We discovered he's wanted in New York and New Jersey, as well as Salt Lake City."

"Salt Lake City?"

"Yup."

"Isn't Salt Lake City full of Mormons? I thought they were all proper and law-abiding citizens."

"They probably are, but this guy definitely isn't."

"Ah. I see."

"And now," Phil continued, "I'm working on a case I can't discuss." He took another gander at his watch. "And Ernie's supposed to be helping with it."

"He is?"

"Yes."

Hmm. I wondered if this case Phil couldn't talk about had anything to do with Mrs. Persephone Chalmers, who seemed like a shady character to me. I was trying to think of a sneaky way to find out when Phil *again* hauled out his watch and gave it a black frown. "Damn it—sorry, Mercy. But Ernie swore he'd be here at nine. It's important."

I didn't know what to say to that, so I said, "I'm sorry," and then wished I hadn't. Heck, it wasn't my fault Ernie was late to keep his appointments. *I* was punctuality itself. "It's only just nine, Phil. Take it easy. I'm sure he'll be here shortly."

"Did he say where he was going?"

"No. That is to say, I didn't speak to him directly. But he left a note for me with Lulu downstairs."

"Huh."

Phil and Lulu weren't fond of each other, although for my money Lulu had more reason to dislike Phil than Phil had to dislike Lulu. He'd arrested Lulu's brother Rupert on a charge of murder, for heaven's sake, and the poor boy hadn't done it. Anybody but an idiot could have seen Rupert didn't have the brains to concoct a scheme like the one that had been perpetrated. Not that Rupert wasn't a bright lad, but he was rather innocent, and had come to the big city directly from a small town in Oklahoma, not that Oklahoma probably doesn't grow crooks, too, but . . . Oh, never mind.

It occurred to me to tell Phil what Ernie's note said, but I didn't, hoping he'd leak some more information about his current, mysterious case.

Phil transferred his frown to me. "Well? What did the note say?"

I thought about telling him that the note had been for me and not him, but that would have been disingenuous. If Ernie hadn't wanted Phil to know where he was, he wouldn't have left a note at all. I'm sure he wouldn't have done it for my sake alone. Which didn't make me feel very important, as you can well imagine. With a hearty sigh, I fished the crumpled note out of the wastepaper basket where I'd tossed it and smoothed it out on my desk.

Phil read it. "Aw, hell." He looked up quickly. "Sorry, Mercy."

I wished he'd quit apologizing every time he said a *hell* or a *damn.* Ernie swore in my presence all the time. I was practically inured to swearing by that time. "It's all right. But why don't you like it?"

"That woman is trouble," Phil grumbled.

I perked up. "Ha! I knew it!"

Phil looked at me oddly, and I think I blushed. At any rate, my face got hot.

"I mean, how interesting," I said feebly.

"Well," Phil said after another few seconds. "When Ernie gets back, tell him to 'phone me."

"I will." In fact, I pulled over one of my very professional-looking message pads and wrote the message on it. By that time in my career as a P.I.'s secretary, I'd already memorized Phil's Los Angeles Police Department telephone number.

He stood. "Thanks, Mercy. I'd better be going now." He glared into space for a moment or two. "Drat Ernie Templeton." And he marched out the door, slapping his hat on his head.

I concurred with him about my dratted employer, actually, although it would have been disloyal to say so. I only sighed and wished I had something to do.

It wasn't until about ten-thirty that I began to worry about my wayward boss. Granted, his note hadn't been specific as to time, but it wasn't like Ernie to disappear like this or miss a specific appointment. He'd never vanished before in the almost three months I'd worked for him, and he'd never been late for an appointment. Of course, I supposed there was always the possibility that he was making mad, passionate love to Mrs. Persephone Chalmers, but I doubted it. Or maybe I just didn't want that scenario to be the truth.

I went out to lunch that day with Lulu. We dined, if it can be called that, at a little delicatessen down the street from the Figueroa Building.

"Where'd Ernie go?" Lulu asked at one point.

"He's consulting with a client," said I, trying to manhandle a rather hefty corned-beef sandwich into submission. Corned-beef sandwiches were another aspect of my new life that I liked a lot. Mother would pitch a fit if anyone so much as hinted at enjoying corned beef, which only proves one more time how snobbishness can get in the way of a fulfilling life. Or a filling one, anyhow.

"All morning? Must be a mighty pretty client." Lulu giggled.

I didn't.

Nevertheless, at about two-thirty that afternoon when, Ernie-less and bored to tears, and after vetoing the notion of visiting the Los Angeles Public Library to check out a novel or two as not being work-related, I decided to do a little detecting of my own. First I called the Los Angeles Police Department and asked to speak to Detective Bigelow.

"Bigelow," came Phil's voice, sounding gruffer than usual. I deduced from his tone that he was not in a good mood.

"Good afternoon, Phil. This is Mercy. Have you heard from Ernie?"

"No, damn it—sorry, Mercy. The son of a . . . um, as I told you earlier, we had an appointment at nine this morning, and I haven't heard from him *yet.* Have you?"

Poor Phil sounded quite annoyed. I didn't blame him, but my mind was uneasy. While Ernie was a casual individual, he wasn't generally *this* casual. Not about his business, at least. "No. I haven't heard a word from him. I don't like his continued absence or this unusual silence, Phil. Do you think something might have happened to him?"

"Happened to him?" Phil snapped. "What the devil could happen to him with the Chalmers woman?"

"You're the one who said she's trouble," I reminded him.

"I didn't mean *trouble* trouble," said Phil, not clearing up the matter one little bit in my mind. "Anyhow, what kind of trouble do *you* mean?"

"Well, I don't know, but don't you think this behavior is un-like him?"

A largish pause on Phil's end of the wire ensued before Phil said, "I don't know, Mercy. Maybe he's . . . um . . ."

I knew what he was thinking. Men. That's all they ever think about, according to Chloe. I wouldn't know from personal experience.

I huffed, but had to admit Phil might have something there, even if I didn't want to believe it. I said, "Perhaps," with as much dignity as I could, and bade Phil good day.

Nuts. I didn't buy Phil's theory. Not that he'd voiced it, but *I* knew what it was. He thought Ernie had decided upon a spot of dalliance with the lovely Mrs. Chalmers. Of course, the fact that I'd thought the same thing didn't cheer me up any. However, I determined I needed to find Ernie. And if he *were* dallying with Mrs. Chalmers without having had the courtesy to keep his appointment with Phil or tell me when he'd be returning to the office so that I could pass the information on to clients who called—not that we had any—I was also going to give him a big, fat piece of my mind.

After thumbing through the client files, I telephoned Mrs. Chalmers' home. No answer. Then, truly annoyed and not a little bit worried, I wrote down Mrs. Chalmers' address and telephoned for a taxicab to pick me up in front of the Figueroa Building. The salary Ernie paid me didn't run to taxicabs, but I figured Great-Aunt Agatha wouldn't have minded. She'd been quite a good old girl, in spite of belonging to my family, which was probably why my mother had disliked her.

Mrs. Chalmers—and her husband if she had one, I suppose—lived on Wilton Place, near Second Street, in Los Angeles. As the cabbie drove me there, I decided it was a very pretty neighborhood, with big houses and awfully pretty yards. I think that, during my first few months in Los Angeles, the landscaping impressed me more than just about anything else in my new home. I suppose it's easier to have lovely lawns, fabulous rose bushes, and all sorts of other flowers when the weather never freezes as it does in Boston. Chloe and Harvey had a gorgeous yard, and, although Chloe complained occasionally about not having a swimming pool—swimming pools were *de rigueur* amongst the Hollywood set, I had discovered early in my stay here—I didn't miss it one little bit. I preferred the wonderful rose garden.

Naturally, neither Chloe nor Harvey worked in the garden. They had a staff of professional gardeners to do the work, but Mrs. Biddle, their housekeeper, made good use of the flowers therefrom.

The taxicab pulled up to the curb in front of a large white

house with a massive porch and a huge double door. The cabbie opened the door for me. I asked him to wait, and I walked up a long paved pathway lined with gardenia bushes whose sweet, cloying fragrance nearly knocked me over. I climbed the short flight of stairs to the porch, crossed the porch to the gigantic doors, and twisted the doorbell. I heard the noise it made, and I waited.

And I waited.

And waited.

Frowning—where on earth could Ernie and Mrs. Chalmers have gone, and if they'd gone somewhere, why hadn't Ernie called me or touched base with Phil?—I decided to take a chance and grabbed the doorknob. It turned easily. Then I hesitated. Did I really want to waltz into someone else's home without having been invited?

Squaring my shoulders, I told myself firmly that I did indeed want to do that, because my boss might be in trouble. In fact, didn't I feel a little tingle up my spine? After thinking about it for a second or three, I decided I didn't.

Nevertheless, I gingerly shoved the door open and walked inside the house. Could this action of mine be called breaking and entering? I wasn't sure, and I also wasn't sure if the fact that I hadn't actually broken anything would count if somebody found me there. Oh, well.

The door opened onto a foyer-type room, kind of like the one in Chloe's house, only Chloe's house has lovely tiles on the floor, and this was polished wood covered with a pretty Oriental rug. The rug looked like a Bukhara to me, although I'm certainly no expert on Oriental rugs.

Because I was still nervous, I cleared my throat and said, "Good afternoon?" in a questioning sort of voice.

No answer. Perhaps that was because I'd almost whispered the words. After taking a deep breath for courage, I repeated my greeting, more loudly this time: "Good afternoon!"

Still no answer.

Well, pooh. Now what?

Although my nerves were jangling like the bells on a Christmas sleigh, I decided it would be cowardly on my part not to finish what I'd started now that I had officially entered the house uninvited, so I set out to look for my boss. And, of course, Mrs. Chalmers.

I didn't know the layout of the house, but having been born and reared in a place remarkably like this one, I didn't have any trouble finding my way around. No one was in the breakfast room. No one was in the kitchen. No one was in the butler's pantry or the dining room. Speaking of butlers, didn't Mrs. Chalmers have any servants? In a place as big as this? I figured that a maid would probably pop up when I was searching a bedroom and screech, so I stopped and said, again loudly, "Good afternoon! Is anyone home?"

Still no answer. My nerves had begun to jump about like the Mexican jumping beans I'd seen people sell on the streets of Los Angeles, but I doggedly decided to pursue my goal. By that time, I was truly worried about my feckless boss.

Retracing my steps, I returned to the morning room and began my search in the opposite direction. There was nothing in the office but a piano and a desk. A library off the office appeared as though Mr. Chalmers, if he existed, used it as a refuge. It seemed definitely a masculine room, with leather sofas and chairs and so forth. From the library, a huge withdrawing room, furnished to the teeth with expensive pieces, opened onto a vast hallway leading to a staircase.

It was there, at the foot of the stairs, that I saw something more frightening even than having walked uninvited into someone else's house: a lumpy bundle of filmy cloth. Not that a bundle of filmy cloth is horrible in and of itself, but this particular bundle was light and frothy and diaphanous. And it enclosed a body. Even before I tiptoed over to see for sure, I knew the body was that of Mrs. Persephone Chalmers.

Once I determined for certain that it was she, I think I screamed, although I'm not sure. If I did, I'm ashamed of myself. After all, I aspire to the position of assistant to a private investigator. Someone in that capacity has no business screaming at the sight of bodies. Still and all, this was only the second dead person I'd encountered in my entire life who wasn't properly laid out and made up and in a coffin. The funeral director in Boston had actually made Great-Aunt Agatha look a good deal better in death than she ever had in life.

Not so Mrs. Persephone Chalmers.

Lest you think I added to my list of failures by running away from my duty as well as screaming, let me assure you that I did not. In actual fact, I mentally braced myself—hard—and knelt beside Mrs. Chalmers' body. I checked the pulse in her neck. There wasn't one. I checked the pulse in her wrist. Again, there wasn't one. And then I saw the blood-caked back of her head and leaped up and away from the corpse. Since I was kneeling at the time of my leap, I ended up in an undignified position on my rump with my legs spread out before me. From that position, I could see the entirety of the late Mrs. Chalmers, and I have to say that every bit of my former envy of the woman vanished. All I saw from this angle was a poor, seemingly silly, woman who had died before her time, and violently at that. I don't believe she was much older than thirty, and while thirty sounded kind of old to me, at twenty-one, it wasn't really. Heck, Ernie was almost thirty.

The smack on my rump seemed to loosen the parts of my brain that had been frozen in horror, and they began working again. If Mrs. Chalmers was dead at the foot of the stairs in her house, and if Ernie had come to her house to visit her before nine o'clock this morning, where in the world could he be now, at . . . well, I wasn't sure what time it was. Maybe three or three-thirty? I decided I needed to get myself one of those new wrist-watches Chloe and I saw at the Broadway Department Store.

Could Ernie, too, be . . . ?

No. I didn't want even to think of such a thing. Not Ernie. Not the man who'd given me my very first job. Not the man whom I'd come to . . . like a lot.

But where the heck was he?

Steeling my nerves—they needed a whole lot of steeling that day—I rose to my feet, tiptoed around the recumbent Mrs. Chalmers, and silently padded up the stairs, keeping my eyes and ears pricked. While I was no expert on the various causes of death available to a person, it sure looked to me as if someone had given Mrs. Chalmers a wicked bash on the head before she'd fallen—or, more likely, been hurled—down those very same steps. I allowed myself a couple of peeks at the carpet runner on the stairs, but it, too, was patterned in an intricate Oriental pattern, so I couldn't tell if any of the reddish splotches of color might have been made by blood. If they were, they'd fallen in a remarkably regular pattern.

Boy, what I didn't know about the art of criminal investigation could fill a book! Actually, it probably did. Maybe more than one. Perhaps I should visit the Los Angeles Public Library again soon, and this time my visit *would* be work-related.

But my insufficient knowledge of criminal investigation was neither here nor there. As I've already mentioned, as I climbed those stairs, I listened hard, trying to detect any movement in the upstairs part of the house. I'd already ascertained there was no one in the downstairs. No one alive, at any rate.

Silence as deep as that ought to be outlawed, because it's terribly nerve-wracking. To be fair, I suppose my nerves would have been wracked even more drastically if a criminal had hurtled out of a room and hollered at me or, worse, grabbed me. Still and all, I had the creeps and the willies and the heebie-jeebies as I reached the top of the stairs and looked both ways down the hall where the stairway ended.

Nothing.

I glanced down the staircase. Mrs. Chalmers was still there. Oh, goody.

So I headed down the hallway to my right, determined to snoop until I'd found my boss. Or not found him. I hoped for the former result.

I suppose it's considered good housekeeping to shut all the doors in a house when no one's in the rooms behind them, but it's really, really intimidating to open one closed door after another in a house where you suspect a murder has recently been committed. I say *recently* because of the relative warmth of Mrs. Chalmers' body when I checked various parts of her for a pulse. Of course, the September heat might account for some of that warmth, but I still didn't believe she'd been dead for too awfully long. The notion made me shudder, and I did a bit more nerve-steeling.

My gasp when I opened the last door at the end of that infinitely long corridor might have awakened the dead, although I later learned that Mrs. Chalmers hadn't stirred in spite of it.

"Ernie!" I regret to say I squealed the name.

Ernie, who looked as if he might be dead, too, didn't stir. Sprawled across a big bed covered with a crimson brocade throw, he lay on his stomach with his head turned to one side—the side toward me—only his eyes were closed. Oh, good Lord, he couldn't be dead! Could he? Not Ernie!

My hand pressed to my thundering heart and with, I'm sorry to report, tears in my eyes, I hesitatingly approached the bed. As I did, I noticed something rather odd about Ernie that I hadn't at first taken in: he was bound and gagged. I'd read books in which people had been bound and gagged, but I'd never seen anyone who had been. He also seemed to be out cold. I peered closely at him, praying he still breathed. When one of those eyes of his opened, I darned near screamed again.

"Grmph!" said Ernie.

"What?" said I.

"Grmph!" he repeated, with more emphasis this time.

I decided it might be a good idea to get the gag out of Ernie's mouth before I attempted further communication with him. So I did. Doing so wasn't easy. Whoever had tied the knot had been quite thorough. I didn't have a knife with me, so I had to work the knot free with my fingers, and by the time I finally succeeded, two of my fingernails had broken and Ernie's temper wasn't at its best.

"God damned son of a bitch!" were the first words out of his mouth. Then he clutched his head and groaned.

While rather shocked at his language, I decided I'd better not call him to task for it. I could tell he was in a foul mood. Anyhow, I supposed he deserved to swear a little, given the circumstances.

Rather, I did my level best to untie the bonds holding his wrists together. "Darn it, these are too tight." I was surprised, in fact, that his hands hadn't swollen and turned blue from lack of circulation.

"Use the pocketknife in my back pocket," he suggested in a surly voice.

Undaunted by his mood, I gingerly reached into his back pocket where, sure enough, I found one of those knives with all sorts of blades, screwdrivers, and bottle openers and things attached to them. Handy tools, those. Then, trying my very best not to draw blood, I slit the rope binding Ernie's hands. I only slipped once or twice, to wicked grumbles from my boss. Once his hands were free, Ernie flapped them in the air, I presume to get the circulation back. Then he said, "I'll cut the rest of them myself. If I let you do it, you'll probably slit one of my veins."

Although I didn't appreciate his comment, his suggestion was fine with me, so I handed him the knife with only one small "hmph." As he sawed at the rope binding his feet, swearing softly the while, I cleared my throat and said, "What happened, Ernie?"

"How the hell should I know?"

"If you don't know, who does?" I asked. By that time, I wasn't in the best frame of mind myself. Here I'd risked life and limb—or at the very least, arrest and imprisonment—to find this man, and all he could do was swear at me. I was not amused.

"Dammit, Mercy, what are you doing here? What the hell time is it?"

"Stop cursing at me, Ernest Templeton, darn you! I came looking for you when you didn't return to the office by two-thirty this afternoon—with, I might add, not a telephone call or a note to tell me when you'd be back. What did you expect me to tell any clients who called?"

"Huh," said Ernie. "I suppose there were thousands of those."

I scowled at him and didn't rise to his bait. "And I came here because you said you'd *be* here! And I don't know what time it is. When I left the office, it was early afternoon. Why don't you look at a clock if you want to know what time it is? Or your own pocket watch?" I turned, intending to leave my irritating employer to his own devices.

Then I remembered the body at the foot of the stairs and stopped in my tracks. I did not, however, turn around to face Ernie. What I was attempting to do as I stood there was think of another way out of that stupid house.

"Listen, Mercy, I'm sorry I yelled at you."

"So am I." I still didn't turn around. Maybe there was a back staircase. Servants were supposed to use back staircases. At our family home in Boston, Chloe and I used to think it was fun to ride up and down the dumbwaiter, but I was littler then. These days I probably wouldn't fit in the dumbwaiter, even if I could find it in this mansion. No. There simply had to be another set of stairs somewhere.

"Mercy, please. Don't you have any idea what time it is? I don't remember anything since this morning. God, is it really afternoon already?"

Very well, since he sounded repentant, I turned. Still glaring, I said, "Really? You truly don't remember anything since morning? I left the office to look for you at about two-thirty."

I think he'd have rolled his eyes if he'd felt better. "Good God. *Two-thirty?* Really? I don't remember a thing. Is it honestly two-thirty in the afternoon?" He shook his head, but I could tell he instantly regretted the gesture. "But it can't be that late. I was supposed to meet Phil at nine."

"I know. He came by the office. When I called him this afternoon, he said he hadn't heard from you, and he wasn't very happy about it, either."

Ernie shook his head again, then grasped it between both of his hands and let out a moan of pain. I began to suspect he'd either overindulged in spirituous liquor, been bashed over the head himself, or had been drugged somehow or other. The latter, while bizarre, seemed a trifle more logical than the first two choices, since Ernie hadn't, to my knowledge, a taste for alcohol. He did take the occasional sip from a flask every now and then, which had shocked me until I found out he carried apple cider in the silly thing. I also hadn't noticed any kind of wound or bump on his head.

Because I'm a compassionate person when not being hollered at for no good reason, I returned to the bed. "Do you have a headache?"

"Yes. My head hurts like hell, my mouth is as dry as the Sahara Desert, and I feel like I've been run over by a trolley car. Damn, I need a powder and some water."

"You were drugged," I said.

He squinted at me unpleasantly. "Now who in the name of God would drug me?"

"Probably the same person who killed Mrs. Chalmers," I said before thinking the matter through.

Ernie stared at me as if it were I and not he who'd been drugged. "What did you say?"

Realizing that what I'd just said had probably shocked Ernie a good deal, I sighed and explained. "I found Mrs. Chalmers dead at the foot of that staircase out there. I think she was hit on the head and then pushed down the stairs. Unless she fell and knocked her head on something along her way downstairs, although it didn't look like that to me, since the back of her head looked . . . well, as if it had been bashed. Not," I admitted reluctantly, "that I'm an expert at things like that."

"She's dead?" Again Ernie shook his head. Again he clutched it as if it hurt when he did that.

"Yes."

"You're sure?"

I pressed my lips together, exasperated. "Yes, I'm sure! Why do you think I roamed through this huge, blasted, *empty* house looking for you? I found the front door unlocked, nobody else in the entire house, her dead at the foot of the stairs, and you nowhere. So I climbed the stairs—worrying the entire time, mind you, that some revolting criminal would leap out at me— and I found you tied up in here." I looked around the room and added drily, "Mrs. Chalmers' bedchamber, I presume."

He looked around the room, too. "I don't know what the hell room this is. It looks like something out of the Reign of Terror with all that damned red."

"Ernest Templeton, if you don't stop swearing at me—"

"I'm not swearing at you, for God's sake. I feel like I've been kicked in the head by a mule, and you can't think of anything better to do than criticize my language. Have some mercy, Mercy."

"Your language is deplorable," I said because I felt I should.

"I know it. It always has been. You should be used to it by this time." He groaned and struggled to stand. "Oh, God, my head hurts!"

I pinched my lips together into a tight line, but sympathy got the better of me. "Here. Lean on me if it'll help."

"Thanks, Mercy."

"You're welcome. I suppose there's a telephone in this house somewhere. I imagine we should call the—"

A piercing scream interrupted my suggestion, and I feared it was too late for us to be the bearers of the news of Mrs. Chalmers' death to the Los Angeles Police Department.

Cringing—from pain, I presume—Ernie said, "Shit."

Ever efficient, I said, "I'd better go see who's here and explain what happened. Not that I know what happened." I looked up at my wobbly boss. "Can you walk on your own?"

Through gritted teeth, Ernie said, "Yes."

"Hold on to the door frame until you get your feet balanced sufficiently under you."

Ernie grunted.

Leaving him to his own devices, I ran out of the room, down the hall, and stopped at the head of the staircase. There below me huddled the reason the house had been empty when I arrived. Two women, clutching each other and with faces streaming with tears, stared down at the dead body of Mrs. Persephone Chalmers. The housekeeper and maid, I presumed. Unless one of them was the cook. Or the crook.

But that was silly. Neither of those two women looked

threatening to me, although I'd been fooled before, much to my chagrin.

Anyhow, the situation, as you can fully imagine, was terribly awkward. The poor things appeared to be already distressed, and I was sure that finding two strangers in the house where their employer lay dead wasn't going to make them feel much better. However, I'd been bred to handle difficult situations among servants with aplomb, so I cleared my throat.

Both women gasped and looked up the staircase to where I stood. They, not having been bred under the same circumstances as I, screeched again.

CHAPTER THREE

I descended the staircase as quickly and with as much dignity as I could muster, hoping Ernie would take his time joining us downstairs until I'd conveyed my story to the two women and they calmed down some. They backed away from me, still clinging to each other, as if I were a demon incarnate.

"Please," I said to the older of the two, "my name is Miss Mercedes Allcutt, and I found Mrs. Chalmers this way when I came to visit her. The front door was unlocked, and I was worried, so I entered the house." I didn't mention that I'd been looking for my fugitive employer at the time.

They continued to stare at me. I sighed.

"Will you please tell me where the telephone is? We need to telephone the police department. I believe Mrs. Chalmers was done to death by a criminal."

The older woman bellowed, "*What?* You think she was *murdered?*"

The younger woman let out another cry of alarm, although it wasn't quite so loud as her last couple had been. "She told us this would happen," she said to the other woman, much to my interest. "Didn't she tell us, Mrs. Hanratty? She told us, didn't she?"

"She did, Susan. She did."

Now I was confused. "You mean Mrs. Chalmers feared for her life?"

"Yes!" wailed Susan.

Oh, dear. This was *such* a pickle. And here I'd been told Ernie was only interested in finding some stolen jewelry. Why hadn't he told me this part of the story? Probably because he didn't want me doing what he calls *snooping* into the matter. Idiotic man. He'd left me out of things, and just look what had happened to him. Not to mention Mrs. Chalmers. One of these days, I told myself, I'd teach him what an asset I was. Until then . . .

"Please tell me where the telephone is, Mrs. Hanratty, and I'll 'phone a police detective I know. In the meantime, I believe you should go to the kitchen and prepare a nice pot of tea. That might calm the two of you somewhat."

Mrs. Hanratty, rather than taking my sensible suggestion and acting upon it, looked around the hallway. "Is the mister here?"

It was my turn to stare. "There's a mister? A Mr. Chalmers?"

Mrs. Hanratty nodded. Then she seemed to gather control of herself, straightened, set Susan aside, and said, "Susan, I don't know why this young woman is in the house, but I think you'd best telephone the mister at his place of business." To me she said, "I think it's mighty fishy to find a stranger in the house along with the body of the missus, young woman."

I didn't blame her for feeling as she did. However, I also wasn't guilty of doing anything more grievous than entering a house uninvited.

It was then when Susan chose to scream again. I knew what had caused this latest outpouring of terror without even turning around to see Ernie, but I did anyway, mainly because I wasn't sure he was steady enough on his pins to negotiate the staircase.

"Do you need my help?" I asked politely. I had to ask the question rather loudly because Susan was in full rant by that time. I heard a sharp smack, and she shut up, from which I deduced that Mrs. Hanratty had slapped Susan's cheek to quell her hysterics.

"And just who in blazes are *you?*" Mrs. Hanratty demanded of Ernie. I got the feeling she'd been shepherding the members of this household for quite a few years, because she had a tone of command that almost rivaled that of my mother.

Ernie, pale, pasty, and looking sick, reached into his jacket pocket and produced a card, which he handed to Mrs. Hanratty, who stared at it as if she expected it to bite her. Then she took the card and read it. "You're the fellow who's been looking into the theft?" she asked, as if she didn't believe it. She stared at Ernie as she said the words, and I have to admit that her doubtful tone was justified. Ernie looked perfectly awful.

"Yes, I am. I'm also the fellow to whom Mrs. Chalmers came when she suspected someone was trying to kill her." Then he knelt beside the body.

I heard Mrs. Hanratty gulp.

"Has anyone called Phil?"

"Not yet. I was trying to calm down the servants."

"Well, for God's sake, go call him! What the devil are you waiting for?"

"I'm waiting for someone to tell me where the telephone is, Ernest Templeton!" By that time in this circus of events, I'd become downright cranky.

CHAPTER FOUR

Mrs. Hanratty and I finally got Susan to shut up and sit down—she continued to weep, but less noisily than before—and Mrs. Hanratty led me at last to the telephone room, a small nook under the staircase.

"I really think I should telephone the mister first," she told me.

"You may call Mr. Chalmers as soon as I telephone the police," I said sternly, following Ernie's instructions. *He* knew what he was doing. Usually.

"Well . . ."

"Mr. Templeton was employed by Mrs. Chalmers because he's a professional, and he knows in which order these things need to be undertaken."

I was proud of that sentence, mainly because it seemed to do the trick with Mrs. Hanratty, who heaved a huge sigh and said, "Well, I'll go make a pot of tea. Susan isn't going to be worth spit for the rest of the day."

Interesting description. Wrinkling my nose in some distaste, I dialed the number for the Los Angeles Police Department and asked to speak with Detective Bigelow. To my unutterable relief, Phil was there at his desk. I had feared he might be out chasing criminals. In a very few words, I told him what had happened.

"She's dead?" he said, a note of incredulity in his voice.

"You did say she was trouble," I reminded him.

"Yeah. I know I did, but I didn't think the trouble would

happen to her. I thought she was it and it would happen to Ernie."

"Oh. Well . . . well, so did I, actually. But she's really and truly dead—murdered, if I'm not mistaken—and I found Ernie bound and gagged in an upstairs room." I didn't mention that I suspected the room to be Mrs. Chalmers' bedchamber.

"You found Ernie? Bound and gagged?" Phil sounded even more incredulous than he had before.

"Yes. And I believe he was drugged into the bargain."

A significant silence on the other end of the wire let me know Phil was attempting to digest the information I'd just imparted. At last he said, "I'll be there as soon as I can be. Don't move anything. I wish you'd left Ernie the way you found him."

"Phil!" I cried, agog at his callousness. But he'd already replaced his receiver on the cradle, so I couldn't ask him for an explanation of what I considered to be a particularly cruel wish on his part.

By the time the police arrived at the Chalmers' residence, Mr. Chalmers had been notified of the trouble at his house, and he'd arrived, too. A tall, stout man with striking silver hair, he wore a handsomely tailored business suit in light gray wool. His collar was clean and starched, and he looked much too respectable to have been married to the wafty Persephone Chalmers. Or to any other woman who'd been murdered, for that matter. He looked kind of like my father, who wouldn't hear of anyone being murdered in *his* family. I soon learned, however, after talking to him, that he was a much more gentle gentleman than any of the men in my family.

Considering that, in the case of a murdered spouse, the extant spouse is generally the first person suspected of having done the deed—Ernie had taught me that—Mr. Chalmers appeared truly grieved by his wife's demise. I got the feeling he'd have felt bad even if she'd died of natural causes, although I also wondered if he were faking his feelings. If so, he was a mighty good actor. He appeared positively sick.

Phil and Ernie were busy discussing things over the body of Mrs. Chalmers, and I'd helped Mr. Chalmers to an easy chair, where he sat with his face in his hands and his elbows propped on his knees, patently miserable—again, unless he was faking. Feeling useless, I said, "Is there anything I can do to help you, Mr. Chalmers? I'm so very sorry about all this."

He glanced up at me, and I saw that tears stood in his eyes. "Thank you, Miss Allcutt"—I'd introduced myself—"I can't think of anything. I'm so . . . so . . ." His words trailed off.

"If you do think of some way I can be of help to you, please don't hesitate to ask me."

"Thank you. Oh!" He straightened in his chair. "There is something you can do for me. You can telephone my son."

"Your son?" Another suspect, by gum! Maybe the son of this family had decided to do away with his mother so that he'd inherit more money. Or something like that. I'd have to work out the details later.

"Yes. I . . . I'd call him myself, but . . ." He gulped loudly, and I deduced he was having a bit of trouble keeping his emotions in check. My sympathy was instantly aroused, and I began to believe he wasn't faking anything.

"I'll be very glad to telephone him for you, Mr. Chalmers."

"Wait a minute, you," a gruff voice said at my back.

I turned, surprised, to find a uniformed member of the Los Angeles Police Department scowling at me. "Yes?" I said in my mother's most austere voice.

The policeman seemed unaffected by my hauteur. Breeding will tell, as my mother is fond of saying. Curse this man, he had none. Nevertheless, I lifted my eyebrows to let him know what I considered his place in the universe to be, even if he disagreed with my assessment.

To my relief, my Mother imitation seemed to be having an effect at last. The officer swallowed and said, "Er, I just need to know who it is you're going to telephone. That's all."

Mr. Chalmers responded to this almost-civil statement. "I asked Miss Allcutt to put a call through to my son. He needs to know what happened, and I need him here to . . . to . . ." He couldn't go on. Folding up like a fan, he again buried his face in his hands, and his shoulders started to shake slightly.

With a grimace for the officer, I expressed my opinion of a servant of the public who would make a grown man cry. The policeman only looked slightly abashed. I knelt beside Mr. Chalmers. "What is your son's number, sir? I'll call him for you." I spoke very gently.

So Mr. Chalmers gave me his son's telephone number, and I headed to the 'phone nook under the staircase and put the call through. After what seemed like a hundred rings, at least, a voice on the other end of the wire answered at last with, "Sierra Vista Golfing Association."

I was a little startled to learn that the younger Mr. Chalmers worked at a golfing establishment. Or perhaps he only played golf there. My awful brother, George, played golf. I think all bankers are required to learn the game. George looked positively ridiculous in his golfing knickerbockers. But that's neither here nor there. "I need to speak with Mr. Chalmers, please."

"One moment, please," said the polite voice at the other end of the wire.

It wasn't much more than a moment later when another, lighter, more playful voice said, "Simon here. Who's calling?"

"Mr. Chalmers, my name is Miss Allcutt, and I fear there's been an . . . accident at your parents' house. Your father requested that I telephone you and ask you to come home as soon as you possibly can."

"An accident?" He sounded alarmed. "Is the old man all right?"

The old man? Exactly how callous was this fellow, anyway? "Your father is well, sir. It's your mother who has had . . . an accident."

"My mother? My mother's dead!"

I reeled at his words. Had he just confessed to murder? Over the telephone? To me? Before I had a chance to react, he spoke again.

"Who did you say you were?"

Good Lord. Complications upon complications.

Thinking fast, I said, "My name is Miss Allcutt. I'm here with representatives of the Los Angeles Police Department."

"Good God! The police are involved?"

"Yes."

"Tell the old man I'll be there in five."

And he hung up the receiver on his end before I could ask five what or get him to repeat his confession. Perhaps I'd misunderstood him. With a sigh, I replaced the receiver on my end and turned to find Ernie scowling at me.

"What the hell do you think you're doing?" he demanded. He still looked sick.

However, his looking sick was no excuse for his abominable behavior. "I was telephoning Mr. Chalmers' son for Mr. Chalmers is what I was doing. What are *you* doing, standing there and glowering at me?"

Ernie's scowl faded. "Don't get mad, Mercy. I still feel like hell. That was nice of you to call the man's son for him."

"Thank you." My voice was stiff and icy.

"It turns out I'm their chief suspect, you know."

The ice melted at once, and I stared at him in horror mixed with more than a little disbelief. "You? Why on earth do they—?"

"I told you that you should have left him tied up," said

another voice. This one belonged to Phil Bigelow. "You unwrapped him, and now there's nobody but you to swear that he was bound and gagged."

"What?"

"He's right, Mercy," said Ernie, grimacing. "Please don't yell."

I transferred my stare of astonishment to him. "I'm not yelling! I don't believe this!"

"Listen, Mercy, it's just that the police pretty much have to see for themselves that what people involved in a murder say is true," Phil said. "They can't just take anybody's word for anything when it comes to murder."

It took me a second to untwist those sentences. When I did, I nearly exploded with wrath. "Do you mean to tell me that the representatives of the Los Angeles Police Department don't believe *me?* Mercedes Louise Allcutt? From Boston, Massachusetts? Does that disbelief extend to *you,* Detective Philip Bigelow?" Except for a couple of times when dealing with my mother, I don't think I'd ever been that angry in my life.

Phil held up a hand. The gesture was meant to be one of placation, I think, although I wasn't in a mood to be particularly discerning at the time.

"It's not that they don't believe you," he said. Then he instantly reversed himself by saying, "But you have to understand that most people don't want to be involved in situations like these, and the police must be very careful about who they believe and who they don't believe."

"Your grammar is as hideous as your logic!" I told him. I'm not generally so mean to people, but I was truly quite angry at the time. "Anyhow, the woman was hit on the back of the head! Why would Ernie hit her on the head?"

"I don't think he did, Mercy," said Phil. He appeared as frustrated as I felt.

"Well, then," I said, "if there's no good reason for Ernie to have hit her on the head and thrown her down the stairs, why do the police suspect him?"

"Mercy, it's just a fact of life in a situation like this," said Ernie. I noticed he had a hand pressed to his head as if he were trying to hold it together.

"But it's insane not to believe that what happened happened!" Indignant as all get-out, but conscious of Ernie's pain, I lowered my voice and told Phil, "Just go upstairs and look at the ropes and gag yourself if you don't believe me!"

"We've got everything in evidence, but the ropes and gag alone don't mean anything. We don't know what they were used for or who used them. You're the only who saw him in them."

"And nobody believes me? Or Ernie? Just look at him! He looks terrible!"

"Thanks," Ernie said. I frowned at him, but all he did was grin back at me. I was right, though. He looked terrible.

"I believe you, Mercy," said Phil, sounding as if he wished he were elsewhere. "But the police department has a big job to do, and we have to corroborate all the evidence that's discovered at a crime scene. Unfortunately, there's no corroboration of Ernie's condition when you arrived at the Chalmers' home, because no one but you saw him." He eyed me for a second and said, "You said the servants were out?"

"Yes. The house was unlocked, and because I was worried about Ernie, I entered. I suppose *that's* a crime too?"

Phil sighed. "No. I understand why you entered. I only wish you'd had someone with you and that the someone else had seen Ernie. The only story we have is yours, and you work for him. For all we know, you're the one who tied him up in order to divert suspicion from him."

"I *beg* your pardon?" My voice came out like sharp, pointy icicles.

"They think we staged the thing," said Ernie wearily.

"They *what?*" That time my voice was more like a shriek. Both men winced.

Phil shrugged. "I know you wouldn't do anything like that, but I'm not the only detective on the case."

"But look at his wrists!" I said, lowering my voice slightly. "There are marks there! I wouldn't tie him up so tightly! In fact, I doubt that if I'd tied him up there would be any marks at all, because the ropes wouldn't have been on his wrists for very long."

Phil appeared disgruntled, as well he should. "Listen, all of this is relevant. But the fact is I'll probably be taken off the case, since Ernie and I are good friends. I suspect Detective O'Reilly will be assigned to lead the investigation."

"Which is bad for me," said Ernie wearily. "O'Reilly hates my guts. And vice-versa."

"But that's not fair! If you're Ernie's friend and they won't let you handle the case, why would they give the case to a man who hates his guts?" Gee, I don't think I'd ever said the word *guts* before.

Another shrug from Phil. "That's just the way these things work sometimes."

"And why would I tie up my own boss? For that matter, why would I have to? Why would Ernie kill Mrs. Chalmers? There's no motive!"

"Well, one of my colleagues suggested that Ernie and Mrs. Chalmers had been . . . engaged in some sort of . . ."

Phil's face turned a dull, brick red. I didn't understand what he was trying to convey, so I prompted him. "Engaged in what?"

"Oh, Christ, Mercy," said Ernie disgustedly. "Some cop thinks the Chalmers dame and I were playing sex games, and I must have accidently pushed her down the stairs."

I was speechless. In fact, I don't think I could have uttered a word if I'd tried.

Fortunately for me, Phil said, "You don't have to be so blunt, Ernie." He nodded his head toward me. In other words, he considered me too innocent to hear such things.

The awful truth was that I seemed to be exactly that. I gave myself a hard mental shake. "If they were playing . . . those kinds of games, why would Ernie hit her on the head?"

"*I* don't know, Mercy!" Phil said, throwing his hands in the air in a gesture of futility and frustration. "Somebody only mentioned the possibility, is all."

A silence descended among the three of us that lasted a good year or two. Then I asked, feeling desperate, "Well, what about fingerprints? Wouldn't there be fingerprints on the ropes and gag? And has anyone found the weapon she was bashed with?"

"No weapon has been found. The only fingerprints they're liable to find on anything in that room are yours and mine and those of Mrs. Chalmers," Ernie told me. "Ropes don't take good fingerprints. Anybody have any headache powders?"

I stared at him bleakly and ignored his question. "But . . . but . . ." I couldn't even bring my stern Boston breeding into play in this situation. That's probably because my mother would have preferred to be caught dead than have anything at all to do with the police and, therefore, I had no memories upon which to call. I cast a glance at the body of Mrs. Chalmers, which had finally been decently covered with something that looked like a sheet and recalled the younger Mr. Chalmers' confession.

Somewhat cheered by this recollection, even though I still wasn't sure I'd heard it exactly right, I said, "When I telephoned to Mr. Simon Chalmers, he said he knew his mother was dead." When both men stared at me blankly, I said with some impatience, "Don't you see? He already *knew!*"

Ernie and Phil exchanged a glance. Then Ernie said, "Mr. Simon Chalmers' mother has been dead for years. Mrs.

Persephone Chalmers was his stepmother."

My euphoria at having already tagged the crook evaporated like steam from a teakettle. "Oh."

"So I'm still their chief suspect."

"I can't believe this," I finally said in something akin to defeat.

Ernie patted me on the shoulder. "Don't worry about it, Mercy. I'll figure out who did this. It sure as hell wasn't me."

"Of course, it wasn't," said I in staunch defense of my employer, even if he did swear too much.

With studied nonchalance, Ernie reached into an inner jacket pocket and pulled out the wretched flask that had so upset me the first time I saw him use it, and took a long swallow. I guess I could understand that he might be thirsty after having that gag in his mouth for . . .

"How long has Mrs. Chalmers been . . ." I looked around and lowered my voice. I didn't want to upset Mr. Chalmers any more than he was already upset. Provided, of course, that he hadn't done the deed himself. "How long has she been dead?"

"We won't know that until the coroner gets here," said Phil. He looked worried, which worried me. "I don't like this."

"Neither do I," said Ernie.

"Nor I," I said.

Plaintively, Ernie said, "Doesn't anyone have any headache powders?"

I led him to the kitchen, where Mrs. Hanratty dumped a paper of powder into a glass of water and stirred. Ernie gulped down the resultant cloudy mess with a grimace of distaste.

"Thanks," he said to Mrs. Hanratty.

"Humph," said she. I got the feeling she blamed Ernie for not protecting her employer. I suppose I understood her attitude, although I didn't appreciate it.

Ernie and I returned to the living room and I got my first look at Mr. Simon Chalmers a couple of minutes after that, because a police officer escorted him into the room. I eyed him thoughtfully. He looked like a younger, spryer version of his father, whom he approached with what seemed like touching solicitude. I'd learned early in my career as a private investigator's assistant—I mean secretary—that it was best not to take anything for granted. For all I knew at that point in time, Simon Chalmers had cracked his stepmother on the head and dumped her down the stairs. And then gone out to play golf? I eyed him some more. His current clothes didn't look anything at all like the stupid knickerbockers my brother always wore when he went out to play at golf tourneys. Perhaps Simon Chalmers was an employee of the Sierra Vista Golfing Academy. Or whatever its name was.

"I'd like for you to make a statement to one of our officers who takes shorthand, Mercy," said Phil, interrupting my survey of the younger Mr. Chalmers. "Is that all right with you?"

No. It wasn't all right with me, mainly because I was mad at Phil Bigelow and the entire L.A.P.D. However, for Ernie's sake, I agreed to be interviewed. It would have been easier for me to go back to the office and type out a statement, but I sensed that would be going against another one of the department's idiotic rules.

I tried not to let the young officer who took my statement know exactly how put out I was that my words, which he took down using the same Pitman method of shorthand that I used, might not be believed. His face—I looked at his shield, and it said his name was Officer Ronald Bloom—was about as expressive as a block of granite, so I couldn't tell if he believed my story or not. At any rate, it didn't take long to relate it in its entirety to him.

He closed his notebook, which was just like the ones I used at work, and nodded his head. "Thank you, Miss Allcutt. I'll have this typed up, and then you'll have to sign it. Would you prefer to come to the station or have someone bring it to your home?"

I thought about offering to type it up myself, but didn't. If these people weren't going to believe anything I said, why should I help them? "I expect you or one of the other representatives of the law will be visiting Mr. Templeton's office tomorrow sometime. Just bring it there, why don't you?" I smiled sweetly at him. "I did tell you I was his secretary, did I not? Don't you believe that, either?"

Officer Bloom didn't bat an eye over my sarcasm. "It's not my business to believe people, ma'am. I'm just supposed to get the story."

Oh, brother. He made his job sound like that of a newspaper reporter. "Very well. Bring it to Mr. Templeton's office tomorrow, and I'll sign it—*if* the typewritten version of my report corresponds to the story I told you." I gave him a good, hot frown. "It's not my business to believe people, either, Officer Bloom, but I won't sign any statement that is incorrect in any way."

"You'll have the opportunity to read it over and make corrections," he said. I got the feeling he was accustomed to people being unpleasant to him, which made me wonder why anyone would want to be a police officer, if all they got was guff from folks. Ah, well. Mine was not to reason why, as the poet wrote. That's always sounded redundant to me, by the way. Not that anyone cares. But I really don't think one should put a "why" after the word "reason."

Oh, never mind.

When Officer Bloom walked away from me, I glanced around the room and saw that Ernie was being interviewed by Phil and another fellow who, I presumed, was also a detective because he was wearing a suit rather than a uniform. The fellow who wasn't Phil had an unpleasant grin on his face, and I wondered if he was Detective O'Reilly. For Ernie's sake, I hoped not. O'Reilly looked as if he'd enjoy locking Ernie up for a number of years, and I aimed to ask Ernie exactly why he and O'Reilly didn't like each other. I'm sure the fault, whatever it was, lay with O'Reilly.

I thought the poor fellow—Ernie, I mean—needed to go home and lie down, but I suspected he was going to be detained for some time yet, especially if the police actually suspected him of murder, or wanted to, as I imagined was the case with O'Reilly. I shook my head. Ernie might be lots of things, but I didn't for a minute believe he'd kill anyone. Anyway, how could he have killed Mrs. Chalmers if he'd been tied up and drugged at the time the murder had been committed?

Then I reminded myself that nobody believed me about that, and Phil had actually suggested I might have tied Ernie up myself in order to divert suspicion from Ernie, which was so ridiculous as to be . . . well, ridiculous. What an absolutely *stupid* day this had been.

I noticed Mr. Simon Chalmers sitting dejectedly on a sofa in a corner of the room and decided it might be a good time to speak with him and learn what I could about Mr. and Mrs. Chalmers and how they lived, since there had to be *something* in their lives that had led to Mrs. Chalmers' decease in so disturbing a way. Perhaps the younger Mr. Chalmers had resented his stepmother's presence in his life. Or maybe he feared his father would leave *her* all his money, and had done her in to prevent the possibility. That was a good thought. I strolled over and sat on the sofa beside Simon.

He glanced at me and rose about halfway. Manners. Evidently, Mr. Simon Chalmers had been taught some, too. "I'm sorry. I don't believe we've met," he said politely, if a trifle dully.

"I'm Miss Allcutt. I'm the person who telephoned you with the unfortunate news."

"Oh. Well . . . thank you, I guess." He gave me a wan smile.

"This is a terrible thing, isn't it?" Sympathy oozed from every word I spoke.

"Ghastly," he agreed.

"I'm awfully sorry about your stepmother."

"Thank you."

Hmmm. This conversation, so far, was going nowhere. That was probably because of my own good manners. Therefore, I decided to drop any remnant of Boston from my demeanor and reached out to touch Mr. Chalmers' arm. "It must be simply horrid for you and your father to lose someone so very close to you."

He didn't seem alarmed by my boldness. He only nodded and appeared sad. "Yes. It's terrible. I feel really sorry for Dad. He's crushed."

In truth, it had been Mrs. Chalmers who'd been crushed, but I didn't say so.

"Indeed," I said, virtually bleeding compassion. "How long have your father and Mrs. Chalmers been married?" I braced myself for a rebuff, but evidently the younger Mr. Chalmers was accustomed to Los Angeles behavior and didn't seem to realize how rude I was being.

"Oh, about five years, I guess."

"I see." I shook my head to show how much sympathy I felt for him. "Your father must be devastated."

Simon shot a glance at his father and nodded. "Yeah. He sure is. Devastated is the word for it, all right."

I tried to discern by the expression on his face if he approved of his father's love of his—Simon's—stepmother. The English language really needs another pronoun, although this isn't the place for that discussion, I suppose. "You must have been very fond of her, too. After all, she'd been your mother for five years."

For the first time, a glint of humor appeared on Mr. Chalmers' face. "I was grown up when they met and married. I didn't know her that well, but she was all right."

"All right?" I lifted what I hoped was an expressive eyebrow.

Tilting his head to one side in a sort of considering posture, Simon Chalmers thought for a minute. "Well, she was nice," he said. "I was happy for my dad, because he'd been really lonely since my mother died. But Persephone was a little . . . I don't know."

And then, darned if he didn't lift his right hand, point his first finger, and twirl it beside his head in the classic gesture one makes when one is trying to convey a degree of mental instability about another person. Ha! So he'd noticed that fey characteristic in Persephone Chalmers, too, had he?

I bit my lip for a second and then decided to plunge ahead. "You know," I said softly, "I work for Mr. Templeton, the private investigator whom Mrs. Chalmers hired to find her stolen jewelry."

He made a kind of "pfff" noise. I don't know how else to describe it, although it indicated to me that Mr. Chalmers was as unsure about the stolen jewelry as he was about his late stepmother's sanity.

I lifted another eyebrow. Or maybe it was the same one I'd lifted before. "You didn't believe her jewelry was stolen?"

"Oh, sure, it was stolen—or at least taken—but I don't think there's much mystery about where it went."

"Oh?" Now I was genuinely surprised. "What do you mean? If you don't mind my asking."

"Heck, no. I don't mind. But you see, my stepmother had recently joined that crew of crazy folks at the Angelica Gospel Hall and was a devoted follower of Adelaide Burkhard Emmanuel. *Sister* Emmanuel, she calls her. Called her. I think somebody from the Hall took the jewelry."

"Oh. My goodness. I've read a good deal about Mrs. Emmanuel's work. That's an amazing church she built."

"The money of deluded people like my stepmother is what paid for that building," Simon Chalmers said with a flat note in his voice that told me he'd disapproved of his stepmother's contributions to Mrs. Emmanuel's cause.

"My goodness. Did your . . ." I swallowed, aghast at what I'd almost asked him. Then I told myself that Ernie's very life might be on the line here, and I asked my question anyway. "Did your father mind that Mrs. Chalmers donated a lot of money to the Angelica Gospel Hall?"

One of his shoulders lifted and dropped in what might have been meant as a shrug. "I don't know. I don't live here anymore. Haven't for years. Only visit once in a while."

"I see. Do you work at that golfing academy?"

He stared at me as if I'd said something absurd. "Work? I don't work anywhere. Investments. That's what's needed in today's society. I do like to play golf, though."

"Ah. Yes." A man after my mother's heart. My father probably wouldn't like him, since, according to him, men—even men from his family—should at least try to earn their way in the world. His standards, as I may have mentioned several times before, were different for the women in his family, who weren't supposed to do anything but sit still, look decorative, and attend tea parties. "So you don't know if your father approved or disapproved of your stepmother's religious inclinations?"

"Oh, I don't know. I don't think he minded. Anything she wanted to do was fine with him."

"But you do believe that someone from the church stole her jewelry?"

He heaved a huge sigh. "I don't really know, but I wouldn't put anything past one of those crazy people."

"I see. But Mrs. Chalmers enjoyed her association with the church?"

"Enjoyed it? She loved it. She'd go on about that Emmanuel

character for hours, but Dad didn't seem to mind." Simon Chalmers shook his head. "She'd have driven me nuts, but he loved her."

I hesitated to say what popped into my mind, but I said it anyway. "I gathered a rather odd impression from Mrs. Chalmers when I first met her."

This time he actually chuckled. "Odd? I always thought she was crazy as a coot. But the old man couldn't see it."

"Yes," I said. "I understand love does have that effect on some people."

"She was always good to him. Waited on him. I think she doted on him as much as he doted on her."

"How nice for both of them." I decided we'd drifted off topic, so I said, "But you think someone from the church might have stolen Mrs. Chalmers' jewelry? Do you think that, perhaps when she confronted the culprit, he or she . . ." *Bashed her on the head* sounded so undignified. "Um, did her in?"

Again he shrugged. "I don't know. What I wonder is if she sold the jewelry and gave the money to *Sister* Emmanuel. Or maybe she just gave her the jewelry and then told Dad that it had been stolen."

Merciful heavens! Now there's an idea I hadn't thought of before. Perhaps Mr. Chalmers, disgusted with his wife's extravagance, had, in a moment of sublime rage, killed her!

"My goodness, that doesn't sound like very Christian behavior on her part."

Simon Chalmers sighed again. "I'm probably wrong about that. I don't know."

But I wasn't so certain he was wrong. I couldn't wait to tell Ernie what I'd learned.

CHAPTER FIVE

"I'm only going to tell you this once, Mercy. Stay out of the Chalmers business. Don't pretend to be an investigator. Don't even talk to anyone concerned with the case. It involves a vicious murder, and it might well be dangerous for you to do any snooping. Do you understand me?"

Ernie was furious. And all I'd done was propose my well-thought-out theory of what might have happened at the Chalmers residence the day before. I must say that he looked a wee bit better today than he had on the day mentioned. Still, that didn't mean he could dictate to me what I could and couldn't do on my own time.

"I understand you, Mr. Templeton, believe me. You want me to butt out, as you once so eloquently put it. However, I'm not willing to do that. Why, if we don't find the true culprit in this crime, the L.A.P.D. might pin it on you. I'm not going to sacrifice my employment because you don't want me looking into a murder that might well be blamed on you."

"Your employment." Ernie's sneer was a work of art. "I don't know why you want to work anyway. You're already richer than God."

Drat the man! He'd pegged me for a rich man's daughter the moment he saw me. I guess they teach things like that at the police academy. You know: how to differentiate among the classes we in the United States aren't supposed to have. Still, that piece of detection had convinced me that he was good at his job and that I could do worse than to emulate him. In some ways. In others, he was the last man on earth I'd want to copy.

"Nonsense. Why, I've already interviewed Mr. Simon Chalmers, Mr. Chalmers' son, and learned that the late Mrs. Chalmers was crazy as a coot."

At Ernie's ironic expression, I amended my statement. "Those are Mr. Chalmers' very words. They're not mine."

"Of course not. You'd never be so unrefined as to call anyone crazy as a coot."

Blast the man. "Anyhow, Mrs. Chalmers had recently joined the Angelica Gospel Hall, and was spending vast quantities of money there. It's quite possible that either the younger or the older Mr. Chalmers did her in to curtail her extravagance."

"If either of them did it, they curtailed her extravagance with a vengeance, I'd say. There are a lot of easier ways to curtail a woman's spending habits than by killing her."

"I agree, but perhaps someone didn't see it that way. Remember, it was you who taught me that the first people to investigate in a case of murder are family members."

"It's good to know that you take some of the things I tell you to heart."

I ignored that jibe. "Anyhow, you knew about her activities with that church, didn't you?" I actually hoped he hadn't known, because then I would have proved to him that I could ferret out information with the best of them.

"Sure. She told me all about it."

Nuts. "Well, do you think someone from the church might have had something to do with her death?"

"At this point, I don't know anything at all about her death, Mercy Allcutt, and neither do you, except that she is definitely dead. And this is one case where you're *not* going to become involved. Let the L.A.P.D. and Phil do their jobs for once without your interference, will you? For God's sake, Mercy, you're a pampered young lady from Boston! You have no business fiddling with murder."

"But Phil said some detective named O'Reilly would lead the case, and you told me yourself that O'Reilly hates you."

"Yeah, well, I don't like him, either."

"Why not? What did he do?"

Ernie's grin was wry. "You're sure our animosity is all his fault, are you? How very loyal of you."

I felt myself flush, blast it. "Don't be ridiculous. You've already told me most L.A. coppers are as dirty as old laundry. Is O'Reilly a dirty cop? Is that why you don't like him? And he doesn't like you because you're not dirty?" Oh, boy, if my mother ever heard me talk like that, she'd have a fit—or, which is more likely, she'd give *me* one.

"He was one of the policemen on the Taylor case. They really botched that case. So badly that it's never been solved. Some of them were paid off. I'm as sure of that as I am my own name."

"I see." Ernie had told me he'd decided to leave the L.A.P.D. after William Desmond Taylor's murder and its resultant deplorable investigation by the police. They did such a lousy job that the case isn't solved to this day. "So you suspect O'Reilly might be on the take? And maybe you told him so? And that's why he hates you?"

"Yeah, yeah. It doesn't matter."

"Nonsense! It might matter a whole lot, Ernest Templeton. If there's a dirty cop who hates you investigating this case, it could mean the difference between the real culprit being caught or you being blamed for a crime you didn't commit. You can't leave it to O'Reilly to solve this crime, Ernie. We'll have to investigate it ourselves."

Ernie let out a huge gust of air, as if he didn't want to pursue this matter anymore. "Hell, let O'Reilly hate me. He's a good cop. More or less. No worse than most, at any rate. All I'm saying is that *you* need to butt out of this case. It has nothing to do with you."

If I'd forsaken my roots as much as I liked to pretend I had, I'd have sworn at him. But I couldn't make myself form a swear word at that moment in time, even in my head. I was standing there, feeling totally furious but impotent to express myself when Ernie continued.

"And if you *do* continue to interfere, I'll damned well fire you!"

My mouth dropped open in astonishment. I snapped it shut and said, "You wouldn't!"

"I would."

He appeared to mean it. I was so angry I could have spat railroad spikes. Since I was unable to do that any more than I could curse, I said, "Good. Fire me. Then I'll have all day, every day, for however long it takes, to investigate Mrs. Chalmers' murder!"

I left Ernie's office while he was still rolling his eyes and muttering swear words—he didn't have my personal qualms against cursing, blast him—slamming the door behind me. I was sorry about the slam, not because I thought Ernie deserved a silently closed door, but because my mother and Chloe had managed to enter the office while I'd been arguing with Ernie inside his office.

Sweet Lord, have mercy on Mercy, please. I know: you're not supposed to pray as if you're asking Father Christmas for things, but I couldn't help myself at that moment in time. Stopping in my tracks from what had been a pretty nifty flounce, I gaped at the two women in consternation. For once in my life, I didn't know what to say.

Mother never had that problem. "Mercedes Louise Allcutt, your behavior since you moved from your home in Boston to this city of sin becomes more deplorable every day."

I swallowed. "Good morning, Mother. Hey, Chloe."

My sister and I exchanged a grimace of mutual sympathy. In truth, Chloe was worse off than I as far as dealing with our mother went, because she didn't have a lovely job as a private investigator's secretary to which she could escape Mother's presence. See? There you have yet one more good reason for women to seek employment.

"Um, I didn't know you were in Los Angeles, Mother."

"I arrived today. The trip was grueling, but one must endure if one is to prevail."

Exactly the point I'd been trying to make with Ernie. However, I didn't appreciate my mother talking about enduring and prevailing after grueling. For heaven's sake, all she'd had to do was take a train from Boston to Los Angeles. *I* had to solve a ghastly murder. Well, I didn't actually *have* to, but . . . Oh, you know what I mean.

"You're coming to luncheon with us right this minute, Mercedes Louise," my mother went on to say. "We have a number of things to discuss."

Uh-oh. This didn't sound good. Mind you, I'd stood up to my mother before, but it had been a hair-raising experience, and I didn't relish having to do it again. I suspected this luncheon idea was being proposed to me—I mean demanded of me—because she wanted to bully me into moving to Pasadena to live in the home she and my father had bought a month or so ago as a winter residence.

I looked at the clock on the wall. It was almost twelve-thirty. Just about time for lunch, unfortunately, so I couldn't get out of this demand by pleading work to do. Nevertheless, since I really didn't want to dine with my maternal parent, I said, "Let me see if Mr. Templeton needs me for anything, Mother. We run an extremely busy office here, you know."

Very well, so I'd just lied to my mother. You'd have lied to her, too, if she were your mother.

"Nonsense," Mother said. "This *job* idiocy has got to stop."

"No," I said firmly. "It does not have to stop. I like my job, and I intend to keep it."

"In that case," said a voice from Ernie's office door, which now stood open revealing Ernie in his coat and hat—his coat and hat were the first garments he removed in the morning after he arrived at the office—"you won't be messing around in the current case, will you?"

His smile was positively evil.

"I don't *mess around* with any of your cases, Mr. Templeton, thank you very much."

He ignored me. Removing the hat he'd so recently donned, he bowed to my mother. It was an ironical bow, but I'm pretty sure my mother didn't know that. "How do you do, Mrs. All-cutt? How nice to see you again."

Very well, so Ernie lies, too. He's had more practice in the activity than I, so his lie didn't count.

"And good day to you, too, Chloe. Good to see you."

He wasn't lying that time. Chloe and Ernie liked each other.

"Hey, Ernie. Good to see you, too."

Our mother said, "I'm perfectly exhausted, young man, and I intend to take my daughter to luncheon." She added an imperious "Now," to her command.

"Be my guest," said Ernie, plopping his hat on his head once more. "See you back at the office after *luncheon,* Mercy, unless you decide to use the sense God gave a flea."

And he left the office with one of his more insouciant waves.

"Deplorable manners," Mother muttered. "I don't know how you can work for such a man, Mercedes Louise."

And I didn't know why Mother persisted in calling me *Mercedes Louise* every time she spoke to me. It's not as if I didn't know who I was, for heaven's sake.

"Manners in Los Angeles are less rigid than they are in Boston, Mother." Resigning myself to my fate, I fetched my hat—a cunning cloche that went well with the white shirt, blue blazer, and gray flannel skirt I wore—and handbag from my drawer.

"Yes. I noticed that the last time I was here. Shocking. Absolutely shocking."

Shocking, my eye. If she wanted shocking, I could tell her some really shocking stories. Not that I ever would. I had enough trouble with Mother already, and she only knew a mere tenth or so of what my job entailed.

"Then I'm surprised you and Father wish to spend half the year here," I said, knowing as I did so that I was provoking the dragon.

"You know very well why we plan on spending our winters in California. For one thing, the weather in Pasadena during the winter months is more salubrious than that in Boston. For another thing, Pasadena, unlike Los Angeles, is a civilized city."

So much for me.

In silence we took the elevator down to the lobby where Lulu wasn't. She'd gone to lunch, too, I suppose. It was just as well. I could tell her all about my *luncheon* with my mother when I came back to the Figueroa Building and garner much sympathy from doing so. Lulu had met my mother, too.

In silence Chloe drove us to the Ambassador Hotel, which was fairly new, and where all the so-called stars of the moving-picture industry dined. I'd just as soon grab a tamale and a lemonade from a street vendor or a corned-beef sandwich with Lulu, but today I was with Mother, and Mother didn't do things like that. She'd undoubtedly faint if faced with a tamale, and I believe I've already mentioned her feelings about corned beef.

Chloe entered the restaurant first, which was a good thing since the place was packed and the maître d', who smiled

69

warmly at us, knew her and Harvey. Evidently she'd telephoned ahead for a reservation, because he said, "Please come this way, ladies. It's a pleasure to see you again, Mrs. Nash."

"Thank you, Houston. This is my mother, Mrs. Allcutt, and my sister, Miss Allcutt."

Houston, a tall, dignified fellow who looked rather oldish, with white hair and moustache and a perfectly splendid black suit, bowed to us both. His bow wasn't ironical at all. His living depended on kowtowing to people who considered themselves important, so he probably didn't dare be anything but absolutely respectful until after he got off work. After that, I suspected he and his cronies laughed a lot at the airs and graces some people adopted. I did notice that Chloe slipped something into his hand as she stepped aside to introduce Mother and me, so I have a feeling he'd had to make room for us, probably by ousting some other, more deserving, diners. Money talks. Even I know that.

He held chairs for Mother, Chloe, and then me. I smiled at him, and he smiled back, which was nice.

Naturally, as soon as we were seated, Mother started in on me. "You're deplorably underdressed for dining in this restaurant, Mercedes Louise." She looked around the room with an upper-crust sneer. "Even if it is in Los Angeles."

"I didn't know you were going to make me go to the Ambassador for luncheon, Mother," said I, snapping my menu open.

"*Make* you go to the Ambassador? I should think you'd be grateful for a nice meal instead of devouring one of the corned-beef sandwiches Chloe has informed me you feed on regularly."

I shot a scowl at Chloe, but I couldn't really blame her for telling on me. After all, she had to say something to our mother, who was a difficult conversationalist at the best of times. Therefore, my scowl only lasted a second before I grinned at my sister. "I adore corned-beef sandwiches," I said to Mother.

"With sauerkraut, especially."

Mother would have shuddered had she been another sort of woman. She wasn't. Instead, she pressed her lips together and decided to save her guns for the bigger battle, which, I suspected, would be that of forcing me to move in with her and Father.

Talk about grueling! I'm surprised I survived that luncheon with Chloe and our mutual mother with my skin intact. The entire meal, except when we were chewing, was devoted to my lack of family feeling, disgraceful behavior, and general moral laxity.

I more or less staggered into the Figueroa Building at one-thirty or thereabouts, having left Mother steaming in Chloe's machine, and not from the heat of the day, but from the heat of her anger with me. Thank God Lulu LaBelle had returned from her own lunch (short form) and occupied the desk in the lobby, where she sat in one of her more astonishing costumes, filing her nails. She filed her nails almost constantly. I'm not sure why.

As soon as Lulu saw me, she jumped to her feet. "Oh, Mercy! Ernie told me about your mother. I'm so sorry!"

Removing my hat and sinking slowly into the chair before Lulu's desk, I whimpered, "It was awful, Lulu."

"Where'd she take you?"

Lulu asked the question almost avidly, and I might have resented her tone except that I understood Lulu knew I'd come from "money," as Ernie so inelegantly put it, because she'd told me Ernie'd ratted on me. Lulu came from the same small town in Oklahoma where her brother had originated. I'm sure she expected me to have gone somewhere grand. And I had. Not that I'd wanted to.

"The Ambassador," I said, still whimpering.

"The Ambassador? Oh, my!"

Lulu's breathy voice told me how much she'd like to go to the Ambassador for a meal someday. Next time my mother ordered me to go to luncheon with her, maybe I'd send Lulu in my stead.

But no. I couldn't do that to Lulu. She didn't deserve my mother any more than I did.

"Did you see any stars?" Lulu asked.

"Stars?" Had I seen any? Boy, I hadn't even dared look around. I'd pretty much just tried to choke down my lobster thermidor and not wither under Mother's blistering scorn. "I'm sorry, Lulu. I didn't notice."

Lulu gasped. "You didn't *notice?*"

I'd have felt guilty except that . . . well, Lulu had met my mother. I only stared at her.

She gazed sorrowfully upon me. "I'm sorry, Mercy. I'm glad my mother isn't like yours."

"For your sake and Rupert's, I'm glad, too."

As I've already mentioned, Rupert Mullins was Lulu's brother. Mind you, Lulu's last name was LaBelle, but she'd chosen it for herself, figuring LaBelle would look better on a theater marquee than would Mullins. She aimed to be discovered one day by a talent scout or a director or a producer. I wasn't sure this was a sound plan on her part, since it didn't seem to me that talent scouts were thick on the ground in the Figueroa Building, but I'd already carved out my own career. If sitting behind the receptionist's desk was how Lulu planned to carve hers, who was I to judge? Anyhow, Rupert was employed by a dear friend of Chloe's and, now, mine, Mr. Francis Easthope, one of the world's most gorgeous men—but a really nice one.

"But didn't you even see one star? Not one little teensy little star?"

I gazed as woefully upon her as she'd gazed upon me seconds earlier. "I'm sorry, Lulu. Would you like it if I took you to lunch at the Ambassador one of these days? I'm sure I'll have a better time with you than with my mother, and it would be fun to look around and see if we recognize any picture people."

She gawked at me as if I'd lost what was left of my mind. "*You* can't get into the Ambassador! You have to be famous to go there."

Puzzled, I said, "I'm not famous, and they let me in there today."

"But your sister is married to *Harvey Nash,* one of the picture business's most important people! The Ambassador would let a Nash in."

Was Harvey really that important? Gee, I hadn't known that. How fascinating. "Oh," I said, befuddled for a moment. Then I thought of an answer to the Ambassador problem. "I can still take you. I'll just ask Chloe to call for a reservation." And then I'd bribe Houston when we got there, but I didn't need to tell Lulu that part.

Lulu clutched her clasped hands to her heart. I hoped she hadn't just applied a coat of varnish to those pointy nails, or her alarmingly fuchsia dress might be ruined. "Would you do that, Mercy? Really and truly?"

"Really and truly."

"You're a real pal, Mercy." There were honest-to-God tears in Lulu's eyes.

For some reason, having made Lulu happy lessened the debilitating effect of having spent the better part of an hour being vilified by my mother. It was a brighter Mercy Allcutt who climbed the stairs to the third floor of the Figueroa Building to begin my afternoon's work. The understanding that Mother would soon be on her way to Pasadena as I climbed helped my mood, too. With any luck, she wouldn't be marring the atmosphere in Chloe's house when I got home from work, and I wouldn't have to deal with her again for a few days, at least.

When I entered the office, I saw that Ernie's door was shut. Darn. He must have someone in there with him. I hoped it wasn't an L.A.P.D. officer like that O'Reilly character who'd come to arrest him. I removed my hat and put it and my handbag and gloves into the drawer where they always resided when I was at work and wondered if I should knock on the door and ask if Ernie needed me.

He very seldom needed me, but that didn't mean he didn't need me at that particular moment, particularly if the L.A.P.D. was giving him the third degree. Whatever that was. Or whatever mean-tempered L.A. coppers did to people.

Mind you, having held my own against my unreasonably formidable mother for an hour didn't exactly make me yearn to deal with yet more difficult people. Still and all, Ernie was my boss, and as a loyal employee it was my duty to make his working life easier in any way that I could.

Steeling my nerves—I seemed to be doing that a lot in those days—and squaring my shoulders, I retrieved my secretarial notebook and a sharpened pencil from the cunning little pencil cup I'd bought in Chinatown and headed for Ernie's door. There I rapped sharply. If the police had Ernie tied to a chair and were shining a bright light in his eyes, I aimed to stop them, by gum.

"Yeah?"

Hmm. Ernie's voice didn't sound as if he were being coerced into confessing to a murder he hadn't committed. Nevertheless, I took a deep breath for courage and opened the office door.

Phil.

Well, nuts. Here'd I'd had Ernie being tortured, and the only person in his office was Phil Bigelow, detective with the L.A.P.D. and Ernie's best friend. What's more, Ernie's feet were propped on his desk and he had his hands behind his head, cupping it as he lounged back in his swivel chair.

"Good *luncheon,* Mercy?" Ernie's grin was positively wicked.

I wanted to heave my secretarial notebook at him, but even I realized the impulse to be unfair. After all, Ernie couldn't have known of my worries on his account.

"My luncheon was hellish, thank you, Ernie." I don't believe I'd ever used a word like *hellish* before. For some reason, saying so shocking a word bolstered my courage. I turned to Phil. "Have you caught Mrs. Chalmers' murderer yet, Phil?"

A duet of heavy sighs filled the air.

Phil answered first. "Not yet. But we will. We're working hard on it. Don't forget, it's not my case. It's O'Reilly's."

I huffed my opinion of that circumstance.

"And they don't need any help from you, Mercy," Ernie added, as if he hadn't already told me that six or seven hundred times already.

"I'm sure," I said, using as much sarcasm as I was able to use, which wasn't a whole lot. No matter how much I wished it were otherwise, I had been reared by my mother, after all.

"Have a seat," said Phil cordially.

I eyed him suspiciously. "Why?"

"She can't add anything to what she's already told you, Phil." Ernie's voice exuded peevishness.

Feeling the need of a target at the moment, although I don't really know why, I turned on my boss with fury. "And how do you know that, Ernest Templeton? I'm the one who found Mrs. Chalmers, after all, not to mention *you.* For all either of you know, *I* killed the stupid woman!" For the life of me, I don't know why I said that.

Ernie had the everlasting gall to burst out laughing.

When I squinted at Phil, I could tell he was trying not to do likewise.

75

Very well, I knew I was a most unlikely suspect as a cold-blooded murderer. Still, I didn't like being laughed at. Sniffing, I took up Phil's offer to sit and sat.

You may have noticed that I neglected to mention that the men in the office rose from their chairs upon my entry into it. That's because they didn't rise upon my entry. They remained seated solidly on their chairs. I think this behavior, rather than being ungentlemanly in terms prescribed by my mother and father, only means that secretaries were considered by the populace in general not to be ladies. Not that secretaries were thought of as scarlet women or anything else in that sense, but rather that we weren't considered the types of ladies for whom gentlemen rose politely upon their entry onto a scene. We secretaries were of the working classes—or most of us were, anyhow—and, therefore, not ladies in the gentlemen-rising sense of the word.

But that's neither here nor there, although the behavior of the two men helped solidify my opinion that people like my mother didn't know anything at all about the real world.

I sat, and Ernie and Phil remained seated. Then, sensing Ernie was a lost cause, I turned my attention to Phil. "You did know, did you not, that Mrs. Chalmers was a recent convert to the Adelaide Burkhard Emmanuel school of religion and spent tons and tons of money there? Mrs. Emmanuel is the one who built that gigantic Angelica Gospel Hall."

"*Sister* Emmanuel," Ernie corrected snidely.

"Right," said Phil. He did not say it as Ernie might have: that is to say with biting sarcasm. He only said it.

"And that Mr. Simon Chalmers, Mr. Chalmers' son, resented her spending a lot of his father's money at the place."

Phil's right eyebrow rose. "He did?"

Aha! I'd managed to tell him something he hadn't known before! I'd have smirked at Ernie, but I didn't do things like that. Very often. "That's the impression I got when I spoke to him yesterday. That he resented it. He sounded quite scornful about her affiliation with the place, anyway."

"Hmm," said Phil. "I didn't get the impression that the elder Mr. Chalmers minded his wife's involvement with the Hall. In fact, he said he didn't mind at all."

A little deflated, I said, "Mr. Simon Chalmers told me the same thing. He said his father loved his stepmother and didn't care what she did."

With his left eyebrow lifting to join his right one, Phil said, "He didn't express that exact sentiment to us when we spoke to him."

"I imagine he didn't," I said, and rather drily, too, I admit.

"Damn it, Mercy, will you stay out of this investigation?" Ernie. Mad at me. Again.

I sighed.

Phil said, "Face it, Ernie. She was an important witness at the scene. She's the *only* witness, in fact. She's the one who found the body. And, according to the two of you, you. You know darned good and well that O'Reilly will pin this on you if he can. He's hated you ever since you told him what you thought of him during the Taylor investigation. The more people we can get on your side, the better off we'll be. Under the circumstances, Mercy almost has to be involved in the solution of the case."

Exactly what I'd said. So why was it, I wondered bitterly, that Ernie would probably agree with Phil when he absolutely refused to agree with me?

But I was wrong about that.

"Damnation, Phil! You know how she butts in! For God's sake, she's almost been killed twice in the past couple of months because she insists on getting herself mixed up with suspects in murder cases. I don't want her any more involved with this one than she absolutely has to be!"

"I'm right here, Mr. Templeton. You can just as easily speak to me as to Phil."

"I've already spoken to you!" Ernie roared. "Talking to you is like talking to a pile of rocks. You don't listen!"

Rolling my eyes, something I don't believe I'd ever once done in Boston, I tutted.

Phil, the rat, said, "He's right, Mercy. You really don't need to be involved any further in the case than you already have been unless O'Reilly needs to question you again. We have your statement, and if you remember anything else you might have seen or heard there, just telephone me. All right? Don't do any running around on your own."

"Running around on my *own?*" Indignation swelled my bosom. Well, I didn't see it actually swell my bosom, but you know what I mean. I stood so quickly, my chair almost fell over backward. Phil caught it and righted it. "I don't plan to do any *running around on my own,* Detective Bigelow. Thank you *so* much for your tender concern for my welfare!"

Right before I slammed the office door, I heard Phil mutter a quiet, "Whoops."

Ernie's office door opened even before I'd managed to sit in my chair. I glared at it to see Phil standing there, looking sheepish.

"I'm sorry, Mercy. I don't know why I said that."

"I do," I said grumpily. "Neither you nor Ernie think I have a lick of sense."

"That's not true." He seemed to hesitate for a minute before pulling a folded paper from his inside coat pocket. "Um, I brought the statement you gave Officer Bloom. I'd appreciate it if you'd look it over and sign it."

I heaved a big sigh. "Very well. Hand it over."

So he did. I waved at the chair next to my desk, and Phil sat while I read every single word of Officer Bloom's report on the statement I'd given him the day before. I had to correct his punctuation once or twice and his spelling a few times, but other than that the statement seemed complete.

I eyed Phil narrowly. "So where do I sign it?"

He pointed to the bottom of the page. "Right there, please."

So I signed my full name, Mercedes Louise Allcutt, and thrust the paper at Phil.

"Don't be angry with Ernie, Mercy. He's only concerned about your welfare."

I said, "Huh," and pretended to type something.

Phil sighed, rose, and left the office.

CHAPTER SIX

Thank the good Lord and distance, our mother had already left for Pasadena by the time I got home from the office. According to Chloe, she didn't plan to grace us with another appearance until Sunday evening, when she'd invited herself to dinner.

"She expects to see motion picture stars when she dines with us," Chloe said upon a deep and mournful sigh.

Hugging Buttercup to my bosom, I said, "I thought she deplored stars and everything else about the motion-picture industry."

"Of course she does," said Chloe, still mournful. "That doesn't mean she doesn't want to meet some stars anyway."

"Hmm," I said, thinking the matter over. "That's probably so that she can deplore them to their faces."

"Probably." Chloe plopped herself down on the sofa. "May I borrow Buttercup for a moment? I need some comfort."

Although I, too, needed comfort, I handed Buttercup over to my sister. All things considered, Chloe probably needed more solace than I at that moment. After all, I'd only been peeved by luncheon with my mother and conversations with two idiotic men. Poor Chloe had endured our mother almost the entire day. She not only deserved Buttercup; the woman deserved a medal of valor or something.

"How about I get you and Harvey a toy poodle for Christmas?" I asked, thinking the idea a particularly bright one even as it occurred to me.

Chloe actually cheered up, so I guess I was right. "Oh, Mercy, would you? I'd love that! Then our little tyke can grow up with a dog. Every child needs a dog."

I pondered her statement for a second or two. "Neither of us ever had a dog. Neither did George."

Chloe only looked upon me with something akin to derision in her expression.

"You're right, of course. But *real* children do need dogs."

"I couldn't agree with you more," said Chloe. "And I would love to have a little Buttercup of my own. Or my child's own."

"You know, it's actually fortunate for the dog that George never had one."

"Too true. Can you imagine what the poor creature would have endured if it had been entrusted to George's tender mercies?"

"Hideous thought."

"Any dog worth its salt would have died of boredom," Chloe said.

"Precisely."

"Can you imagine that a woman actually went so far as to *marry* him?"

"Well," I said after pondering the question for a heartbeat, "yes. I knew her better than you did, so I do understand. She's every bit as ghastly as George."

"Hard to imagine."

"I know, but it's true."

With another sigh, Chloe said, "No wonder Mother approves of her."

She was right about that, so I went on to a more pertinent subject. "So where are you going to get stars to come and dine with us on Sunday?"

"Oh, I don't know. I'll ask Harvey. He's probably got some of them hanging around the studio somewhere."

"They aren't all on location somewhere?" I was beginning to get the hang of the picture industry lingo. "On location" meant that the actors, cameramen, directors, and so forth were filming at a remote spot some distance from the studio, generally in the desert somewhere in San Bernardino County.

"Heavens, no. They've built an entire western town in back of the studio. That's where they film most of the western pictures these days. It's cheaper than transporting them all to the Mojave Desert."

"Interesting. But do you think Mother would be happy with a western actor? I suspect she's more the John Barrymore type."

"Not likely," Chloe scoffed. "He's always got a drink in his hand."

"Oh, dear. No. Mother wouldn't like that one little bit."

"But I'll find one or two of them somewhere. Harvey's crews are always building sets at the studio. They don't just film westerns there."

It occurred to me that we were discussing human beings as if they were some sort of exotic species of animal, and I decided to change the subject. "Do you know what time Mother will be arriving on Sunday?"

"No, but I doubt that she'll arrive any earlier than six or seven. I'll set dinner for eight."

"Oh, good. Because I want to do something else in the morning, and I don't want Mother to know about it."

Chloe looked a question at me.

Smiling brightly, I said, "I plan to attend services at the Angelica Gospel Hall!"

Chloe nearly fainted.

Nevertheless, two days after that conversation, and after reading articles about the place and studying pictures of people who attended the Angelica Gospel Hall—it doesn't do to attend a function somewhere unless you know how the inhabitants thereof dress—I got into one of my Boston Sunday suits, a blue number crafted of all-wool Poiret twill. It had no decoration other than bands of striped Poiret twill. It had been wildly expensive—all my Boston clothes were—but unless you knew clothes, you wouldn't know that. The dress was simple and discreet, and it kind of matched my eyes. I wore a simple bone-colored hat, gloves, and shoes, and snatched up my handbag in the same color. I knew Chloe would tell me I appeared dull and drab, but that's exactly the image I was striving for: dullness.

As soon as I descended the staircase, preceded by a rapturously happy Buttercup, who didn't know she was going to be left alone that morning, I saw Chloe in the breakfast room, nibbling on a soda cracker and with a steaming cup of tea before her. She looked me up and down with a frown on her pretty face.

"You really meant it, didn't you? You actually *are* going to that dreadful woman's church this morning. You haven't looked that gawd-awful boring since you arrived here from Boston."

I let her comment slide. "You betcha," said I, going to the sideboard to see what goodies Mrs. Biddle had prepared for our morning meal. No soda crackers for me, by gum, especially since I had to fuel myself for a brand-new adventure. "Didn't I tell you about Mrs. Persephone Chalmers and her association with the Angelica Gospel Hall?"

Chloe nodded. "Yes, but what does that have to do with you?"

I turned upon my sister, astounded by her question. "What does it have to do with *me?* I'm the one who found the woman's dead body! I'm the one whose boss is the prime suspect! If the real killer isn't found, and found fast, the coppers are going to pin the crime on Ernie! The lead detective on the case already hates Ernie's guts." *Guts* was a disgusting word. I'm not sure why I used it on Chloe that morning except that I was repeating what Ernie had told me.

"Well, yes. I know that—about Ernie being at the scene. Not about the detective who hates him. But I bet Ernie doesn't want you prying into the case. He hates it when you do that."

"I know he does," I grumbled. "But I'll bet I can get more information about the Chalmers woman from going to the Angelica Gospel Hall than Detective O'Reilly and all his policemen will get from the members of that congregation."

"Who's Detective O'Reilly?"

"The detective who's going to lead the case instead of Phil Bigelow. The one who hates Ernie's guts." Shoot. There I went again.

Chloe didn't seem to mind about the word. "Lord. Mother will croak if she ever finds out you went to that place."

The thought held some appeal, actually, but I said, "Then don't tell her."

Chloe heaved a large-sized sigh. "I'll try not to. But you know how she gets, and when she stares at me with those eyes of hers . . ." My sister shuddered eloquently, and I forgave her ahead of time for telling Mother about my morning's churchgoing activities.

Mind you, Mother would have been happy if her children were to go to the right church. In other words, if Chloe and I attended services at an Episcopal Church, she'd be delighted—or as delighted as Mother ever got about anything. But she'd have all sorts of vile things to say to me when Chloe told her about my visit to the Angelica Gospel Hall. I decided to change the subject.

"Whom did you get to come to dinner? What stars do you have in mind for our mother's delectation—or deploration, I guess. Is that a word?" I took my plate, filled with scrambled eggs, bacon, and a muffin to the table.

"I don't know." Chloe looked at my plate and shuddered

again, but I was hungry.

Tossing Buttercup a piece of bacon, I headed back to the sideboard to get a dish of strawberries and some coffee.

"Renee Adoree and John Gilbert."

My eyes widened, and I darned near stepped on Buttercup. "My goodness, Chloe! They're *really* famous! I mean, they're really *stars!*"

I got the impression my sister's ennui that morning was unfeigned. She didn't look well, and she eyed me wearily.

"I know it. That's why I invited them. Fortunately, they're both between pictures at the moment."

"Are you going to serve wine?" Although I was still goggling at Chloe, I managed to get some scrambled eggs and muffin into my mouth. There wasn't much that could keep me from my food.

Chloe shrugged. "Have to. It's what you do at a dinner party these days."

"Won't Mother screech?"

"She'd better not if she ever expects to be invited to another dinner party at *my* house."

"I thought she'd invited herself this time." But I smiled broadly at my sister, whose last comment had been spoken with the firmness of strict truth.

"Well, she did, but I'm fully capable of thwarting future attempts if she misbehaves. Especially now, when I feel so puny."

"Good for you! I mean, good for you for standing up to Mother. I'm awfully sorry you're feeling puny."

"It's all right. I know what you meant."

Since Buttercup was performing one of her adorable tricks by sitting on her rump and waving her paws at me, I tossed her a bite of muffin. Which reminded me. "What color poodle do you want?"

"Color? Poodle?" Chloe blinked at me slowly.

85

"What's wrong, Chloe." I was really beginning to worry about her. "Are you sick?"

She shook her head. "No. Not really. I just feel sick to my stomach in the mornings. The feeling usually goes away by ten or so. But I'm tired all the time. I hope that passes."

"I'm sorry."

"Not as sorry as I am."

I'm sure that was the strict truth, too. I also reminded myself once again how lucky I was to have a job to which I could escape. Being around a sick Chloe for several hours every morning would dampen anyone's spirits, even those of a fond sister.

"Well?" I prodded.

"I'm thinking. What colors do poodles come in?"

"Well, I've seen a black one, and I think there are white ones, and rusty-red ones. Besides the blondies like Buttercup, of course." I tossed my wonderful dog another tidbit, telling myself even as I did so that I probably shouldn't feed her at the table. If Mother ever found out, she'd never stop scolding me.

Mother. Ever the problem.

Harvey showed up just then. He hurried to Chloe's chair and rubbed her shoulders. "Still feeling sick, honey?"

Chloe put a hand on his. "Yes, but don't worry about me. They tell me this sort of thing is normal when a woman is in the family way."

Distressing thought. Maybe I'd stick to poodles and never get married and have children.

"I'm so sorry, honey." Harvey meant it. He and Chloe were the perfect couple. I mean that sincerely. They absolutely belonged together, which made me happy since . . . well, since they *were* together, if you know what I mean.

Chloe tried to put on a brighter expression. "Mercy's getting us a toy poodle for Christmas, Harvey. What color do you want?"

Harvey, continuing to massage Chloe's shoulders, looked

from me to Buttercup and back again, his eyebrows lifting, whether in delight or surprise I couldn't tell. "That's nice of you, Mercy, but . . . They come in different colors?"

"Tell him, Mercy." Chloe allowed her head to fall forward as she enjoyed Harvey's massaging fingers.

"Black, reddish-brown, white, and golden like Buttercup."

"I like Buttercup a lot," said the ever-diplomatic Harvey, "but I'd kind of like a black one. Maybe."

"Black is a very sophisticated color," I told him. Chloe had enlightened me on that important reality of life; otherwise I wouldn't have known. "In fact, the very first toy poodle I ever met was black, and she was the reason I decided to get Buttercup."

"Black it is, then," said Chloe.

By that time, Buttercup and I had finished breakfast, so I led her out to the backyard where she did her duty as a dog, and then I left the house for the Angelica Gospel Hall. I'd called ahead for a taxicab, and when I told him my destination, he said he didn't need me to tell him the address.

"Everybody's going there these days," he said, trying, I'm sure, to make friendly conversation on our journey.

"That's what I hear. I figured I'd go and see what all the fuss is about."

I could tell he was grinning even though I sat in the back seat. "Hellfire and brimstone, I imagine."

"Maybe. Actually, I've read that Mrs. Emmanuel preaches more about joy and happiness than hellfire and brimstone."

"Yeah? Well, that'd be a new approach, huh?"

"Indeed it would."

In actual fact, once I got there and Mrs. Emmanuel began preaching, I discovered both the cabbie and I had been right to one degree or another. I'd never seen a minister preach in so . . . boisterous a manner. Boisterousness isn't a word one associates with Episcopalians, and that's what my family is. Was. Oh, bother. You know what I mean.

I'd never been in a church where the members of the congregation felt free to vent their feelings with loud calls of "Amen!" and the waving of hands in the air, either. Sister Emmanuel seemed to eat up the enthusiasm, and I could almost understand the attraction of a happy and loving faith in one's god, although my stubborn Bostonian breeding kept me glued to my pew, and I only opened my mouth in order to sing the hymns, most of which were new to me. The entire experience was most enlightening as far as understanding the appeal to so many of the Angelica Gospel Hall and its leader, but I didn't know how attending this service was going to help me solve the murder of Mrs. Chalmers. There I was, stuck in a pew, and there wasn't an appealing suspect in sight. Even if there had been, I was in no position to interrogate him or her.

The worst part was yet to come. After the final amen sounded from His people again, as the old hymn puts it, people stood up, turned in their pews, and began cheerfully embracing and blessing one another. Never, in my entire life, had I imagined that such activities could take place in a church.

The lady beside me said, "God bless you, sister!"

I gulped and said, "God bless you . . . sister."

Then she grabbed me in a big, fat hug. After a second or two spent being appalled and stiff, I unbent and hugged her back. What the heck. I was there, and this was clearly the conduct expected of anyone who was there. My mother was going to freeze into a block of ice when she heard about this latest instance of what she would term unruly behavior on my part.

The hug knocked my pew mate's hat askew, so when she ultimately released me, she straightened it, smiled brightly upon me, and said, "I haven't seen you here before, sister. Did you hear the call?"

The call? "Um . . ."

She evidently didn't need anyone to respond to her questions in order for her to carry on a conversation, because she went on as if she hadn't expected a reply from me. "So many people are being called by the Lord to come to Jesus through Sister Emmanuel." Enthusiasm. The woman definitely had enthusiasm for this new breed of evangelism.

I tried again. "Um . . ."

"Isn't Sister Emmanuel wonderful? Why, I can hear Jesus speaking right through her! I'm sure you could, too."

"Um . . ."

"The Angelica Gospel Hall and Sister Emmanuel have changed my life since I began coming here." She clasped her hands in a frenzy of worshipful ecstasy.

It had changed Mrs. Chalmers' life a whole lot, too, thought I, rather more cynically than was normal for me. However, I was truly unaccustomed to this sort of freewheeling behavior in church. I knew even then that my distaste was primarily due to my stuffy upbringing, but some personality traits are difficult to change when they've been drummed into one from the cradle. It was one thing for me to move to Los Angeles and secure employment. It was an entirely other thing for me to jump up and down and holler in church, for heaven's sake. Or embrace perfect strangers.

"Please," said the woman, still floating on a cloud of glory, "won't you tell me your name and why you chose to come to the light today?"

"Um . . . why, yes. My name is Miss Mercedes Allcutt. Everyone calls me Mercy. I actually came to this church today because a . . . an acquaintance of mine had started attending here not long ago." That was true. In a way. I'd met Mrs. Chalmers a time or two before she was murdered.

"Oh?" The woman seemed even more enthusiastic at hearing

I had a congregation member as a friend than she was before. I wouldn't have believed such a thing to be possible unless I'd seen it for myself. "Who is that?"

I cleared my throat. "Mrs. Persephone Chalmers."

"One of my dearest friends!" squealed the woman. Then she lowered her voice. "My name is Elizabeth Pinkney. Mrs. Gaylord Pinkney. He—Mr. Pinkney—doesn't attend church with me." She appeared downcast for a moment, as if regretting that Gaylord wouldn't end up in heaven with her when God blew his golden trump. Or was it one of his archangels who was going to blow the trump? Well, I don't suppose it matters.

"I'm sorry to hear that," I said, sensing that perhaps I could actually learn something from this trip to church after all. "I don't believe Mr. Chalmers attended with Mrs. Chalmers, either."

"I don't believe he did, but I don't think he dislikes the place as poor Mr. Pinkney does."

Aha! I was getting somewhere! Maybe. "I'm sorry your husband doesn't . . . appreciate Sister Emmanuel's message." There. That had been tactful, and it was even the truth.

"It's a shame. But I'm sure he'll come 'round in the end. I pray for him every day."

"How very kind of you." I hoped she did her praying in private and didn't do so in front of the poor man. If the latter situation prevailed, it wouldn't have surprised me to discover an article about the decease of Mrs. Gaylord Pinkney in the *Times* one day.

"It's all I can do, pray for him. I think he's weakening."

I said, "Let us all hope so," although I kind of felt sorry for Mr. Pinkney.

Fortunately, Mrs. Pinkney dropped the subject of the prayed-over Mr. Pinkney and looked around at the milling throng. People had begun to exit the sanctuary. "I don't see Mrs.

Chalmers in church today. We usually sit together, so that rather surprises me. Did you say you'd planned on meeting her here?"

Oh, dear. This poor woman hadn't heard about Mrs. Chalmers' death yet. I'd read the obituary in the *Los Angeles Times* this morning, but since she'd died on Thursday and I hadn't discovered her body until the afternoon, and the police were involved and all, I guess the news didn't hit the Saturday paper. Naturally, the obituary hadn't mentioned anything about murder. It had only mentioned a "sudden and untimely" death.

So I decided that, if I couldn't honestly get as excited about this Angelica Gospel Hall thing as Mrs. Chalmers and Mrs. Pinkney, at least I could darned well act. Therefore, I put on a tragic expression, took hold of Mrs. Pinkney's arm and whispered in the most morose tone I could summon, "Oh, my dear, you haven't heard?"

Blinking and losing some of her gusto, Mrs. Pinkney said, "Heard what?"

I glanced around as if to make sure we weren't being overheard and then whispered even more morosely, "Mrs. Chalmers has passed on."

"P-passed on?" Mrs. Pinkney swallowed. "Whatever do you mean? I spoke with her on the telephone last Thursday morning."

"The very day of her death," said I in the voice of doom.

Mrs. Pinkney's hand flew to her bosom, where it remained. Her eyes widened, and I felt awful when I saw tears building in them. "How . . . how did she die?"

After glancing around one last time, I leaned toward Mrs. Pinkney and muttered, "She was *murdered.*"

Mrs. Pinkney let out a scream that might have torn the ceiling off the Angelica Gospel Hall. Then she fainted.

CHAPTER SEVEN

"Oh, dear, I'm so very sorry!" I whispered, appalled as I stared down at the gentleman who'd rushed over at Mrs. Pinkney's blood-curdling scream.

"Whatever in the world happened to her?"

A deacon, or whatever the folks at the Angelica Gospel Hall called those fellows, was chafing Mrs. Pinkney's hands and looking worried. It was he who'd asked the question, and he looked none too pleased. As for me, I was wishing frantically that I'd followed my mother's strict instruction always to carry a vial of smelling salts with me. Since I'd never fainted in my life and didn't intend to begin doing so any time soon, I hadn't thought I'd needed to follow her orders on my way to church that morning. Shows how much I knew.

"I . . . um, I told her that Mrs. Chalmers—she attended services here, and I guess Mrs. Pinkney knew her—had passed away. Then she screamed and fainted." I left out the part about Mrs. Chalmers having been murdered, which was what had actually brought on the shriek and the faint. I hoped God would forgive me for committing the sin of omission in church.

The deacon's neck nearly snapped when his head jerked up and he stared at me. "You know Mrs. Chalmers?" He was a gaunt-looking fellow, and my news didn't do a thing for his looks. I felt guilty. "You mean Mrs. Persephone Chalmers?"

There it was again. The Mrs. Persephone Chalmers thing. I'd wondered ever since I'd met her why Mrs. Chalmers didn't call herself Mrs. Franchot Chalmers, Franchot being her husband's first name. Not that I'd want to be called Mrs. Franchot anything at all, but I didn't think Franchot was any worse than Persephone. Or Clovilla or Mercedes, for that matter.

However, that is neither here nor there. I knew to whom he referred, and I nodded unhappily. "Yes. Mrs. Chalmers was . . ." Should I use the M word? Well, why not? I doubted this fellow would scream, and if he fainted, he was already pretty close to the floor. "She was murdered, actually. Last Thursday. In the late morning or the early afternoon." I didn't know the time of her death yet, but I'd deduced it from Ernie's statement.

"Murdered! Surely, you're mistaken." The word had so shaken him, he allowed poor Mrs. Pinkney's head to drop onto the tiled floor once more. I winced in sympathy at the dull *thunk,* but answered, annoyed by this fellow's suggestion that I was a liar.

"I am not mistaken," I said, bringing a little Boston ice to bear in my voice. "I found her body myself. It was a most unpleasant discovery, I can tell you."

"Oh, my dear Lord."

"Indeed."

"Whatever is the matter, Brother Everett?" said a new voice.

It was a voice I recognized. Turning in astonishment, I beheld, standing before me in her white robe and looking every bit as dramatic up close as she had upon the chancel behind her pulpit, Sister Adelaide Burkhard Emmanuel. I admit to being a trifle tongue-tied and star-stricken for a moment. I, who had been introduced to John Barrymore, Mary Pickford, and Douglas Fairbanks, and who would be dining with Renee Adoree and John Gilbert that very evening, for Pete's sake!

"Sister Emmanuel," said Brother Everett—I mean Mr. Everett, "this lady just told me that Sister Chalmers has been . . . murdered." He hadn't wanted to say the word any more than I'd wanted to.

"Sweet Lord, have mercy!" cried Sister Emmanuel, lifting her arms toward the church's ceiling and, therefore (I think), toward heaven. I also think she didn't mean the Lord to have me personally, which is why I didn't capitalize "mercy." "Let us pray, Brother Everett. Let us pray. Please join with us, young woman."

And darned if she didn't take my hand and pretty much force me to my knees. Personally, my attention was divided. I mean, Mrs. Pinkney might well be as dead as Mrs. Chalmers, as she still lay on the floor in a faint, but having my hands held by Sister Emmanuel and Brother Everett as Sister Emmanuel sent up an eloquent and very loud prayer also captured my interest.

I don't know how long Sister Emmanuel would have continued praying if Mrs. Pinkney hadn't let out a pained-sounding moan.

"Amen!" shouted Sister Emmanuel. Then she reached for Mrs. Pinkney and lifted her head into her lap.

Did you understand those pronouns? The English language suffers from severe pronominal deficiencies in my opinion. Not that my opinion matters. What I meant was that Sister Emmanuel lifted Mrs. Pinkney's head and placed it on Sister Emmanuel's lap. I thought that was quite a generous and democratic thing for her to do. Yet another difference between Sister Emmanuel and my mother, who wasn't democratic about anything at all. Dictatorial is what she was. And she wasn't even a preacher. My mother, I mean, not Sister Emmanuel. Pronouns. They can be *so* confusing.

But enough of that. Mrs. Pinkney was beginning to come around. She blinked once or twice, and her eyes looked kind of blank for a moment, and then she caught sight of me. I was still on the floor, kneeling, confused about what to do since I wasn't sure it would be polite to stand before Sister Emmanuel did—

kind of like you wouldn't stand in the presence of a queen if she were sitting or, as in this case, kneeling. When Mrs. Pinkney saw me, she snapped to attention, cried, "Oh, my goodness gracious!" and fainted again.

I was beginning to think I'd never get out of that place.

But I did. Eventually.

"Please lift our fallen sister, Brother Everett," said Sister Emmanuel, achieving remarkable results with a sugar-and-honey voice. This points out another reason one needn't be impolite to get one's meaning across. If I dared, I'd have mentioned this salient tip to my mother. "You may take her to my office and lay her on the sofa there until she's feeling better. I believe I have some smelling salts in the desk drawer. And I'm sure a strong, sweet cup of tea won't be amiss."

"I will, Sister Emmanuel," said Mr. Everett.

He was kind of a scrawny fellow, but he was certainly obedient. He lifted Mrs. Pinkney right up off the floor and staggered up the central aisle of the sanctuary, where he made a right turn and disappeared from sight.

Sister Emmanuel turned to me and I stiffened, expecting some sort of rebuke for having caused a ruckus in her sanctuary. But I'd underestimated Adelaide Burkhard Emmanuel. She held out her hand and said, "My poor dear woman. I'm so very sorry you had to bring us this distressing news. Won't you please come with me to my office and take a cup of tea?"

My goodness, I was actually going to be allowed into the inner sanctum! This turn of events was a far better one than I'd hoped for. In fact, there had been times during Sister Emmanuel's fervent sermon when I'd considered trying to sneak out of the place. No longer. By gum, this was my chance to do some honest-to-goodness sleuthing. I hoped. I followed in her regal wake as she walked in the same direction Mr. Everett had carried Mrs. Pinkney, turned right down another hallway, and made another right turn into an office.

Sister Emmanuel's office was fairly large, which didn't surprise me, as the Angelica Gospel Hall itself was an immense structure. She hadn't gone overboard on the furnishings, though, which comported with the message she tried to impart to her congregation, which was one of cheerful service to the Lord and not the accumulation of personal wealth. It was pleasant to discover that the woman practiced what she preached, in her case literally. There was a desk, a telephone, a couple of easy chairs and a sofa, upon which resided poor Mrs. Pinkney, who was stirring and looking as if she were embarrassed about that faint. I mean those faints.

"Brother Everett," said Sister Emmanuel when she ushered me into her office, "will you please ask Sister Everett to bring some tea here? I believe these two ladies could use a brace-up, as can I."

"I certainly will," said Brother Everett, ever helpful, and he bustled off.

"Please, my dear," said Sister Emmanuel to me. "Won't you please tell me who you are and what you know about this terrible business regarding Sister Chalmers? I was surprised when I didn't see her face in the congregation this morning."

She was? Shoot, the place was so big and so crammed with people, I didn't know how she'd ever keep track of one smallish woman. However, if she'd just told me the truth, and I had no real reason to doubt her, her words impressed me. You know, she being the shepherd and the congregation being her lambs, it was her duty to look out for them and know where each one was. In a way. It seemed a pretty large task to shepherd a flock of several hundred human beings who might occasionally behave like sheep, but not so often that you'd notice if the people I knew were any example.

I cleared my throat and glanced at Mrs. Pinkney, thinking

Sister Emmanuel should be spending her time comforting her rather than questioning me. But that was the Boston in me thinking. I was here on investigatorial duties, and Sister Emmanuel had just given me an opportunity to practice the few skills I'd learned from Ernie.

"Yes. My name is Miss Mercedes Allcutt, Mrs. . . . er, Sister Emmanuel."

She bestowed a sweet smile upon me. "We don't care to use earthly titles here, Sister Allcutt. We're all equal in God's eyes and, therefore, in our own eyes. You'll become accustomed to our ways if you join our flock. And I most earnestly pray that you will."

"Um . . . thank you, ma'am. Sister Emmanuel, I mean." Oh, boy. This was going to be tougher than I'd expected. "To get back to Mrs.—I mean Sister Chalmers. I paid a call on her on Thursday afternoon, around three or three-thirty, I believe it was. No one answered the door, which I thought was rather odd, since—"

"You mean Mrs. Hanratty wasn't there?"

It was Mrs. Pinkney who'd interrupted my narrative. When I glanced at the sofa, I saw that she'd managed to sit up, although she was rubbing the back of her head. I imagine that part of her anatomy hurt a good deal, having come into sudden and painful contact with a tile floor not once, but twice, in the recent past.

Before I continued my narrative, I asked, "Are you feeling better now, Mrs. Pinkney? I'm awfully sorry to have caused you such distress. I shouldn't have broken the news to you so abruptly."

Sister Emmanuel took over. I guess she didn't like losing the limelight for too long at any given moment.

"Yes, Sister Pinkney. Sister Everett will be bringing some tea for us in a moment. I'm sure that will perk you right up."

"Yes. Thank you." Mrs. Pinkney's voice sounded weak. Shock

and pain will do that to a person.

"Please, Sister Allcutt, continue with your story."

"Very well." I cleared my throat again. "Anyhow, I rang the doorbell and no one answered my ring." Deciding I might as well throw another name into the room to make these women think I knew Mrs. Chalmers better than I did—and, anyhow, Mrs. Pinkney had asked—I added, "Neither Mrs. Hanratty nor Susan was there. I thought that odd, as I'd believed Mrs. Chalmers was expecting me." There it was: a bald-faced lie right there in the middle of a church. Oh, well. I'd ask forgiveness later. "For some reason—I know it was bold of me, but I was beginning to worry a bit—I turned the doorknob, and discovered the door was unlocked. I thought that was strange, too."

"Goodness, yes," said Mrs. Pinkney, whose voice, while still a trifle breathy, was stronger now. "Especially now, since she's been having so much trouble."

I managed to keep my eyebrows from soaring. "Oh, my, I didn't know about that. What kind of trouble?"

"What? You mean she didn't tell you?"

Mrs. Pinkney squinted at me. I think the squint was from pain and not suspicion, but I decided I'd better make myself clear. "Well, I knew she'd lost some jewelry—"

"She'd had some jewelry *stolen*," declared Mrs. Pinkney. "And then there were the threatening letters."

"Oh, my," I said, my own voice a trifle weak at this news. "I didn't know about any threatening letters."

Mrs. Pinkney nodded once vigorously, then grabbed her head again and stopped doing that. I grimaced in sympathy.

"How many threatening letters did she get?" I asked, feeling as though I might have finally stumbled upon a real, honest-to-goodness detectival trail for once in my life as a P.I.'s assistant . . . I mean secretary.

"Two or three, I think."

"Goodness gracious," I said, hoping Sister Emmanuel wouldn't butt in any time soon. "What did they say? The letters, I mean."

"That she'd better stop throwing her money at the Angelica Gospel Hall, or she'd regret it."

"*Throwing* her money at the Angelica Gospel Hall?"

I couldn't honestly blame Sister Emmanuel for hopping into the conversation at that point.

"Oh, dear," I said, hoping to mitigate Sister Emmanuel's rage.

But I'd wronged the woman. She wasn't enraged. In fact, when I glanced at her, I saw genuine grief on her countenance and tears in her eyes. "Oh, my dear, sweet Lord, I can't believe that anyone could take our message and twist it so horribly that they'd threaten a lovely woman for supporting such important work. If our work played any role whatsoever in her death . . ."

I decided to plop something into the conversation that might cheer her up some. "You never know what the devil will do next. Satan is right here among us, twisting people's minds and souls." I'd read that Sister Emmanuel believed Satan was real and did stuff like that.

It had been the right thing to say. Although she still appeared horrified that someone might have been harmed because of an affiliation with her church, Sister Emmanuel did bestow a nod and a smile upon me. "You're very wise for someone so young, Sister Allcutt."

Fortunately for me, who doesn't accept compliments very well from sources I don't know, Mrs. Pinkney spoke next. "I wonder if the person who wrote the letters is the one who killed her."

"How did the poor woman die?" asked Sister Emmanuel.

We were interrupted by Sister Everett, who didn't look at all like Brother Everett, so I assumed they were husband and wife and not literally brother and sister. Much more heavily built than her husband, she was a good deal taller than he, and had a face that reminded me of a withered peach, perhaps because it was wrinkled and she had yellowish-gray hair. She looked as though she might heave a good-sized cow over a fence if she'd been of a mind to, and it was difficult for me to imagine the couple as . . . well, as a couple. You know. Because her husband was such a weedy-looking fellow. Ah, well. There's no accounting for when and where love will strike, I reckon. I also reckon she didn't believe in using bluing to whiten her hair. She laid a tray on Sister Emmanuel's desk. I expected her to pour tea and hand teacups around, but she didn't. It was Sister Emmanuel herself who said, "Thank you so much, Sister Everett. You may go on about your duties and I'll pour. These poor ladies have suffered a severe shock."

Sister Everett shook her head in sympathy, although her face didn't betray the same emotion. She sounded sincere, though, when she said, "Brother Everett told me about Sister Chalmers. I'm so sorry." And she backed out of the room like a trained maid. My mother would have approved.

As she poured and handed out teacups—they were pretty although not, I could tell, anything out of the ordinary, but probably purchased at a five-and-dime somewhere, which constituted prudent use of the church's funds to my mind— Sister Emmanuel said, "Please continue your story, Sister All-cutt. You say you found poor Sister Chalmers yourself? That must have been a terrible shock for you."

I nodded and said with real feeling, "It was." I took a sip of tea and continued my interrupted story. "I spoke her name when I entered the vestibule, but the house was strangely silent." Might as well put a little drama into my story, after all. Besides, it had been an eerie experience, so why not say so? "Everything was so quiet. I learned later that Mrs. Hanratty and Susan—the hired help—had gone out, which explains the silence, but I didn't know that at the time. I didn't know what to do, but I was feeling rather ill at ease by that time, so I . . . well, I tiptoed from room to room. There wasn't a single soul there. That much I could tell, and I wondered where the servants were. Then I got to the hallway, and . . ."

And I couldn't go on for a moment. The memory of that huddle of filmy cloth at the foot of the staircase stopped my tongue. I swallowed another sip of tea, and then another one, and cleared my throat.

"I'm sorry, my dear. I can tell this recitation is difficult for you."

Chalk up another point for Sister Emmanuel. She knew what to say to people. I was impressed anew. "Thank you."

"Can you go on now?" she asked kindly.

I nodded. "Yes, I think so. Anyhow, I finally walked into the big hallway—" I shot a look at Mrs. Pinkney and said, "You know the one I mean? The one where the staircase comes down?"

She nodded mutely, staring at me in what I presumed was horror or dread or some similar emotion.

"Well, there I found her. Mrs. Chalmers. At the foot of the stairs. I . . . at first I thought she must have tumbled down the stairs, but then I . . ."

Boy, I hadn't realized how difficult it was going to be to relate this string of events to strangers. At the time, when I'd been talking to Phil and Ernie, I was so caught up in the moment that I just blurted it all out. But a couple of days had passed since then, the memories were coming back, and I didn't like them one little bit.

"But . . . well, I went over to see if she was all right, and I saw that she . . . she'd been struck a vicious blow to the back of the head. There was . . . a good deal of blood. On the carpet.

Under her head."

That was it for Mrs. Pinkney. Fortunately, when she fainted this time, she did so on a soft surface. Sister Emmanuel rushed over to her and administered soothing words and tea. And smelling salts, too, which I presume she'd got from one of her desk drawers. Wherever she'd retrieved them from, they did the trick. Mrs. Pinkney sat bolt upright and sneezed. Then her hands flew to the back of her head again. Poor thing. She'd had a hard day, and it was barely after one o'clock in the afternoon. Again, I felt guilty, even though I'd only been doing my job. A job my boss had strictly forbidden me to do.

Oh, dear . . .

At any rate, after she'd administered first aid, Sister Emmanuel returned to her desk and sat once more. "I'm so very sorry about all of this," she said softly. "Will you please pray with me? We must pray for the soul of our dear departed loved one and for the quick apprehension of the person who committed the dreadful deed. I don't believe anyone, however wicked his acts on this earth, is beyond redemption. We can pray that the perpetrator will come to see the light."

Sounded about right to me. And if whoever the perpetrator was didn't see the light, I'd be happy if he was caught quickly, then locked up and fried. Boy, that sounds terrible, doesn't it? Perhaps my stint as a private I's secretary was beginning to have a deleterious effect on my character, even as my mother believed.

Yet again, Sister Emmanuel demonstrated her strength of character. Rather than making the shaky Mrs. Pinkney come to her, Sister Emmanuel went to her. "You just sit there, dear. Sister Allcutt and I will join you."

So there I was, on my knees again, only this time we knelt on a carpeted surface, and the prayer didn't last very long.

My goodness. When I finally managed to extricate myself from Sister Emmanuel and the Angelica Gospel Hall, my head was positively spinning, and I could scarcely wait to go to work the next morning so I could tell Ernie what I'd learned. Which, I thought, frowning, wasn't a whole lot. Still, maybe he didn't already know about the threatening letters Sister—I mean Mrs. Chalmers had been receiving.

I took a taxicab home, thereby having spent my entire week's pay on transportation by Sunday afternoon. And I'd only been paid on Friday. I decided I really needed to economize if I truly wanted to become an honest member of the working classes.

I'd begin doing that very thing after we caught Mrs. Chalmers' killer. Providing, of course, I survived dinner with my mother that evening.

CHAPTER EIGHT

As I'd guessed she would, my mother was fit to be tied that I'd sullied the Allcutt name and not merely ventured into the Angelica Gospel Hall but had actually spoken to Sister Adelaide Burkhard Emmanuel herself.

"Why, the woman is nothing but a vulgar shill for that so-called religion of hers," Mother said, her nose in the air. If she ever did that in the rain, she'd probably drown. Too bad it didn't rain much in Los Angeles, not that it would have mattered then since we were indoors. "If anyone finds out that one of *my* daughters was lending her support to that trashy institution, the entire family will be disgraced."

"I wasn't lending my support to any institution," I said. "I was trying to figure out why some people are so enthralled with the Angelica Gospel Hall and Sister Emmanuel. One of our clients was a member of the church, so you can call it firsthand investigation, if you will." That's what I hoped Ernie would call it.

"*Sister* Emmanuel." My mother made the name sound like a curse. "Horrid woman!"

"She was actually very nice to me," I said in a quiet voice, hoping to teach by example. Silly me. "She was awfully concerned when she learned about Mrs. Chalmers' death. And she was kindness itself to poor Mrs. Pinkney, who was Mrs. Chalmers' good friend."

"And that's another thing, young woman," Mother ranted

on. Well, what I mean is that she continued talking. My mother would no more rant than she'd attend the Angelica Gospel Hall. "Why you keep getting mixed up with dead people is absolutely beyond my understanding. Nothing like that ever happened in the family before you disobeyed your parents and began behaving in so outrageous a manner. Why, the way you stumble over dead people is an absolute disgrace. I want you to quit that so-called job of yours immediately!"

"You know I'm not going to do that, Mother." I held on to my sigh, since to sigh in front of people was another Boston sin. Never mind that Boston was two thousand miles away and on another coast. "I love my job."

"You consort with the lowest sorts of people." Mother sniffed to let me know she was ashamed of me. Since I'd known that for years, her sniff didn't bother me a whole lot, although what did bother me was why it was a sin to sigh and not a sin to sniff.

"Mother, why don't you dress for dinner?" Poor Chloe must have been desperate, since she seldom interrupted our mother in full scolding mode. "Our guests will be arriving soon."

"Oh. Oh, certainly."

Chloe and I exchanged a relieved glance as Mother marched toward the staircase. She'd been given the Green Room, the room allotted to visiting royalty or our mother. Why anyone needed to change for meals was beyond *my* understanding, but I'd not dare fate and tell Mother so.

Mother turned on the staircase. "Whom did you say were going to grace your table this evening, dear?"

Chloe was a dear. I was a monster. Oh, well . . .

"John Gilbert and Renee Adoree," said Chloe.

"Oh, my goodness. I did so enjoy Mr. Gilbert's performance in *The Big Parade*. And Miss Adoree's, too, although I must say

I don't understand that name. It sounds odd to me, and rather vulgar."

To the astonishment of her two daughters, our mother giggled. She didn't stick around to confound us further, but left to accept Chloe's suggestion that she dress for dinner.

Another speaking glance passed between Chloe and me. After peering up the steps to make sure enough distance existed between our mother and us to preclude Mother overhearing, I whispered, "How many times has John Gilbert been divorced?"

"Lord, I can't even remember. He and Leatrice Joy were divorced last year. I do know that."

"So how come Mother gets wobbly knees and giggles about a divorced man, and gets mad at me for attending church?"

"Everyone gets wobbly knees about John Gilbert," Chloe said with some justification—except that we were talking about our mother. Chloe frowned, realizing what a silly thing she'd just said. Then she admitted it aloud. "I don't know, Mercy. I think she's mainly upset that you refuse to toe the line and continue to live the way you want to and not the way she wants you to."

This time I allowed my sigh out into the open, since I knew Chloe didn't give a hoot if sighs were considered unrefined in Boston. "You're right, of course."

Chloe made as if to bustle out of the living room. "I'm going to see if Mrs. Biddle needs any help. I've hired a couple of girls to help out with the serving. Lord, I hope Miss Adoree speaks English."

"Mother will never forgive her if she doesn't," I said.

Chloe laughed, but we both knew I was right. Mother didn't approve of languages other than English.

With another sigh, I said, "Well, I suppose I'd better change for dinner, too. Stupid custom."

"It is, but with Mother here, we'd best conform."

"Amen." I guess my church experience hadn't entirely left

me by that time.

Chloe continued her interrupted bustle, and I climbed the stairs to my own suite of rooms.

Fortunately, I had a perfectly splendid dress to wear for the evening and it was exactly suitable to the occasion, so Mother at least wouldn't be able to complain about my appearance at table. Unless, of course, she wanted to, and then my suitable appearance wouldn't deter her.

The dress, a tubular-shaped one (that was the current mode—I couldn't do much about it), was beaded and had wide shoulder straps, a knee-length skirt with a scalloped hem, and was in the very first stare of fashion. The straps were lined with silk and bound with velvet, so the dress was amazingly comfortable, except that I had to wear an elastic, waist-length bust-flattener. If I didn't have any of the lumps and bumps considered unseemly at the time, I wouldn't have had to wear it, but I did. Have lumps and bumps, I mean. Since I enjoyed my meals, I expected to have to continue using the bust-flattener until the fashions changed. Anyhow, the beading on the dress was green and gold, so I wore my gold, pointy-toed shoes and gold hoop earrings. I even had a gold evening bag to go with everything, but since I was at home, I didn't bother with that particular accoutrement. After I'd donned my evening clothes and checked myself in the mirror, I decided the ensemble was charming, and Mother couldn't complain about it unless she cared to stretch the point a good deal.

She didn't, thank God. When I entered the room, I saw Mother in the far corner of the room, giving orders to Mrs. Biddle, who didn't look as if she appreciated them. Then to my great joy, I discerned Chloe, also dressed to the nines, in the living room chatting with one of my favorite people, Mr. Francis Easthope. As far as I was concerned, Mr. Easthope was even more handsome than John Gilbert, but he had none of Mr.

Gilbert's buccaneering ways with women, being a polite and courteous bachelor who paid no undue attention to either Chloe or me. I tried not to take his disinterest personally. Ernie didn't like him for some reason I didn't understand, but Ernie wasn't there that evening, so it didn't matter what he thought.

"Mr. Easthope," I cried enthusiastically, thinking at least I had one friend on my side. Chloe was on my side, too, as was Harvey, but they were hostess and host, so they'd be too busy contending with their guests to deflect Mother's attentions from landing on me.

Mr. Easthope smiled attractively and held out his hand. "How lovely to see you this evening, Miss Allcutt. You look perfectly charming, too."

He ought to know, since he was the chief costumier at Harvey's studio. So there, Mother.

Speaking of whom, she suddenly loomed behind me. I couldn't see her, but I knew she was there because . . . well, just because I was used to her looming over me, I suppose.

I gave Mr. Easthope a hasty, "Thank you," and turned to face Mother. I even forced a smile. "Good evening, Mother."

"Good evening, Mercedes Louise." She looked me up and down, searching for imperfections, I have no doubt. "You do appear quite presentable this evening."

Boy, I bet it hurt her to say that. I only smiled sweetly and said, "Thank you. You look grand yourself."

And she did. For Boston. For a hot Los Angeles summer evening, she was overdressed. But it was Mother who would suffer for her refusal to adapt to change and not I, so what did I care?

"I do love your dress, Miss Allcutt," said Mr. Easthope. I presume he and Mother had greeted each other earlier, because otherwise he'd never have intruded into our conversation—not that we were having one. "Who designed it, do you know?"

"I'm not sure. Chloe's seamstress, Mrs. Martinez, made it. I like it, too. It's awfully comfortable." I left out the part about the waist-length breast-flattener. "And the colors are my favorites. I love green."

"As do I," said Mr. Easthope. "Green is a marvelous color for you."

"Thank you." I think I blushed, which was stupid of me.

Very well, so it wasn't exactly an inspired conversation; at least Mr. Easthope had diverted my mother's attention from her survey of my person, and for that I appreciated him. I believe I've already mentioned that he was a swell person. He also had mother problems of his own, so he understood Chloe's and my problems with our own mother.

At that moment, a woman squealed. I can't imagine who it was, since most of Chloe's guests were inured to the presence of moving-picture stars, or pretended to be. Maybe it was one of the maids Chloe had hired for the evening. Anyhow, that little screech announced the entry of Mr. John Gilbert into our midst.

Oh, my goodness. Even *my* heart fluttered a bit when I beheld him, and I'd seen actors and actresses aplenty since I'd moved to Los Angeles.

But Mr. Gilbert was what one would call a major star in Hollywood's firmament, and he was absolutely gorgeous. In actual fact, I believe Mr. Easthope outshone him in the looks department, but Mr. Easthope was a costumier. Mr. Gilbert was a *star.* He also has a certain sparkle about him that one just doesn't see on the rest of us merely normal mortal souls. I'd noticed this phenomenon before. There are lots of good-looking people in the world, but people like Mr. Gilbert were folks other people *noticed.*

The perfect hostess, Chloe hurried over to him, bade the maid—she was probably the squealer—to take his hat, coat, and stick, and led him into the fray. I mean the living room.

Clutching his arm—they knew each other from before—Chloe guided him in the direction of our mother, which meant that she led him in my direction, too. My thumping heart sped up a good deal.

"Mother, please allow me to introduce you to Mr. John Gilbert. John, this is my mother, Mrs. Allcutt."

Executing an absolutely stunning bow, John Gilbert took our mother's hand and almost kissed it. It was the "almost" part that won our mother over to his side, I think. Hand-kissing is all well and good for European nobility, but it was gauche for Americans. That's according to our mother. At that moment, it occurred to me that Chloe might well have warned Mr. Gilbert whom he'd be up against that evening. His twinkling eyes hinted that he knew all about our mother and was planning on charming her anyway. I liked him instantly.

Then Chloe said, "John, you simply must meet my sister, Mercedes Allcutt. We call her Mercy, she's recently moved to Los Angeles to live with us, and she loves it here."

Oh, my. To have such a fellow as John Gilbert bestow his entire attention upon one is . . . well, the sensation was almost overpowering. I nearly screeched myself.

He gave me one of his perfect bows, did the almost-hand-kissing thing again, and then gave me a wink for good measure, as if he and I were in some conspiracy together. I couldn't restrain my smile. Here was a nice man, I told myself. And he was.

I have to admit that his speaking voice wasn't altogether what one might want the hero of one's dreams to possess. It was more of a tenor than a bass or a baritone, but it was nowhere near as high and squeaky as people would claim a few years later when he attempted to move from the silents to the talkies. I think someone deliberately undermined his career at that point, and I think whoever did it was mean and hateful and a real stinker.

Then Renee Adoree appeared upon the scene. This time the maid didn't scream or faint, but she did catch Chloe's eye, so Chloe hurried away, leaving John Gilbert with Mother, Mr. Easthope, and me. I tried not to flutter or stutter.

"Mother and I both enjoyed *The Big Parade,* Mr. Gilbert. You played your part wonderfully," I ventured.

"Thank you, Miss Allcutt and Mrs. Allcutt." He turned to Mr. Easthope. "You created the costumes for *The Big Parade,* didn't you, Mr. Easthope?"

I could tell Mr. Easthope was pleased to have been praised. "Indeed I did. It was a pleasure to work with such charming people."

One of Mr. Gilbert's eyebrows lifted. "Was Miss Adoree charming to you? She was rather a cat once or twice on the set."

Chuckling softly, Mr. Easthope said, "She was charm itself at fittings. I guess I was lucky."

"I guess so." Mr. Gilbert turned to me. There went my heart again, battering away at my bound bosoms like crazy. Stupid heart. I didn't even know this man, for Pete's sake. "Say, Miss Allcutt, your sister has told me all about your little poodle. I was thinking of getting a dog for myself, and would enjoy meeting your little Buttercup, if you don't mind."

Would I *mind?* Is my mother an overbearing Bostonian? The answers to those questions, in order, are no and yes. Trying not to gush, I said, "I'd love to introduce you to Buttercup."

So, arm in arm, Mr. John Gilbert, one of the most famous men in the world (after bowing politely to my mother and Mr. Easthope again), and I, Mercedes Louise Allcutt, an absolute nobody from Boston, walked out of the living room and down the hallway toward the sun room, where poor Buttercup had been confined for the evening.

"I'm planning to get Chloe and Harvey a poodle for Christmas," I told him, in order not to appear tongue-tied. "They want a black one."

"Chloe told me about the Christmas present. She also told me about your mother."

I couldn't help myself; I laughed. "I wondered if she'd done that!"

"I figured I'd do my best to rescue you," he said, thus proving himself to be a hero off the screen as well as on it.

"Thank you very much. You can't imagine how much I appreciate being rescued."

"Still, I really would like to meet this Buttercup of yours. I like dogs. Truth to tell, I have a dog already. An English setter. I like to do the occasional bit of hunting, and she's a great bird dog."

"I believe poodles were originally bred to do that sort of thing. Retrieve birds and so forth." That the notion of my precious Buttercup carrying a mangled bird corpse in her mouth made me shudder, I didn't let on.

"I believe you're right. I also think Germany claims them as their country of origin as does France."

"We'd probably better not tell Miss Adoree that," I said.

He chuckled, and I went all giddy for a moment. Good heavens, how silly can one girl get? Then again, if the notion of John Gilbert could make my mother giggle, I suppose I could be forgiven a certain giddiness in his company.

At that moment, I opened the door to the sun porch, and an overjoyed Buttercup leapt out of the bed in which she'd been moping and dashed over to me. Before she could jump up and rip any of the pretty beads from my gown, I bent and picked her up. "Buttercup, I would like you to meet one of the most celebrated men of our time, Mr. John Gilbert."

Then Buttercup did a trick I'd taught her, as if on cue, and held out a paw to Mr. Gilbert. If she wasn't the sweetest thing on the face of the earth, I didn't know what was.

Darned if the man didn't bow and take my dog's paw and shake it as if she were a human being instead of a canine!

"It's as great a pleasure to meet you, Miss Buttercup, as it was to meet your mistress, Miss Allcutt. I must say you're both delightful ladies."

Buttercup returned the compliment by licking him on the chin. Fortunately, Mr. Gilbert had a sense of humor and only laughed.

After petting Buttercup and reassuring her that I'd rescue her eventually, I put her back into her little bed. She whined once, then gave it up. She knew who was boss. Poodles are smart that way.

"An admirable pooch, Miss Allcutt," said Mr. Gilbert as we walked back to the crowded living room.

"Thank you. I'm ever so glad I got her." It occurred to me that Mr. Gilbert might know if any of his fellow actors had been moved to join Adelaide Burkhard Emanuel's cause, so I asked him.

He blinked once or twice, letting me know that I hadn't exactly warmed up to the subject but had rather dumped it on him out of the blue, so I hurried to explain. "I'm sorry to be so abrupt. But that church or some of its members might have a bearing on the case my employer and I are working on." I suppose I should cringe at admitting it, but I was becoming more adept at lying every day. I know that's a bad thing, but it didn't seem like one at the time.

"Ah, yes. Chloe told me you'd chosen to retreat from your ivory tower and pursue honest employment."

The way he said it made me understand he wasn't teasing, but understood that a person might get bored and crave new

113

adventures. I appreciated him for it. "Indeed. And working for a private investigator is most interesting."

His eyes thinned and his brow crinkled. "Say, you're not talking about this Chalmers thing, are you? I heard that Persephone had passed away suddenly, but I didn't realize it was a case. In that sense of the word, I mean."

"You knew her?" I was surprised.

"Not well, but we'd met at a couple of parties. Her husband is a bigwig in some business or other, and his money has helped finance some pictures."

"I didn't know that."

"Well, as I said, I didn't know her well, but I was sorry to hear of her death."

By this time, we'd almost come to the living room, so I said quickly, "She was murdered."

"Dear God!" He stopped in his tracks for a moment and appeared to be honestly shocked.

But then we had to give up the topic because we'd reached the living room and, therefore, the party. Just when I might have been getting somewhere on the case, too. That would teach me to allow my mind to wander from work to Hollywood screen idols.

I had no time to fall into a melancholy, however, because Chloe was on me in an instant with Miss Renee Adoree at her side.

"Mercy!" cried my sister. "You must meet Miss Renee Adoree." So she introduced us.

Renee Adoree, a simply beautiful woman whose looks had been bestowed upon her by God rather than the paint box, had a rather languid air about her, but she wasn't as wafty as Mrs. Chalmers had been. In truth, she seemed a very nice person, if a little standoffish. Not too long after that, and after several more impressive performances in the flickers, she was diagnosed with tuberculosis. That would make me sad, especially as she died only a short while after her diagnosis.

That evening in Chloe's living room, Renee Adoree was stunning, dressed to kill and extremely polite. I soon discovered, however, that while she had a lovely speaking voice—marred, my mother would say, by an unfortunate French accent—she didn't know beans about the Angelica Gospel Hall or its minions or converts, so I didn't bother with her much after learning that.

Dinner was, naturally, a great success, with all sorts of delicious courses and wines and so forth and so on. I'd come to understand shortly after my arrival in Los Angeles that everyone who was anyone had his or her own bootlegger. Chloe was right in that she would have been considered a very odd hostess indeed not to have served wine with dinner that night, Mother or no Mother. Not that this bit of information adds to the tale. I only mention it.

After the meal was finished, we gathered once again in the living room, where I scouted out Mr. Gilbert. I didn't want to appear too obvious, for fear Mother would think I was pursuing the man. Telling her I was only doing so for the sake of my job would, as you must know by this time, not have softened any rebuke she'd fling at me.

"Your sister and brother-in-law sure know how to entertain," said Mr. Gilbert with a smile and a drink in his hand when I approached him. He'd been chatting with Harvey, who winked at me. Have I mentioned that Harvey was a great fellow? Well, he was.

"Harvey and Chloe are two of the very best people on earth," I declared to Mr. Gilbert, which earned me a wide grin from Harvey.

"It's good to see siblings who are so close," Mr. Gilbert said, and I think he meant it. "So often families aren't affectionate.

For good reason, in some cases."

I cast a quick glance at my mother, but she was safely ensconced on the other side of the room, holding forth with Mr. Easthope and another woman who was prominent in both literature and the flickers, Elinor Glyn. I'd met Miss Glyn before, and she intimidated me, although I think that was only because my own aspirations seemed so tepid when compared to her accomplishments. Still and all, I was relatively confident that the likes of Elinor Glyn wouldn't have anything to do with the likes of Sister Emmanuel or Persephone Chalmers, so I saw no reason to fight my feelings of inferiority in order to question her. Besides, Mr. Gilbert was ever so much more my cup of tea, if you know what I mean.

It was obvious that Mr. Gilbert and Harvey had seen my desperate glance Mother's way because they both laughed.

Harvey said, "Don't worry, Mercy. I think the storm has settled for a while."

"Oh, dear," said I, embarrassed.

"Don't think anything about it," recommended Mr. Gilbert. "Remember that old saying, which, I'm sure, is only popular because it's true: one can choose one friends, but one can't choose one's family."

"Amen," I muttered. "But I don't know what I'd do without Chloe."

"And I can add an amen to that," echoed Harvey, which made my heart all warm and fuzzy. While I didn't understand the attraction between Mr. and Mrs. Everett, it was obvious that Chloe and Harvey were made for each other. They also looked good together, unlike the Everetts, who were as mismatched a pair as I'd ever seen.

"Chloe is the best sister a person could have," I said staunchly and meaning every word.

"That's good to hear," said Mr. Gilbert. I got the feeling the conversation was boring him, so I decided to forge onward onto another topic.

"You mentioned earlier that you don't know much about the Angelica Gospel Hall, is that right?"

"Er . . . yes, it is. I know one or two people who've attended services there," said Mr. Gilbert. I decided then and there to practice turning topics more elegantly.

"Do you think any of them might be able to give me any information about Mrs. Chalmers' involvement with the Hall?" I asked eagerly.

"Um . . ." Mr. Gilbert seemed taken aback.

"Mercy went so far as to visit the place this morning," Harvey said.

"Talk about sacrificing oneself for one's role." Mr. Gilbert's eyebrows arched.

I smiled but said, "It wasn't really too awful. It certainly wasn't like anything I'm used to."

"I should hope not," murmured Harvey.

"Well," said I, thinking kindly of Sister Emmanuel because she'd been nice to me and had performed well in a crisis, "I believe their hearts are in the right place. They just . . . get a little carried away. For my taste," I hurried to add, just in case Mr. Gilbert was a secret member of the church or something like that. "In fact, Sister Emmanuel was quite nice to me when a member of her parish fainted."

"Somebody fainted?" Mr. Gilbert's posture straightened slightly from its formerly relaxed state, and I sensed a spike in his interest.

"Well, yes. I'm afraid I startled the poor woman by blurting out that Mrs. Chalmers had been murdered, you see."

"Good God, Miss Allcutt, what kind of work do you do for this Mr. Templeton of yours? Chloe told me you were his secretary, but you seem to be busy ferreting out information in a murder case."

Oh, pooh. I didn't want to admit that I aspired to be an assistant investigator, because that sounded stupid. I was, however, on my dignity when I replied to Mr. Gilbert. "I am his secretary, but I also assist him when I can. Mrs. Chalmers was an enthusiastic member of the church, and I figured attending services at the Angelica Gospel Hall would be an interesting thing to do, definitely not dangerous, and I got to meet Sister Emmanuel and a friend of Mrs. Chalmers, so I don't believe my time was wasted."

"My goodness. You're an inspired employee, Miss Allcutt."

I couldn't tell if he was being sarcastic or not, so I said, "Thank you."

"But I honestly don't know anyone who goes to the place. At least no one's admitted doing so to me." I detected a certain sneer in his mien but didn't blame him for it. Most people had at least read about Mrs. Emmanuel's work, and a good many of the articles published, at least those that I'd seen, hadn't been exactly enthusiastic about her work. I think the most charitable of the pieces I'd read called her misguided. Others weren't so kind, and words like *charlatan, bunkum, fraud, cheat,* and the like had been sprinkled about in the articles.

I wasn't sure I agreed with the doubting Thomases. Mind you, I wasn't about to join the Angelica Gospel Hall myself, and I had found the service rather . . . perhaps *gaudy* is the word I'm looking for. Still, Sister Emmanuel had been nice, and so had been Mrs. Pinkney.

All that aside, however, it looked as if John Gilbert wasn't going to be a mine of information for me, so I gave him up as a lost cause and determined to pursue the investigation from other angles.

CHAPTER NINE

"You did *what?* God damn it, Mercy, stay out of this investigation! For God's sake, a woman's been murdered! Don't you have any sense at all?"

I'd seen Ernie angry before, but I don't think I'd ever seen him *this* angry.

"Don't you dare swear at me, Mr. Ernest Templeton!"

Very well, I admit my temper wasn't any too jolly that Monday morning, either. I'd been all smiles when Ernie'd finally strolled into the office around nine o'clock, and I'd even given him time to toss his coat and hat on the rack and have a good gander at the *Times* before I'd entered his office to tell him the results my weekend's investigation.

"I don't want you anywhere near anything to do with this investigation!"

"Well, that's just too bad, because since you're the chief suspect—and don't tell me you're not, because I know better—I'm going to do my best to find that woman's real killer."

"Let the police do their jobs!"

That command came out as a bellow, and I winced slightly. "So far, their jobs have led them straight to your door, Ernest Templeton, and don't try to tell me any different. Even Phil says you're the chief suspect. And since you have a sworn enemy as head of the investigation—"

"O'Reilly's not a sworn enemy! We don't like each other, is all."

119

"Nevertheless—"

"Besides, Phil doesn't believe for a minute that I killed that woman."

"Yes, I know he doesn't, but he's not the entire police force. You've told me more than once how corrupt they are, and if this O'Reilly person is as horrid as you say, then we need all the help we can get. He's the one in charge of the case, don't forget." I squinted at Ernie, recalling something Phil had said at the scene of the crime. "You were at the Chalmers place to investigate her stolen jewelry, weren't you? I mean you weren't . . . doing what that odious man suggested, were you?"

I thought for a moment that Ernie's eyeballs were going to pop out of his head. "For the love of God, Mercy Allcutt, what kind of man do you think I *am!*"

"Well," I said, feeling hot and definitely bothered, "I felt I ought to eliminate the possibility completely."

"*You* aren't going to eliminate anything! And no, I was not having a sordid affair with that idiotic woman!"

"Are you sure that awful Detective O'Reilly knows that?"

"God damn it, Mercy, of *course* he knows that!"

"But are you sure he'll tell the rest of the police force that? I mean, if he hates you as much as you say he does—"

"Dammit—"

But I'd had enough of being sworn at. "Stop it right this instant!" I held up my hand and spoke in my mother's most commanding voice.

Darned if his mouth didn't flap open and his words dry up. Boy, was I ever surprised.

I took advantage of the situation instantly. "Before you holler another word at me, Ernie Templeton, let me tell you what I found out."

He plunked his elbows on his desk and lowered his head to his hands. "Aw, Christ," said he.

Taking this as an invitation to continue, I did so. "During the service, I sat next to a woman whom I later learned was Elizabeth Pinkney. Mrs. Gaylord Pinkney. Mrs. Pinkney told me her husband hated her own involvement with Sister Emmanuel's church—"

"*Sister* Emmanuel," muttered Ernie.

"Don't worry," I told him drily. "I'm not turning to the dark side. I only attended services there to see what Mrs. Chalmers found so fascinating about the place."

"Yeah?" Ernie still cradled his head in his hands. "And did you?"

"Well . . . yes, I think so. The services are very . . . exuberant."

"Huh."

"But that's not the important thing. The important thing is that Mrs. Pinkney was a close friend to Mrs. Chalmers, and she—Mrs. Pinkney, I mean—told me that Mrs. Chalmers had been getting letters threatening her life."

Ernie's head lifted, and for the first time since we'd begun speaking that morning, he didn't look as if he wished he could throttle me. "Yeah?"

My heart soared. "You didn't know about the threatening letters?"

He hesitated for a second, as if he hated to give me his answer. But he did eventually. "No. I knew the woman had problems, but I didn't know about the threatening letters. She didn't tell me about them, although she did say she feared for her life. Are you sure about this?"

"I'm sure Mrs. Pinkney told me Mrs. Chalmers was worried about having received threatening letters."

Ernie sat up straight. "When you say *threatening letters*, what do you mean exactly? Did the letters threaten her life?"

"Mrs. Pinkney didn't go into details. I don't know if she

actually knows any details. But it occurred to me that perhaps someone resented Mrs. Chalmers' involvement with the Angelica Gospel Hall. Mrs. Pinkney said Mrs. Chalmers donated tons of money there. Perhaps someone wanted her to stop doing that."

"Hmm. That might indicate a member of her family," Ernie said thoughtfully.

"Exactly what I thought. Well, we've already talked about Mr. Chalmers and . . . Mr. Chalmers." I wished those two men didn't have the same last name. It would have made my work much easier. "When I asked her, Mrs. Pinkney said she didn't know what Mr. Chalmers thought about the place, although her own husband didn't like her involvement in it, but I also thought of Mr. Simon Chalmers. He sounded disinterested when I interviewed him, but perhaps he was afraid Mrs. Chalmers would spend all of his father's money before he could inherit it. Or perhaps Mr. Pinkney decided to do Mrs. Chalmers in because he hoped she'd stop attending the church if Mrs. Chalmers was no longer around."

"You have a hell of an imagination, Mercy Allcutt."

"Thank you."

"That wasn't meant as a compliment."

"I figured as much."

Before another fight could break out, I heard the front door to the office open, so I had to depart Ernie to attend to my secretarial duties. I was not best pleased to encounter two policemen and Phil Bigelow in the outer office.

"Good morning, Phil." I eyed his two outriders with suspicion. The one who wasn't wearing a uniform I suspected of being Detective O'Reilly. He was the same sneering fellow I'd seen at the Chalmers' home on the day I discovered Mrs. Chalmers' body, and I didn't like the looks of him at all.

"Morning, Mercy. We're here to see Ernie."

"I suspected as much." My voice was about as dry as the Mojave Desert must have been on that warm September day. "And will you introduce me to your friends, please?"

"Uh . . . oh, sure. This is Officer Mahon, and this is Detective O'Reilly."

Aha! Just as I'd suspected. I gave him a meaningful squint. "Good day, gentlemen. I presume you're doing your jobs with due diligence."

"Yes, ma'am," said the uniformed officer Mahon, who seemed rather nervous.

"We always do," said O'Reilly.

I eyed him, searching for any sign of degeneration or vileness. He only looked like a slightly overweight man with a sneer. Bother.

"Um . . ." Phil fidgeted, and I considered this a bad sign.

"Yes?"

"Well . . . we're going to have to take Ernie down to the station, Mercy. It's just a technical sort of thing."

I'm sure my eyes went as round as saucers. "Take him to the station! Do you mean to tell me you're going to *arrest* him?"

"No." Phil sounded crabby. "But this is an official investigation, and we have to conduct it according to the rules."

"Whose rules?" I demanded.

"Those of the L.A.P.D."

"The same L.A.P.D. that so bungled the William Desmond Taylor investigation that we don't know who killed the man to this day, and from which Mr. Templeton resigned because the corruption therein so disgusted him?"

O'Reilly and Mahon exchanged a look I couldn't interpret, although I got the feeling Phil might have told them something about me and my firm belief in my employer's innocence.

Phil heaved a large sigh. "This isn't helping, Mercy. Ernie will have to come with us and answer a few questions. We won't keep him long."

I said, "Anyhow, I thought you were out of the investigation."

"I'm not out of it. Only I persuaded the chief that my friendship with Ernie wouldn't affect my conduct of the case. I've got O'Reilly breathing over my shoulder to make sure of it."

"Right," said O'Reilly, sounding as if he enjoyed his role.

Looking O'Reilly straight in the eye, I said, "I think it's totally unfair that someone who dislikes Ernie should be involved in the case at all."

"Now, listen here, Miss Allcutt—"

But Detective O'Reilly didn't have the opportunity to defend himself. Ernie appeared in his office door, clad for going out of doors. "Don't mind her, guys. She's still convinced she and she alone can find the murderer."

"I am not! I do, however, believe that I can help the investigation along. I already told you something you didn't already know, if you'll remember." I'm sure my cheeks were blazing with temper. The rest of me definitely was.

"I know, I know." Wearily, Ernie held his hands out, as if waiting for the handcuffs.

I gasped and turned on Phil with horror. "But you said . . ."

"Don't make a damned fool of yourself, Ernie," growled Phil, apparently not appreciating Ernie's gesture. "We're not arresting him, Mercy. We just need him to make an official statement at the department."

"Right," said Ernie, sounding as though he didn't believe Phil's words any more than I did.

"We already gave statements," I reminded him.

"Further statements," Phil said, looking and sounding uncomfortable, which he should be, darn it.

"It's all right, Mercy. None of this is Phil's fault." Then Ernie frowned at O'Reilly and, giving every appearance of disenchantment, left with the three men.

Well.

I sat at my desk and stewed for a bit and then decided to take matters into my own hands. The police department didn't seem to be doing anything but looking at Ernie, while I knew there were other suspects out there. Somewhere. After considering the matter, I decided not to telephone Mr. Chalmers before I hied myself to his house for a chat. Why not do some more sleuthing on my own? There was certainly nothing for me to do on the job in the Figueroa Building.

Of course, this trip entailed another cab fare. I silently apologized to Great-Aunt Agatha. Then I reminded myself that Agatha had been a good old girl and would probably applaud my energies in attempting to prove an innocent man's . . . well, innocence. Small wonder my parents had disapproved of her almost as much as they did me.

A black swag decorated—if that's the right word—the front door of the Chalmers residence when the cabbie pulled up. I asked him to wait for me and told him I'd pay him for his time when he griped and claimed he'd be losing fares. But I wanted to interview all of the household's inhabitants if I could, and that might take some time. So he agreed to wait. More of Great-Aunt Agatha's money. But it was being spent for a good cause, darn it.

I twisted the doorbell. The act itself brought back memories of the prior week, and they weren't happy ones. I prayed like mad that someone would answer my ring this time, because I didn't want to enter the place and find another dead body. Not, of course, that I would.

Be that as it may, my knees almost buckled with relief when Susan, whose last name I never did learn, answered the door. I cursed myself for not thinking to bring flowers of sympathy or something, but it was too late by that time.

"It's you!" she cried.

"May I come in for a moment?"

Susan looked frantically behind and around her, although I don't know why. Heck, *I* wasn't Mrs. Chalmers' killer.

"I just need to ask a few questions," I said in my most soothing tone.

"Well . . . the mister isn't in very good shape at the moment. He's took the missus's death mighty hard."

Nuts. I really had wanted to interview Mr. Chalmers. Still, if I could at least get into the house, I might be able to work my way up from the servants to the master. I said, "I'd like to speak with you and Mrs. Hanratty, actually. This is part of the ongoing investigation, you see."

"You're working with the coppers?"

"And my employer, Mr. Templeton. After all, he was working for Mrs. Chalmers and was injured at the same time she was killed." Stretching points doesn't count as lying. At least I don't think it does.

"Well . . ."

She wavered just enough for me to slip past her. I headed toward the kitchen, where I figured Mrs. Hanratty would be, mainly because I could smell savory odors issuing therefrom and guessed she was preparing luncheon for the master of the house.

"Well . . ." came again, weakly, from behind me.

Susan trailed after me, unsure if this was a proper thing I was doing, but unable to stop me now that I'd gained entry.

Gently, I pushed the kitchen door open. Sure enough, Mrs. Hanratty stood at the stove, stirring what looked like a pot of soup.

"Good morning, Mrs. Hanratty."

The poor woman jumped and whirled around, dropping her

wooden spoon into her pot. "Good heavens! You gave me such a start."

I went to her and took her arm, feeling contrite. "I'm awfully sorry. I didn't mean to alarm you."

She shook her head. "Alarm me? What with the missus falling down the stairs and killing herself and the mister being that miserable and Mr. Simon here underfoot all day long, day after day, and that preacher woman visiting, I don't know what the world's coming to."

Aha. So Sister Emmanuel has visited Mr. Chalmers! Whatever did that mean? Probably nothing. But I didn't have time to ponder the minister's visit.

"I don't either." Sympathetic was the tone I reached for, and I flatter myself that I achieved it. Because I wasn't altogether sure about that, I said, "I'm so sorry to interrupt your work, Mrs. Hanratty, but I do need to ask a few more questions about poor Mrs. Chalmers and her death."

"I don't know anything about her death," the woman said stolidly.

"I'm sure that's true, but you see, in investigations of this sort, we need to discover everything we can about the person who was murdered. Only in that way can we discover the killer."

Mrs. Hanratty's eyes thinned. "I thought it was that boss of yours who kilt her."

"It most certainly was not Mr. Templeton," I declared. "After I discovered Mrs. Chalmers at the foot of the stairs, I discovered Mr. Templeton upstairs, bound and gagged. And drugged."

She sniffed. "Sez you."

"I do say it, because it's the truth."

Mrs. Hanratty tried to hold on to her indignation, but finally let it out on a long sigh. "I suppose he didn't do it. He never seemed the type to me. But if he didn't kill her, who did?"

"That's exactly what I'm trying to discover."

Although she'd gone back to stirring her soup, she eyed me narrowly. "You? What can you do?"

"I can ask questions. That's what investigators do, you see."

She thought about my words for a while.

As she did so, I looked around and discovered that Susan had lingered in the doorway, still looking as if she'd done the wrong thing by not blocking my way when I tried to get into the house. I smiled at her. "Perhaps you can join us, Susan. I'd like to speak with both of you, actually."

Pointing to her chest as if she wasn't sure who she was, Susan said, "Me? Why me? I was with Mrs. Hanratty when some devil threw the missus down those stairs."

"I know. But you see, I need to learn more about the household and its visitors and things like that."

It was Mrs. Hanratty who responded. "Well, sit down . . . What's your name, anyhow? I forgot it."

"Miss Allcutt," said I.

I'd been taking in the kitchen, and it looked pretty well stocked and up to date to me. Not that I knew a whole lot about kitchens, but I'd been in our kitchen in Boston—the cook, unlike our parents, had been friends with Chloe and me— and in Chloe's kitchen. This one looked much like Chloe's, with cheerful curtains at the windows, bright paint, what looked like a new stove and a large icebox. Come to think of it, as I examined it more closely from where I stood beside the kitchen table, it looked as if it might be one of those newfangled electric refrigerators. Chloe had one, and this one seemed remarkably similar to hers.

"Well, sit yourself down, Miss Allcutt. And you, too, Susan. We have a little while before you have to serve the mister and Mr. Simon their lunches. And I just made a pot of tea."

"Oh, is Mr. Simon Chalmers here, too?" Better and better. Maybe I could speak with both gentlemen.

"Yes. He's been here a lot lately. Comforting his pa and all. Tomorrow's going to be a dismal day, what with the funeral and all."

"Yes, I'm sure you're right. I read about the arrangements in the paper." I'd contemplated going to the funeral but had decided that would be too intrusive a thing to do, even for me.

"Mr. Simon didn't want that preacher lady praying over the dead missus, but the mister said that he wanted to do what the missus would have wanted, and she'd want that preacher lady."

"The preacher lady?"

"Yeah. Mr. Simon, he kind of snorted, but he went along with the mister."

"You said that the . . . er, preacher lady visited Mr. Chalmers?" I probed gently.

"Yes. She come Sunday afternoon." Mrs. Hanratty's face squinched up in thought. "Didn't stay long. I think she and the mister prayed together or something."

I imagined Mrs. Hanratty was right, if the visitor was who I thought she was. "Did Mr. Chalmers seem to . . . resent her coming to visit?"

"Resent her visit?" More wrinkles. More thinking. "Naw. He said afterward that he thought it was nice she paid a visit, since his wife was so fond of her. I don't see it myself, but there's no accounting for taste."

Wasn't *that* the truth? "I see. What about Mr. Simon Chalmers? Did he visit his father and stepmother often before Mrs. Chalmers' death?"

Mrs. Hanratty thought about that for a moment as she continued to stir. "Sometimes he did. He has his own place. I got the feeling he didn't like the missus much."

"I got that same impression when I spoke to him last Thursday. It's always a shame when families aren't close," I said, more or less repeating Mr. John Gilbert's words to me. As if I'd know anything about close family relationships. Well, except for Chloe and me. We were very close.

"Oh, don't get me wrong," said Mrs. Hanratty in a hurry. "Mr. Simon was always polite to the missus, and he and his pa have always got on great guns. I don't think he liked it that the missus got herself involved in that new church."

"Ah, yes. The Angelica Gospel Hall. Where Mrs. Emmanuel preaches."

"That's the one!" This, from Susan, who'd hesitated before daring to sit with me at the kitchen table. Class distinctions. Phooey on them, I say.

"And it was Sister Emmanuel who visited yesterday afternoon?" I asked Mrs. Hanratty.

"Yup. That's the one, all right. She seemed kind of nice." She spoke as though Sister Emmanuel's niceness had come as a surprise to her.

To encourage Susan's participation in this conversation, I gave her another friendly smile. "Was Mrs. Chalmers good to work for, Susan? Was she a kind mistress?"

"Oh, yes. She was very good, ma'am."

Boy, if there was one thing I wasn't used to being called, it was *ma'am*. But I didn't say anything to discourage Susan. "I'm glad to hear it. When I met her, she seemed a lovely lady." Very well, I hadn't liked her much. She had been lovely, though, and that was nothing but the truth.

"Oh, yes, ma'am, that she was." Susan's face crinkled up a bit. "Though she did keep on about that new church with me and Mrs. Hanratty."

"Susan," said Mrs. Hanratty in a reproving voice.

Susan flinched slightly, but I rushed to reassure Susan. "But don't you see? This is exactly the sort of information I need. You see, if Mrs. Chalmers annoyed you, perhaps she annoyed someone else, too. Someone with evil intentions."

After chewing this bit of news over for a second or two, Susan said, "Well, it's not so much that she annoyed me or anything. Like I said, she was a very nice lady. But I'm a Roman Catholic, you know, being Irish and all, and I couldn't go to her church. My family would never forgive me."

"I see." I also understood.

I heard Mrs. Hanratty give a deep sigh over her soup pot. "She asked me to go to that place with her, too," she said. "I think she only did it to be kind, but I have my own church. Besides, I like to spend my days off away from my work." She eyed me as if she wasn't sure she could trust me. "If you know what I mean."

"Believe me, I understand you completely." Then I asked, "Who else used to visit Mrs. Chalmers? Did she have special friends who came by regularly or whom she went to see regularly?"

Mrs. Hanratty squinched her eyes up again, I presume to help her think. "Let me see . . ."

"There was that Mrs. Pinkney," Susan said.

"Yes. Mrs. Pinkney was her best friend, I'd say."

"I've met Mrs. Pinkney," said I. "She was very broken up to learn about Mrs. Chalmers."

"I imagine she was," said Mrs. Hanratty with a sad expression. "The missus and her were good chums."

"Did anyone else from the church visit her?" I asked, trying to broaden my investigation.

"Hmm. I don't—"

"Yes!" cried Susan, as if she'd just had a bright thought. This encouraged me a bit, since I'd begun to think of Susan as a rather dim bulb. "There was that other couple. What was their names . . . ?" Again her forehead crinkled.

"Oh, yes. I forgot them. I think their last name started with an I. Or was it an E?" Mrs. Hanratty, too, appeared puzzled.

But I thought I knew to whom the women were referring. "Could they have been Mr. and Mrs. Everett?"

"That's them!" said Susan, pleased.

Mrs. Hanratty nodded. "Yes. That's them, all right, although they called themselves Brother and Sister Everett, like as if they was born into the same family, when they was really married." She shook her head as if she didn't understand or appreciate Sister Emmanuel's brothering and sistering ways. "Liked him. Didn't like her."

Interesting. "Why not?" I asked.

With a shrug, Mrs. Hanratty said, "Don't know exactly."

"I know why I didn't like her," Susan said firmly. "She kept looking around as if she smelled something bad. And she had funny eyes."

"Funny eyes?" I said, hoping for elucidation.

"Yeah. I don't know how else to describe them."

Great. Funny eyes. I hadn't noticed anything particularly funny about Mrs. Everett's eyes, although I must admit I'd only seen her for a moment or two last Sunday. I decided I needed to visit that church again the following week.

Before I could ask the two servants anything else, the kitchen door swung open and darned if Mr. Simon Chalmers didn't stroll in!

"Mrs. Hanratty, could you serve luncheon—" Then he spotted me. "Why, good day to you, Miss . . . um . . ."

"Allcutt," I said. "I'm only here to ask a few questions in pursuit of determining the identity of your stepmother's murderer." At that bold statement, I almost cringed myself, thinking of how Ernie would react if he knew I was here.

"Miss Allcutt. Yes." He walked over to me. "You're an enterprising young woman. I didn't realize you were an investigator, too."

Was he being cheeky? I couldn't tell, so I decided to act as if the statement was a serious one. "Goodness, yes. Why, the police actually think my employer might have done the wicked deed, and I know he did not. Therefore, I'm doing everything I can to solve the mystery, since they seem determined to pin it on Mr. Templeton."

"I see."

"In fact," I went on, greatly daring, "I'd like to speak with you . . . and your father, too, if he's up to it, after you take your luncheon. If you wouldn't mind."

Simon Chalmers blinked at me a couple of times, then said, "Well . . . I guess it's all right. My father is pretty devastated, so I hope you won't ask anything . . . well, you know."

"I know," I assured him. "And I would be most grateful to you both."

"Then, sure. But you might as well come along now. I don't believe Mrs. Hanratty will be serving lunch until around one. By the way," he said, this time speaking to Mrs. Hanratty, "will you please serve lunch in my father's library? He doesn't feel up to moving around much."

"I'll certainly do that, Mr. Simon," said Mrs. Hanratty.

I could tell by the smile she gave him that he was a favorite of hers, and I hoped I wouldn't have to have him arrested for murder. I liked Mrs. Hanratty. I also noticed that Mr. Simon Chalmers only gave Susan a friendly nod. I presume he'd already pegged her as someone not worth conversing with, although whether that was because she was a maid or because she didn't have much intelligent conversation in her, I didn't know.

"Why don't you come with me," he said to me.

So I did.

CHAPTER TEN

Mr. Franchot Chalmers did appear to be suffering a great deal of emotional anguish when Mr. Simon Chalmers opened the door to his library and ushered me in. Slumped in a chair, and with red, swollen eyes, the senior Mr. Chalmers looked honestly heartbroken and bereft. He also looked as if he'd been perhaps taking too much brandy than was good for him, to judge by the almost-empty bottle on the table beside him.

Prohibition? What Prohibition? But I've already covered that issue, I reckon.

Mr. Franchot Chalmers—you know, I'm getting tired of writing out the full names of these two men. Will anyone become annoyed with me if I refer to them by their first names? Well, I don't know who would, come to think of it. My mother will definitely never read this journal.

At any rate, Mr. Franchot rose from his chair at once when I entered the room. Polite and gentlemanly he definitely was, if a little fuzzy around the edges, probably due to his consumption of brandy.

"Pa, this is Miss Allcutt, the one who found Persephone's body and telephoned me at the club. I'm sure you remember her."

"Ah, yes. How do you do, Miss Allcutt?" He bowed politely, and I felt like a rat.

"I'm so very sorry to disturb you, Mr. Chalmers. I understand how distressing this time must be for you."

"It was nice of you to call," he said mechanically. Then he looked at his son as if asking him to clue him in to why I'd been allowed into his presence. I'm pretty sure other visitors were treated politely and dismissed by the house servants or Mr. Simon and were seldom allowed as far as Mr. Franchot's personal library, where he seemed to be attempting to hide from the world.

"Pa, Miss Allcutt needs to ask us a few questions. She's helping the police in solving the crime."

That was nice of Mr. Simon to say and most unexpected, and I smiled to let him know it.

"Ah." Mr. Franchot hesitated, then said with a sigh, "Very well. Have a seat, Miss Allcutt. I hope somebody solves the murder soon. Murder," he repeated with revulsion. "I can't believe this has happened to Persephone. I can't seem to take it in." He buried his head in his hands.

I felt awfully sorry for him. Still and all, I also didn't want Ernie to be arrested for committing a murder he didn't. Commit, I mean.

"Go ahead, Miss Allcutt. The sooner you ask your questions, the sooner Pa can get back to . . ."

Mr. Simon let his sentence sort of trail off. I wondered what word he'd have inserted if he'd chosen to finish it. Finishing his brooding? Finishing his mourning? Finishing his brandy?

Well, I'd never know the answer to that one, so I started my inquiry. "I understand that Mrs. Chalmers had recently begun attending the Angelica Gospel Hall. Is that correct?" In order to add verisimilitude to this question—and also because I wanted to be sure I remembered what these two said—I'd taken out my secretarial pad and a sharpened pencil from my handbag. I hadn't used these accoutrements in the kitchen, sensing their presence would have made the two servant ladies nervous.

"Yes. She'd begun taking a good bit of interest in Adelaide

Burkhard Emmanuel's message. I didn't understand the fascination myself, but Persephone seemed to enjoy it, so I didn't say anything to discourage her. As far as I was concerned, anything that made her happy, made me happy." He sighed deeply, and I felt sorry for him again.

"I understand she spent a good deal of her time and money on the Angelica Gospel Hall. That didn't bother you?" And what a brazen question *that* was!

"Not really. Persephone had money of her own. I didn't even notice, to tell you the truth. I have my own business interests that take up most of my time."

Investments, thought I. Like his son. As a female person, I was supposed to know nothing about such masculine pursuits. As a matter of fact, in the case of investments, I didn't. But it wasn't my fault. My father could have instructed me in investments just as he'd done my awful brother. But had he? Heavenly days, no! Women's brains were too feeble to grasp such concepts. Phooey.

"I see. So she didn't depend on you for her, um, living?"

He shrugged. "I supported her as her husband. That's only proper. But as I said, she had money of her own. And, as I mentioned, her church participation made her . . . I don't know if happy is the right word. On a personal level, she felt she'd discovered something to do that mattered in the world, if that makes any sense." He sighed and shrugged again. "It didn't make much sense to me, but she seemed to love it. She made friends with people there and invited them over for tea and so forth."

"Yes, I believe I understand." Personally, I'd prefer to donate my time and money to an animal shelter or some organization that would help poor people, but I wasn't Mrs. Chalmers— which was a darned good thing, or I'd have been dead.

I continued with my investigation. "My employer, Mr. Ernest

Templeton, was hired by Mrs. Chalmers to investigate the theft of some jewelry. Did you know about that, Mr. Chalmers?"

"Oh, yes. Persephone told me. A jade necklace and bracelet, and a diamond brooch she'd inherited from her grandmother, I believe, were the items stolen. I can't imagine how."

"You don't believe a servant or visitor might have pilfered the gems?"

He blinked at me as if I'd just uttered the stupidest question ever spoken by a human being on this earth. "Our servants have been with the family for years, Miss Allcutt, and I doubt a casual visitor would have known the combination to our safe, or even where it is. The servants, either, come to that. I'm not in the habit of using it in front of the servants."

"I see. But the items were taken from the safe?"

"Yes."

Mr. Simon chimed in at that moment. "That's what Persephone said. They were taken from the safe."

Suddenly, Mr. Franchot looked at his son and said, "Say, you don't suppose one of those people from that church might have taken them, do you?

Mr. Simon hesitated before saying, "Well, I don't know, Pa."

"The jewelry was kept in the safe. How could anyone know the combination to the safe?"

"And she did say they were taken from the safe," reiterated Mr. Simon.

I eyed him for a moment, wondering why he'd repeated the bit about the safe. Did he suspect his stepmother had given the items to someone and then reported them stolen for some fell purpose unknown to her husband? Well, of course he did. He'd already told me as much when I'd spoken to him at the scene of the crime. I asked, "Where is the safe?"

"In this room, as a matter of fact," said Mr. Franchot.

"Hmm. I suppose that if an acquaintance were visiting with

137

her, Mrs. Chalmers might have gone to the safe to take something out to show the acquaintance," I mused aloud.

"Hard to imagine. How often does one need to open a safe when one is entertaining guests?" said Mr. Franchot. "Besides, the safe's behind that picture." He waved at a picture of a horse on the far wall.

Good point. I'm sure my parents had a safe back home in Boston, but I didn't even know where it was, and I couldn't imagine Mother taking a friend to visit the safe.

"Did Mrs. Chalmers entertain guests often?" I asked.

Mr. Franchot shrugged.

Mr. Simon said, "As Pa said, she had her church friends over a lot. I can't believe any of them are thieves, although I wouldn't put much past some of the religious zealots I've met in my day."

Mr. Simon was about thirty years old, and I wondered exactly how many religious zealots he'd met in those relatively few years. I didn't ask.

"Anyhow, she didn't entertain them in my library," said Mr. Franchot. "I don't know how the theft was accomplished." His eyes thinned a bit. "In fact, as long as the thief was pawing around in my papers and her jewels, I don't know why he didn't take a whole lot of other things while he was at it. I keep some bearer bonds in there, along with a good deal of cash."

"Yes. Interesting theft," I said, thinking the same thing.

Mr. Simon cleared his throat. "Pop, I know you don't want to hear this, but don't you think Persephone might have taken the jewelry to sell for that church of hers?"

Father looked at son, not challengingly, but as if Mr. Simon's words had hurt him. "But why, Simon? I didn't care how much money she gave to that silly place. She could have given away all her jewelry, as far as I'm concerned. I'd rather have her back than any of those damned trinkets."

"I know, Pa. I'm sorry." In an aside to me, he said softly,

"They weren't exactly trinkets."

I nodded to tell him I understood. Still, it didn't seem as though I was getting anywhere with the jewelry angle, so I decided to try another tack before these two got sick of me and asked me to leave. "Did Mrs. Chalmers have any particularly special friends she saw more often than others?"

Mr. Simon shrugged. "I didn't know her that well, to tell the truth."

Mr. Franchot thought for a bit. "There was one woman she went places with a lot and who came here quite often. Mrs. Fincher? Mrs. Pincher?"

"Mrs. Pinkney?" I supplied helpfully.

With a slow nod, Mr. Franchot said, "Maybe that was it. Yes. In fact, I'm sure it was, because the woman's husband actually had the gall to telephone me here at home one evening and demand that my wife stop leading his wife astray. Those were his very words, by God. And I'd never even met the fellow, much less had anything to do with him."

"Good heavens. That sounds like an odd demand to make of a perfect stranger."

"I gathered from further conversation that he was ranting about the church both ladies attended," said Mr. Franchot drily. "I told him I had no control over his wife, and if he couldn't handle her activities, how the devil should he expect me to? I beg your pardon, Miss Allcutt."

"Think nothing of it," I said with an airy wave of my hand.

But what he'd said was most interesting. Could Mr. Pinkney have become so annoyed by his wife's involvement in the Angelica Gospel Hall that he might actually kill the woman he believed responsible for that involvement? The notion was certainly something to think about.

However, I believed I'd stayed long enough with these two men, one of whom was clearly bereaved—unless he was a better actor than John Barrymore, which would be a stretch for any man. Therefore, I closed my notebook, placed it and my pencil in my handbag, and rose from my chair.

"Thank you both very, very much for seeing me at such a miserable time for you. I do appreciate your cooperation and hope fervently that the villain who killed your wife will be found shortly, Mr. Chalmers." To Mr. Simon, I said, "Thank you, too. You were very kind."

"Think nothing of it, Miss Allcutt. I wish you and your employer all the best in solving this crime."

So, on that friendly note, I departed the Chalmers house, not a whole lot wiser than when I entered it, although I did most certainly intend to pursue the Mr. Pinkney angle.

By the time I left the Chalmers home, it was past my usual lunchtime, so I directed the cab driver, who had waited as requested, to drop me off at a small tea shop near the Figueroa Building. When I stepped inside, whom did I see but Lulu La-Belle! She hailed me with a wave of those bright red fingernails and a loud, "Mercy! Over here!"

So I joined her at the luncheon counter. She'd almost finished her own lunch, but she waited around for me to order and eat my own, which, probably because I was still annoyed with my mother, was a corned-beef sandwich. With sauerkraut. And lemonade. Honestly, if you haven't tried corned beef, it's well worth the effort, no matter what stuffy people who have grievances—unwarranted, I might add—against the Irish have to say about it.

Lulu, naturally, quizzed me about the events of the morning. "The police led Ernie away, Mercy! Whatever is going on?"

So I told her everything. Why not? Merely because Lulu didn't come from a highly educated family didn't mean she didn't have a workable brain, something else my mother would never believe.

"Golly," she said upon a gust of expelled breath. "What a pickle for poor Ernie. I'm glad you're investigating, Mercy. Wish I could help, but I'm stuck behind the desk in the lobby."

"I wish you could help, too, Lulu. I don't like leaving the office so much, but . . . well, to tell you the truth, we don't have a lot of work at the moment, and I figure nobody will miss me."

Lulu nodded her sympathy. "I know. Ernie's never had much business except when you put that ad in the *Times.*"

I gaped at her. "You know about that?"

"Sure. Ernie told me."

"I thought he'd bite my head off, he was so angry with me for placing the ad."

"I don't know why, since it brought in business."

Morosely, I said, "I think I know why. He was mad because he didn't think of it himself. He is a man, after all, and many of them seem to be like that."

Lulu grinned. "You're probably right." She sobered. "But say, Mercy, isn't there some way I could help you investigate this murder? Investigation sounds ever so much more interesting than sitting at that stupid desk filing my nails and answering the telephone every two hours or so."

My glance slid over Lulu, from her vibrant yellow dress, enlivened with an orange sash around the dropped waist, to her orange hat, to her violently red fingernails. "Well . . . you know, Lulu, one of the primary aspects of detective work is to be . . . well, inconspicuous." That wasn't actually anything Ernie had told me, but it made sense to me. "Um, I don't think you're very inconspicuous."

After giving herself a once-over as I had done, she said, "Y'think so?"

"Well . . . yes. I mean, well, you favor such bright, lovely, *lively* colors. Nobody'd ever forget you once they saw you." I then thought, far too late, to say something kind. "And no one

141

could ever forget your beauty, either. Why, you have a face no man would forget."

"Really?" She cheered up considerably, and I blasted myself for a fool for not mentioning the beauty angle earlier. Not that Lulu was a God-given beauty, but art had done a good deal to perk up what she'd been born with, which wasn't bad to begin with, and she was definitely unforgettable, so that wasn't even close to a fib. "Well, I still wish I could help."

Something then occurred to me that was downright brilliant. Or maybe it wasn't. But it couldn't hurt. "I know! Why don't you attend the Angelica Gospel Hall with me next Sunday?"

Poor Lulu must have thought I'd lost my sanity. "Do what?"

With a laugh, I said, "Don't worry, Lulu. I'm not trying to convert you to Sister Emmanuel's church or anything, but you see, Mrs. Chalmers had recently joined that church, and according to the people I've spoken with so far, she spent every waking hour and nearly every cent she had on the place. I went to church there last Sunday and met some people who knew her. Perhaps you can come with me, and we can both do some snooping."

"Oh, gee, you think so?" Her face almost glowed for a moment before it fell again. "I dunno, Mercy. I don't think I'd fit in very well with those folks."

"I don't fit in, either, Lulu, but they didn't seem to notice."

"But I don't have any church clothes. All my clothes are bright." She sniffed. "Bright colors make me happy."

"I could let you borrow one of my dull working costumes."

Her eyes began glowing once more. "Oh, would you? Really?"

"Sure. We're about the same size." I peered more closely at Lulu's shapely figure. Lulu didn't bother with a bust-flattener. "Or thereabouts."

"Golly, Mercy, that would be swell!"

We were darned near bosom buddies by the time I'd finished

off my dill pickle spear (yet one more thing for my mother to deplore if she ever found out about it) and walked together back to the Figueroa Building. As we walked, something else struck to me, but I decided not to bring it up with Lulu yet since to mention it at that moment would have been premature.

It hadn't occurred to me that Ernie might have come back to the office from the police department, since I'd pictured him there, tied to a chair and with bright lights shining in his eyes while big, ugly coppers smacked him around with their billy clubs. Boy, was I wrong.

"Where the hell have you been?" he yelled as soon as I walked through the door into the outer office. It looked as if he'd been roaming the office searching for me, as if I might be hiding in a desk drawer or something. Oh, dear.

Bracing myself against another of his assaults upon my senses, I told the truth. "I went to the Chalmers house, where I interviewed the two house servants and the two Misters Chalmers."

"Christ." And Ernie, clutching his hair in both hands, staggered back to his office and all but fell into his chair.

I followed him into his lair, which I consider mighty darned brave of me under the circumstances.

"How many times have I told you to stay out of this investigation, Mercy?" Ernie's voice was calm now, but I knew he wasn't.

"Too many to count," I said, standing erect and dignified before his desk.

"And you refuse to obey my direct orders."

"Yes."

"And if I fire you, you'll continue to investigate, right?"

"Right."

"Shit."

"But I discovered some things that I think you ought to know," I said, even though I hadn't really.

He didn't let go of his hair, which was quite a mess by this time, but he looked up at me. "Yeah?"

"I know, for instance, that Mr. Simon Chalmers thinks Mrs. Chalmers took her jewelry and sold it to give to the church and only called you in as a cover-up. I know that the jewels were kept in a safe behind a picture of a horse in Mr. Chalmers' library, and that nothing but the jewelry was taken. I also found out that none of the servants know where the safe is or what the combination to it is."

"So he thinks."

"Exactly. So he thinks. However, I also learned that Mrs. Gaylord Pinkney's husband—Mrs. Pinkney was evidently one of Mrs. Chalmers' greatest friends—called Mr. Chalmers and demanded that he stop Mrs. Chalmers from leading Mrs. Pinkney astray by involving her in the Angelica Gospel Hall."

Ernie said, "Huh."

"Naturally, since he was perfectly content with his wife's involvement with the Hall, Mr. Chalmers ignored Mr. Pinkney's demand and told him not to call again."

"Going to church being better than running around with another man, I guess," grumbled Ernie.

I decided to ignore this salacious comment. "I also learned that Mrs. Chalmers entertained people from the Hall at her home quite often."

And then I couldn't think of anything else to say, so I shut up.

Ernie lifted his head and tried to smooth his hair down. His attempt was not awfully successful. "That's it?"

"That's more than we knew before," I told him sharply. "And I fully intend to pursue my own inquiry with Mrs. Pinkney. Perhaps she knows something she hasn't told me, but that will emerge with shrewd questioning."

I ignored Ernie's "huh."

"What's more, I'm going to her home, and I'm going to attempt to meet her husband and find out exactly why he's so adamant against his wife's involvement in that church. Mind you, while I can almost appreciate Mrs. Emmanuel's message of love, I'm no convert. But attending church services does seem a fairly innocuous thing for a woman to do, and I don't understand her husband's strenuous objections to it. She could be out robbing banks or something instead, don't you know."

I resented that blasted eye-roll Ernie was so fond of employing in my presence. Rather than reacting to it, I sat myself down on one of the chairs in front of his desk and said, "How long did the police keep you? Were they kind to you? They didn't hit you or anything, did they?" My worry leached into my voice, and I was embarrassed to hear it.

"Hit me? Hell's bells, Mercy, we live in the twentieth century. People don't torture people in order to get information nowadays."

"That's not what I've read in certain books," I told him.

"Books," he dared to grumble, as if he thought my statement was idiotic because I'd read about such things in books. Ernest Templeton, in whose desk I'd discovered, my very own self, an issue of *Black Mask,* in which appear many, many stories featuring the police giving innocent citizens less than lovely treatment in their departments. *Huh,* himself, blast the man.

"Nevertheless, I want to know what happened at the police station," I told him, my voice registering the fact that I was serious and would brook no nonsense from him.

"Not much. I told them I arrived at Mrs. Chalmers' house about eight o'clock last Thursday morning. She'd called and said she needed to tell me something important, and I had to get to her place early because I had an appointment with Phil at nine. I don't know what she wanted to tell me, because I don't think we got that far, although I honestly don't remember. The last thing I remember is drinking tea, of all things, with her on her living room sofa."

"You don't remember anything else at all after that?"

"That's right. I don't."

"But how did you get upstairs?"

"How the hell should *I* know? The last thing I remember is sipping that damned tea. Disgusting stuff, tea."

"Temper, temper," I said, trying to hold on to my own.

He sighed. "I don't know how I got upstairs."

"You had no bruises on your back or anything?"

"Bruises? What the hell would bruises prove?"

Pinching my lips together for a moment, I reminded myself that here was an innocent man who was suspected of murder, and who, if we didn't learn the name of the real murderer, might well be tried and convicted of said murder. Therefore, rather than screaming at him, I said quietly, "If someone drugged you downstairs and then hauled you upstairs by your feet, you'd probably have bruises on your back and perhaps your lower limbs. Maybe even the back of your head. Of course, you might have staggered up the stairs yourself, but I should think you'd remember that." Unless he was under the influence .of drugs and Mrs. Persephone Chalmers. I decided to keep that bit of unpleasant thought to myself.

Ernie's eyes opened a little wider, and he rubbed the back of his head. "Say, you might just have something there, Mercy All-cutt. The back of my head has hurt like hell for the past few days, and my back has felt like shit, too."

Ignoring his foul language was putting a tremendous strain on my nervous system. However, I controlled myself. "Did you bother to look at your back in a mirror?"

"Well . . . no. My head hurt and . . . well, it was lower than my back that hurt, actually."

"Lower than . . . Oh. I see." His posterior had bumped

against the stair steps, I presumed from his modest hesitation. That surprised me, actually, since I didn't consider Ernie Templeton to be a particularly modest man. "Well, did you look at your . . . lower regions in the mirror?"

"Hell, no! I don't go around looking at my butt in the mirror."

"Well, you might want to do so this time, if it means clearing you of a murder charge." My voice had risen in spite of my concerted effort to keep calm.

He didn't speak for a moment, although his lips writhed as if a number of oaths were squirming to get out. At last he said, "You're right."

"If possible, you should have Phil take a look at you, too, just so he won't think you're making it up. In fact, it's a shame they didn't take pictures of your back at the scene of the crime at the appropriate time."

"I'll be damned if I'll have Phil Bigelow or anybody else looking at my ass! And I'll be double damned if I'll have anybody take pictures of it!" roared Ernie.

This latest outburst was too much for me. I rose stiffly from my chair and said, "Fine. In that case, I'll continue my own investigation in my own way, without your help."

As I marched toward the door into my own office, Ernie said, "Damn it, Mercy. Give a fellow a break, can't you? You wouldn't want me looking at your ass, would you?"

Would I? Well, that might just depend . . .

So shocked was I when that thought entered my mind, I stopped dead in front of the office door and whirled around. "Ernest Templeton, if you aren't the most aggravating, horrible—"

He held up a hand, effectively stopping me in mid-rant. "I'm sorry. You're right. I should get a doctor or someone to look and see if I have any bruises. Not that bruises would prove that anyone hauled me up those damned stairs."

"Nevertheless," said I, regaining my control and my thoughts, which had scattered momentarily, "I shall place a telephone call to Dr. Vernon Piper, whose office is on the second floor of this very building, and set up an appointment for you. You can tell him why you want to know about bruises or not, as you choose, but it certainly wouldn't hurt you to have that head of yours examined."

With that skillful jab, I left Ernie's office, sat in my chair, grabbed the Los Angeles telephone directory, looked up Dr. Piper's number, and made an appointment for Ernie for that very afternoon. After that, I told Ernie about his appointment and went back to my desk.

From there I telephoned the Pinkney residence and asked to speak with Mrs. Pinkney. Curse Ernie and the entire Los Angeles Police Department. If *they* didn't intend to prove Ernie didn't kill that idiotic woman, *I* did.

"Oh, Miss Allcutt," said Mrs. Pinkney in a breathy voice. "I'm so glad you telephoned!"

She was? My goodness, I hadn't expected this. "Um . . . well, I wanted to know how you were getting along, you know," I said, thinking it a feeble thing to say.

"I miss Persephone dreadfully," she told me with meaning, "and I just discovered something I think you should know. Perhaps I should telephone the police, but—"

"No!" I cried, interrupting her. Rude, I know. "Please, Mrs. Pinkney. I . . . I'm sure I'll be happy to hear what you've discovered. Then, after we've discussed the matter, we can decide if the police should be told."

Curse Ernie and the entire L.A.P.D., *I* wanted to be the one to break this case.

"Oh, thank you, Miss Allcutt. You relieve my mind. Won't you please come to tea tomorrow afternoon, then? It will be such a relief to get this off my chest."

"I will be delighted to take tea with you tomorrow afternoon, Mrs. Pinkney," I said, meaning it absolutely.

CHAPTER ELEVEN

Lulu went home with me that night. I think Chloe was surprised, but she was as gracious to Lulu as she was to all her guests. So was Buttercup, who loved visitors from all stations in life. Shoot, Buttercup even welcomed my mother when she came to visit, although her enthusiasm had not thus far been returned, my mother being who she was.

"We're only here to get Lulu some boring clothes to wear to the Angelica Gospel Hall on Sunday," I explained.

Chloe waved her hand in an airy gesture. "Well, that should be easy, given your wardrobe."

"She doesn't like my taste in clothes," I said in an aside to Lulu. "I keep telling her my wardrobe is suitable to my profession, but she still doesn't approve of it."

But Lulu wasn't listening to me. Or to Chloe, either, for that matter. She was gazing about her as if she were looking upon some kind of royal castle in Europe. I guess Chloe's house was pretty fancy, but I was used to fancy. Lulu, clearly, was not.

"Golly," she whispered, as if she didn't want to speak too loudly for fear of disturbing any lingering angels. "I've never seen such a great place before, much less been inside one."

Chloe took this comment in stride. She'd met Lulu before when I'd introduced the two of them at the Figueroa Building, and she knew all about how Lulu and her brother had come to California from some dinky little town in Oklahoma. "Thank you. I'm fond of our home here on Bunker Hill, but I'm afraid we're going to have to move before too long."

"You're going to leave all *this?*" Lulu was dumbfounded.

I explained. "Mr. Nash's company is going to be moving to a place called Culver City, which is west of here, and he wants to build another house closer to his business. In Beverly Hills, I think." I looked to Chloe for confirmation, and she nodded.

Lulu's mouth fell open for a second before she breathed reverently, "*Beverly Hills?* Where Douglas Fairbanks and Mary Pickford live?"

"Yes. And tons of other motion-picture folks, too," I said crisply, wishing to move the conversation ahead. My opinion, not that it matters, was that Lulu was far too in awe of moving-picture people, who were, after all, only human beings like us, except they were luckier and looked better on the screen than most of the rest of us do. "Let's go upstairs to my room, Lulu, and we'll find you something to wear to church on Sunday."

"Okay."

Lulu's voice was very tiny. I got the impression she felt small in such grand surroundings. That was silly of her, too, if she knew it. Chloe had related to me the stories behind lots of motion-picture people, and I could have told Lulu about many so-called stars who'd come from backgrounds similar to her own. Or worse, even, although the picture companies' publicity people generally lent them romantic backgrounds in order to thrill their fans. Telling other people's stories wasn't my business, however, so I restrained myself. Still, I didn't think Lulu needed to be quite so overcome with the glory that was Chloe's home, especially if the plan that had begun churning in my noggin came to fruition.

We walked up the staircase, Buttercup scampering ahead of us, and came to my room, where Lulu stopped in the doorway and looked around. She remained stunned, if I were to guess by her demeanor. "Gee, Mercy, this is . . . this is . . ." Her words trailed off.

It was? I glanced around, too, and had to agree that the room was quite pleasant. Very well, it was more than pleasant. In truth, Chloe's upstairs had suites of rooms, one on the east wing, where Chloe and Harvey slept; one in the middle, the so-called Green Room, where my mother and other guests were lodged when they visited, and which was kept empty most of the time; and one in the west wing, which was where I lived. There were two other bedrooms upstairs, one flanking each side of the Green Room.

Anyhow, my suite included a sitting room, where I had a sofa, chair, desk (upon which sat my trusty typewriter), and a fireplace; a bedroom, which was smaller than the sitting room; a walk-in closet where I kept my minimal wardrobe; and a bathroom of my own. As I gazed about me, I realized the Nash house truly must seem like a dream-fantasy home to Lulu.

And that only reinforced my own belief that we Allcutts were not naturally good people, but had been darned lucky. What if the first Allcutt's bank had failed? What if another Allcutt had been a flagrant drunkard or wastrel who'd squandered the family's fortune? No one, including my family, could tell me that people, *any* people, were born to their stations in life because of some decree from God, blast it! The King of England would just be Joe Blow from the docks but for a quirk of fate, for Pete's sake.

And no matter what my mother might say, I'm still not a Socialist. So there.

But that's neither here nor there. I did acknowledge Lulu's flabbergastation (is that a word?), since I felt obliged to do so.

"It really is a pretty swell place, isn't it?"

"Swell?" Lulu kept goggling. "It's fantastic. Fabulous. I've never seen anything like it in my life."

"It's nice to have money, I reckon." My voice was uncharacteristically dry.

"Well, you should know." So was Lulu's.

Her words humbled me. "Yes. You're right. I should, and I do. And it is nice to have money, Lulu, but I swear to you, money isn't everything."

"Yeah. That's what everybody who has money says. You'll never hear somebody who doesn't have enough to eat saying that money isn't everything."

I thought about that for a moment. "You're right. You're absolutely right."

With a deep sigh, Lulu said, "But it's not your fault I was born poor and you were born rich. Let's see your boring clothes, Mercy."

"Good idea." I took her to the closet, and there we selected several outfits that would work nicely for Lulu's stint as a visitor to the Angelica Gospel Hall.

By the time she'd tried on about three different things, we were both nearly hysterical with laughter. I'd never realized how much fun it was to have a friend to do things like this with. I'd always enjoyed Chloe's company, but this was different. In spite of the differences in our backgrounds, Lulu and I had become real, honest-to-God friends, and I valued her.

"Oh, my sweet aunt Fanny!" Lulu gasped at one point, holding up a gray worsted suit in front of her and staring into the full-length mirror on the door of the closet. "I look like a Salvation Army lady!"

Dabbing my eyes, I said unsteadily, "I don't think Salvation Army ladies wear bright red lipstick and nail polish. But the suit is perfect."

Lulu turned and stared at me. "*Perfect!* I look like an undertaker's assistant!"

We both whooped at that one, but eventually that was the

outfit we selected for Lulu to wear on Sunday.

By that time, Chloe had come upstairs to see what all the hilarity was about, and she, too, started laughing. But Mrs. Biddle interrupted us to tell us that dinner was ready.

Instantly, Lulu stiffened. "Oh. Hey, I don't want to butt in or anything. I didn't mean to stay this long."

God bless my sister. She said, "Nonsense. If you're going to be working with Mercy to solve this crime and are actually going to wear that monstrosity to church on Sunday, the very least we can do is feed you."

So Lulu stayed for dinner. Only the three of us partook of the meal, since Harvey had to attend a business dinner at the Ambassador.

"Say, Chloe, how about you make reservations for Lulu and me to have lunch at the Ambassador one of these days? I told her all about our luncheon with Mother there, and she'd love to see the place."

Lulu's eyes went big. I'd have bet anything she'd thought I'd forget about my promise to feed her at the Ambassador. But not Mercy Louise Allcutt. By gum, I stick by my friends.

"Sure. I'll call Houston tomorrow. When do you want to go?"

So we set a day—the following Wednesday, to be precise— and by the time dinner was over, Lulu and Chloe were as thick as thieves, which made me happy. Chloe's chauffeur drove Lulu home after dinner—yet another first for her, and one she cherished and couldn't stop talking about at work for weeks— and Chloe, Buttercup, and I were left to ourselves, staring at each other in the living room.

"If Mother ever finds out . . ."

"I don't care if she does find out," I said defiantly. "It's far past time Mother stopped thinking of herself as better than the rest of the world and believing she knows precisely what everyone in it should think and do. The only thing Mother has is more money than most of the rest of the world, and that doesn't make her any holier or better than anyone else. I like Lulu, and she hasn't had our advantages."

"I'm not arguing with you," said Chloe with a grin. "I like her, too."

That made me happy.

The first thing I did when I got to the office the next morning was telephone Mrs. Pinkney's house to confirm our appointment for tea that afternoon. If anything, she sounded even more eager to see me than she'd been the day before. I wasn't sure Ernie would approve of my plans, but by that time I didn't care what he wanted.

He strolled into the office a little past nine, as usual, only looking a trifle more haggard than was normal for him. I guess being suspected of a heinous crime will do that to a fellow.

I followed him into his office. "What did the doctor say yesterday?" I asked him before he'd had time to shed his hat and coat and fling his feet onto his desk.

Before he answered, he followed his morning routine, then sat in his chair and glowered at me. "I have bruises."

"Did the doctor write that down in a report for the police to see?"

"A report? How the hell should I know?"

Sweet Lord, give me patience, I prayed, not awfully sanctimoniously. In an even voice, I said, "How do you expect the police to understand that you were bound and gagged and dragged upstairs in that pernicious house if the doctor or someone else doesn't tell them about the injuries you incurred during the process?"

"I'll tell Phil. He can talk to the doc."

Well, that was a little better, although I was far from satisfied.

"Did the doctor say the bruises were consistent with my conjecture?"

"I don't know if he's ever seen anyone who'd been bound and gagged and hauled up some stairs, but yeah. He said they probably were consistent with your *conjecture*." He spoke the last word in a nasty tone, which left me unimpressed.

"I'm the one who thought of it," I reminded him. "And I'm also the one who made the appointment for you to see the doctor." Then I remembered something I hadn't done, and I burst out with the worst words I'd ever uttered in my life: "Hell and damnation!"

Ernie blinked at me.

I turned as hot as a roasted potato and slapped my hands over my face. But what an idiot I'd been! "Darn it, Ernie, we should have had the police take photographs of your wrists. They were all red and chafed from that stupid rope. Oh, for heaven's sake, why didn't I think of this then, when it might have done some good? If they'd taken photographs of your wrists, anybody with a lick of sense would understand that I couldn't have tied you up! You'd been tied up for hours, not the short time I was in the house. And *that* can be proved by telephoning the taxicab company." I was pleased that I'd thought of the cab company.

"Well, they didn't take pictures, so that's that," said Ernie.

I turned my fury on him. "Or why didn't *you* think of having them take pictures? *You're* the so-called detective in this outfit!"

He blinked again. Very mildly, he said, "I was still under the influence of whatever drug I'd been given."

"If you're going to blame—"

He interrupted me by raising his hand and saying. "I'm not blaming you for anything, Mercy. You're right. Somebody should have thought to take pictures of my wrists. Or at least look at them. I don't know why Phil didn't do that at the time."

"I don't, either. He should do his job better than he does, Ernie Templeton. I don't care if he is your best friend. Stupid policemen. No wonder you quit the force if they're all such idiots that they don't do things like take pictures of injured people when a suspicious death has occurred."

"Now, wait—"

"Show me your wrists," I demanded. "There might still be rope burns on them."

Without a word or a protest, something that only later astounded me as obedience to my orders was uncharacteristic for Ernie, he actually did as I'd asked without quibbling. He held out both wrists, pushed up his shirtsleeves, and we both bent over them, squinting like mad.

"It looks as if there's still a little redness here." I touched the inside of his left wrist.

Ernie bent closer. "I think you're imagining that. Do you really think it's still red? It doesn't hurt any longer."

My head snapped up. "So it did hurt at the time?"

"Of course, it hurt. I'd been twisting in that damned rope, and my wrists hurt like hell for a few days. There were even a few drops of blood." He sounded as if he wanted sympathy, but I was in no mood to be handing him any. I was peeved as all get-out.

"You should have told the police that at the time, for heaven's sake. Ernest Templeton, I don't know what's going to become of you."

Ernie only let out a sigh.

So did I. "Well, I still think it looks as if it's chafed or chapped or something. That could have been caused by the rope. Can't those people—what do they call them? Pathologists or something like that? Can't they tell if the chafing is due to rope burns?"

"I don't know."

We bent over his wrists again, staring. I was trying to discern

157

anything that looked even vaguely rope-like in the faint redness remaining.

"Gee, I hope I'm not interrupting anything," a voice came from behind me, making me leap up and utter a cowardly squeal.

"Damn it, Phil! Why'd you want to do that for?" Ernie didn't seem any more pleased than I that his best friend had sneaked up on us. "Knock first, will you? Christ, you almost gave Mercy a heart attack."

Well, I liked that! As if he hadn't been as startled as I. But I decided it would be useless to quarrel about the point since we had bigger fish to fry.

Phil appeared a little abashed. "Sorry, guys. But what were you doing?"

I was still mad as a wet hen, as a maid of ours in Boston used to say, so I spoke first, and not kindly. "We were doing something *you* should have done last Thursday, Detective Philip Bigelow! We were looking for traces of rope burns on Ernie's wrists. You wouldn't believe *me* about finding him bound and gagged, but you couldn't have denied evidence you could see with your own blind eyes, now, could you? And there was no way on this green earth that I could have tied him up as a cover, either, since I'd only been in the house for a short time when I found him. *Which* can be verified by placing a call to the taxicab company!"

"Uh—"

I honestly don't know if it was Phil or Ernie who had tried to interrupt, but I was having none of it. "And, what's more, Ernie saw a physician yesterday—at my insistence, by the way—and the doctor found bruises upon his body that are absolutely consistent with his having been tied and hauled up a flight of stairs!"

This time it was Phil who blinked at me.

Ernie said, "She's right, Phil. On both counts."

"Oh, my God," said Phil, as if that would do any good. "I'm sorry, Ernie. We should have taken more notice of your health at the time. Although, in our defense, we generally concentrate on the corpse in situations like that, you know."

"Well, you might have better spent some of your time by concentrating on the fellow who's going to be blamed for creating the corpse, if you don't start doing your job better!" I was still blazing with fury. Can you tell?

"Mercy," Ernie said. "Simmer down, will you?"

Ooooh. I could have killed him myself in that instant. Since I couldn't do that, I ranted on. "No! I will not simmer down. I won't simmer down until I find the murderer of that ridiculous woman and you're cleared absolutely of a crime you didn't commit. If neither you nor the Los Angeles Police Department cares about justice, *I* do!"

And with that, I flounced out of the room and into my office, where I plunked myself down into my chair and darned near burst into tears. But I wouldn't give either of those awful, officious, *stupid* men the satisfaction of seeing me cry.

Therefore, I decided to go down to the lobby and talk to Lulu. Maybe by the time I got back upstairs, I'd have calmed down some. I ran down the stairs as if pursued by demons, but was brought up short when I saw Lulu behind her desk in the lobby, filing her nails and talking animatedly with Mr. Emerald Buck, who'd propped himself on his push broom whilst he listened.

"I tell you, that house was like a castle or something," Lulu told him. "I've never seen anything like it."

She was telling him all about Chloe's house, no doubt. Ah, well. At least it was a change of topic from murder and mayhem. And at least Emerald Buck was a kindhearted gentleman who never told me to simmer down. Striving to attain some sort of inner peace, I strolled over to Lulu's desk.

"Oh, hey, Mercy!" Lulu said happily. "I was just telling Mr. Buck about your sister's house."

"Sounds like a grand place," said Mr. Buck. He had a lovely voice, deep and velvety. He'd told me once he sang in his church's choir, and I could well believe it.

I said, "It's nice, all right. Too bad they're going to have to sell it."

Lulu heaved a huge sigh. "Yeah. Boy, I'd give anything to live in a place like that."

And that, as they say, was that. I decided then and there that if none of the men in my life gave a rap about what I did, said, or discovered, at least it might be possible for me to make Lulu happy. So I sat myself down in the chair facing Lulu's desk and said, "I've actually been thinking of buying the place myself, Lulu. If I did, I'd have to get some tenants, since I don't think I could make the payments all by myself."

That wasn't strictly the truth, since Great-Aunt Agatha had been most awfully generous in her gift to me after her death, but I didn't want Lulu to know that. What I wanted was for Lulu—and perhaps another working girl or two—to have a chance to live as I'd lived my whole life long and had believed the rest of the world did, too, until I'd learned otherwise.

I think Lulu had been stricken dumb, because she stared at me with her mouth open, and no words emerged.

It was Mr. Buck who broke the silence. "That's a right kindly thing to do, Miss Allcutt."

"I don't think of it as being kindly," I told him truthfully. "I just really like the house and the location, and would hate to live there all by myself. Well, with Buttercup, I mean." I'd told Mr. Buck all about Buttercup. He approved of dogs, so I approved of him.

Which reminded me of something else. "Say, Mr. Buck, didn't you mention once that your wife works as a cook and housekeeper for some folks on Carroll Avenue?"

"She do that," Mr. Buck agreed, nodding.

"We'd need a cook and a housekeeper if I bought the house, wouldn't we, Lulu?"

But Lulu still sat at her desk mute, her fingernail file held loosely in her hand, and stared at me as if I'd just offered her the moon and the stars and all the diamonds at that big jewelry store in New York. What's the name of it? Tiffany's? I think that's it.

Unfortunately, it now looked as if Mr. Buck had been stricken with Lulu's muteness. I hadn't realized until that moment that such things were contagious. Or perhaps I'd been too precipitate again. I really had to work on moving up to things in a roundabout way so as not to shock people.

Well, it was too late for that now. I rose and said, "Please think about it, both of you. I'm going to talk to Chloe and Harvey about buying the house from them, and I'd love to have people I already know to share it with me."

I figured I'd better get back to the office now that I'd calmed down a little, although I wasn't sure I wouldn't explode again if Ernie or Phil said or did something else to annoy me. It seemed I was a trifle touchy that day.

CHAPTER TWELVE

Lulu and I went to lunch together at twelve-thirty. We decided to stop at the little hot dog stand on the corner of Broadway and Sixth. I had sauerkraut and mustard on my dog to spite my mother, Ernie, Phil, and everyone else in the world who'd ever aggravated me. I don't know what Lulu had on hers, but we sat on a bench in Pershing Square, listened to the street preachers rant, and my own personal lunch was very tasty.

Naturally, Lulu wanted to talk about my plans to buy Chloe's house, so we discussed that. I wasn't awfully interested in the topic, since I was more concerned about the case of Mrs. Chalmers' murder, but I let Lulu rhapsodize. Although this is kind of embarrassing to admit, I think one of the main reasons I wanted to buy the Nash home was so that I could continue taking Angels Flight down to Broadway every day. But that sounds so trivial a reason to buy a house that every time I thought it, I was ashamed of myself. Imagine buying a house because of a tiny railroad line! I'd bet money, if I ever bet on anything, that poor people didn't use inane reasoning like that when they set about to buy houses. Anyhow, I didn't divulge my reason to Lulu, so I guess it doesn't much matter.

I also couldn't use the excuse that I needed to keep my job and that's why I wanted to buy the house, because I didn't really need my job. I didn't tell Lulu that, either. Besides, she already knew it.

"Oh, boy, it would be fun to have a friend to go to work with every day," said Lulu.

"I think so, too."

"I wonder if Mr. and Mrs. Buck would like the idea."

"I don't know, but I do know there's a lovely apartment off the kitchen that has a bedroom and a bathroom and a sitting room. Do you know if they have any children?"

Lulu shrugged. "I think Mr. Buck told me about a daughter going to school back east somewhere. I think I heard him talk about a son, too, but I'm not sure."

"Hmm. I wonder what school she goes to that it has to be back east. There are lots of schools around here." I wiped mustard and sauerkraut on a napkin and wished my spite hadn't been quite so great, since the napkin was small and the mess was largish.

"Well," said Lulu. "She's going to college, and there aren't a whole lot of colleges that take Negro students. Especially girl Negro students. I suspect they found one in the south somewhere. Mr. Buck says she wants to be a teacher."

It was my turn to gape mutely at someone. Don't ask me why, but it had never once occurred to me that colleges might not accept students because of their race. That didn't seem fair to me. "But . . ."

"Face it, Mercy. You've lived in heaven all your life. This is the real world. Mr. Buck is a nice man, but he's a Negro, and his kids are Negroes, and there's nothing you or me or him or anyone else can do about it."

"But . . ."

"Would you want your kids to go to school with his kids?"

Her question stunned me. I thought it over. Presuming I ever had children, would it bother me if they were in classes with students of other races?

Oh, dear. I didn't like it that I was thinking what I was thinking.

163

Lulu smirked at me. "See?" She, not having had my type of manners shoved down her throat from birth, licked the mustard from her own fingers. "Personally, I think Mr. Buck is a heck of an improvement over that Ned creature who used to kill women, and I also think he's smarter than Ned ever was. But he's still not white. And *that*, Mercy Allcutt, is the only thing that matters, when push comes to shove."

"Good heavens," I whispered, feeling depressed and defeated. Then it occurred to me to wonder if Sister Adelaide Burkhard Emmanuel would allow Negroes into her Angelica Gospel Hall. I hadn't seen a single one there that first week I'd gone. Did God judge people by their color, too?

I didn't believe it.

"When did the Civil War end?" I asked, still feeling kind of faint.

"How the heck should I know? I was never any good at history."

"Eighteen sixty-five, I believe. And the Emancipation Proclamation was passed a couple of years before that."

"What's the Emancipation Proclamation?" Lulu didn't sound as if she much cared.

"It was the proclamation freeing the slaves." But it hadn't freed all of them. I remember being shocked when I'd learned that.

Bother. My heart gave a big twist. In that moment I wished . . . But I didn't have the time, money, or energy to save the entire world from its follies. My purpose in life at this moment was to clear Ernie of murder charges. Therefore, I attempted with my whole self to shove the question of prejudice and unfairness out of my mind and concentrate on the problem at hand.

I even gave myself a shake, as if by doing so, I could shake irrelevancies out of my head. If they were irrelevancies.

But no. *Stop it, Mercy Allcutt,* said I to myself. And I did. Stop it, I mean.

Therefore, I said to Lulu, "I'm going to be visiting a lady named Mrs. Pinkney this afternoon for tea. She was a friend of Mrs. Chalmers."

"That's the lady who was murdered, right?"

"Yes. Mrs. Chalmers was, not Mrs. Pinkney."

"Uh-huh."

"And I'm going to ask questions and see if I can discover anything with relevance to the case. Mr. Pinkney doesn't like his wife's involvement with the Angelica Gospel Hall. He even called Mr. Chalmers to see if he could get Mrs. Chalmers to stop inviting Mrs. Pinkney to go to church with her, and I'm wondering if he might be a suspect."

"Gee, Mercy, be careful, okay?"

"Don't worry, Lulu. I'll be very careful."

"Does Ernie know you're doing this?"

"Um . . ." Did he? I thought over my morning and, although I could remember Ernie and even me shouting and swearing a good deal, I didn't remember telling Ernie I was taking tea with Mrs. Pinkney. "I think I forgot to tell him. I was so mad at him by the time Phil Bigelow got there, I just stormed off."

"Phil Bigelow," said Lulu in a tone that left no doubt whatsoever what she thought of him. I didn't blame her, Phil having once arrested her brother and all.

"Well, it doesn't matter. If Ernie's still in the office when we get back from lunch, I'll tell him then." I turned to look at Lulu and grinned. "Did I tell you he threatened to fire me if I didn't stop investigating the Chalmers case?"

Lulu gasped. "No! He didn't!"

"He did. So I told him to go right ahead. That would leave me all day, every day, to investigate the case."

I was glad when Lulu laughed, because her amusement did

something to brighten my thus-far gloomy day.

By the time we got back to the office, Ernie had left it again. With the police. My heart crunched when I read the note he'd placed on my desk: *Gone with Phil and O'Reilly to the station. Stay out of trouble.*

I didn't mind the *stay out of trouble* part, because I'd become accustomed to Ernie telling me stuff like that. It was the *going to the station with Phil and O'Reilly* part that bothered me. A lot. Why had he gone to the station again? Had Phil made him go? Had O'Reilly? Had Ernie decided to go on his own for some reason beyond my understanding? Since he never divulged anything of importance to me, I had not a clue in the world about anything at all.

However, that was a situation I intended to change that very afternoon by deft inquisition of Mrs. Pinkney, and even her husband if he was there at home with her.

The Pinkneys didn't live in as grand a neighborhood as the Chalmerses, but on a neat little street with a bit of charm called Hoover. I decided not to have the cabbie wait for me, since I didn't anticipate any trouble from Mrs. Pinkney, a woman I'd pegged as rather meek. Not that my judgment when it came to people had proved correct one hundred percent of the time in the past, but I still didn't believe Mrs. Pinkney a deranged murderer. Of course, her husband might be a different matter entirely, but he was probably at work somewhere, so I still told the cabbie not to wait.

Before I even got to the front door, Mrs. Pinkney had opened it and stood there, a beaming smile on her face, as if my visit was one of the most looked-forward-to events in her life. She wore a pretty, pink flowered day dress and looked as if she'd dressed especially well for my visit, which touched me. I figured she probably didn't get out much. My heart twanged again when I realized her not getting out much probably had a good deal to do with her best friend's death.

"I'm so glad you could come over today, Miss Allcutt," she said, grasping my hand and all but tugging me into her house. "Since Persephone's death, I've been so lonely. And I did so want to tell someone of my discovery."

And darned if she didn't start crying. I swear. This woman cried or fainted at the drop of a hat—or the drop-in of a guest.

"Please, Mrs. Pinkney," I said in my most sugary voice, "please don't weep. Remember that Sister Chalmers is in a better place now. And you'll see her again one day. Don't forget that." Until Ernie Templeton hired me as his secretary, I hadn't understood the true meaning of a detective's job. So far, for me, it had been mainly acting, yet one more form of employment my parents would deplore.

She hauled out a hankie and mopped her eyes. "Yes, yes. You're right. I know that. But I still miss her so much."

"It's those of us who are left behind who hurt, I know. But you can take heart from knowing that Mrs. Chalmers is singing in the heavenly choir now."

I could hardly believe those words had come out of my mouth. Still, I felt sorry for Mrs. Pinkney, and my insipid comments seemed to be giving some comfort to my hostess, so I didn't worry too much about them.

"You're right. And Persephone was such a cheerful, optimistic person. She always looked on the bright side. She'd hate it that I grieve so for her."

Boy, doesn't that just show you that perception is everything in this world? The Persephone Chalmers I'd met had been virtually insubstantial, with her wafting ways and tiny, breathy voice. Yet one of her best friends had known her as a cheerful and optimistic person. You just never know, do you?

"But please, Miss Allcutt, do come into the living room. I've tea things all set up for us there. We can have a comfortable coze."

Whatever that was. I was glad her husband wasn't home, though, since I considered him a likely murder suspect. "Sounds lovely," I gushed, and allowed myself to be led to her living room, which was a bit too full of overstuffed furniture with doilies flung everywhere. I sat on a chair facing a sofa. A table in between the chair and sofa had indeed been laid with tea things, along with bread and butter sandwiches and some cookies my grandmother used to call Scotch shortbread. I guess everyone does, although that points out yet one more thing I'd learned since my move to Los Angeles: different ends of the country call things by different names. For example, where I come from, we have ponds. Californians refer to those same-sized bodies of water as lakes. See what I mean?

Tea and food aside, I learned a great deal about Mrs. Chalmers' association with the Angelica Gospel Hall. Mrs. Pinkney confirmed that Mrs. Chalmers had sold her so-called stolen jewelry and given the money to the church. Truth to tell, that kind of shocked me.

"But didn't she think it was . . . well, a sin to lie like that? To her husband, I mean."

A huge sigh preceded Mrs. Pinkney's next words. "Yes. And she confessed her sin to Sister Emmanuel. Sister Emmanuel told her to confess to her husband, and I think she was going to, although I don't know if she'd got around to it by the time . . ."

She stared out of her front window—which was clean as a whistle, by gum—for a moment, and I said, "I don't think she did. He still seemed under the impression that the jewels had been stolen."

With a melancholy sigh, Mrs. Pinkney said, "Frankly, I don't know why she didn't tell Franchot to begin with. He'd probably have donated the money to the church himself, let her keep her jewelry, and been happy to do it. He was ever so fond of her and was forever giving her jewelry and furs and things like that."

She sounded more than a little bit wistful, and that prompted my next words. "When I spoke to him, I got that impression, too. That he loved her dearly, I mean."

"Oh, my, yes."

"It's too bad we all can't have marriages like that, isn't it?"

Mrs. Pinkney's eyes, which were small and blue, snapped to mine. "Oh, my dear, you have *no* idea. I love my Gaylord, but he can be such a . . ."

I guess she couldn't think of a polite word for what her Gaylord could be. "He dislikes your association with Sister Emmanuel's church, I remember you telling me."

"Yes. He certainly does. He's violently opposed to my going there."

Aha! That word struck me hard. I tried not to sound like it when I said, "Violently?"

She nodded sadly. "Yes. He's even thrown things and told me he'd forbid me going, but I told him you can't stop a person from worshiping God in his or her own fashion. That's the law of this country, after all."

By golly, I think she was right about that. I hadn't memorized the Constitution, but it's what my teachers always said: that our country was founded because people needed freedom to express their religious beliefs.

"Why is he so opposed to your going to the Hall?" I asked, genuinely puzzled. Going to church seemed like such an innocuous activity.

"Gaylord grew up in a Roman Catholic family. I did, too, but I saw the light, thanks to Persephone. Still, I can't convince Gaylord that Sister Emmanuel's message is the correct one. He thinks I'm going to hell. Sister Emmanuel is more forgiving than he."

Because she didn't consign Gaylord Pinkney to hell? I thought stuff like punishment and forgiveness were God's jobs, but I didn't say so. What I said was, "I'm so sorry you have such opposition from such an important person in your life," I told her, meaning it sincerely. She was an average-sized woman, with mouse-brown hair drawn up into a bun, a slim figure, and a face that held a world of unhappiness. Or perhaps it was disappointment, as if all of her dreams had crashed around her.

"Thank you. You're very kind. Sister Emmanuel and I pray about Gaylord all the time. So far, he hasn't softened, but at least he no longer—"

Her teeth snapped together like a metal trap closing. So I said, "He no longer what?"

Another sigh, this one even bigger than her last. "That's what I wanted to talk to you about, actually. I told you Persephone had been getting threatening letters, didn't I? They absolutely terrified her."

"Yes." My heart started beating wildly. "You don't mean to tell me that . . ." I decided I *would* let her tell me. And she did.

Tears began leaking from her eyes again, and I felt sorry for her. She nodded. "Yes. Gaylord thought it was Persephone who was 'leading me astray'—that's what he called it. I believe it was he who sent her those foul letters. I found one in his desk not long after Persephone was killed. Until then, I didn't know he was the one who was terrifying her so. If I'd known, I'd . . . well, I don't know what I'd have done. But I found that letter. I guess he didn't send it because . . . well, he didn't need to anymore. If you see what I mean."

"Yes, I understand completely." Speaking of seeing what she meant . . . "I don't suppose you could show me that letter, could you? I'm not merely being snoopy, Mrs. Pinkney.

Unfortunately, my employer, whom Mrs. Chalmers hired to look into the stolen jewelry situation, is under suspicion of the murder. Now, I don't believe your husband had anything to do with Mrs. Chalmers' death, but it might clear up some things if Mr. Templeton, my employer, could see one of those letters."

If she bought that lousy reasoning, she was a whole lot more stupid than I thought she was. But she surprised me.

With shoulders sagging, she said, "You might as well take it with you. I don't believe Gaylord had anything to do with Persephone's death, but if he did . . . Well, if he did, then I hope he hangs for it! By the good Lord's name, I do! And then I hope he rots in hell!"

Oh, my. I guess that put marriage and friendship where they belonged, at least in Mrs. Pinkney's estimation. I said humbly, "I'm sure he was only trying to frighten her and hoping that by doing so, he'd influence her to withdraw from the church. He probably figured that if she left, you'd leave, too." Yet another big, fat lie to add to my growing list of sins. Still, I was going to get that letter, by gum!

"I hope you're right. But we'd best hurry. Mr. Pinkney will be coming home soon."

"Thank you."

She led me to what Mr. Pinkney probably thought of as his sanctuary from the overstuffed life he lived with his wife, a small room sparsely furnished with an easy chair, a floor lamp by which he read to judge from the pile of newspapers and books stacked on a side table, and a desk. She opened the top desk drawer, withdrew a piece of paper, and handed it over. "Here. Please do whatever you think is best with it."

So I tucked the letter away in my handbag without even reading it first, thanked Mrs. Pinkney heartily for the delicious tea and shortbread, and decided to skedaddle out of there before the possibly murderous Mr. Gaylord Pinkney returned to his home.

"Would you like to call a cab?" Mrs. Pinkney asked. "I'm sure you don't want to be here when Gaylord returns." She sounded so sad, I felt bad about leaving her.

On the other hand, I wanted to get out of there. Fast. Therefore, I thanked her politely and declined the use of her telephone. Rather, I walked as fast as I could to Venice Boulevard, where I was lucky enough to hail a cab.

As I sat in the backseat of the cab, I withdrew the letter from my handbag. It was an ugly thing, in regard to its appearance and its words. In big, bold, black letters, Mr. Pinkney had written: STAY AWAY FROM THE ANGELICA GOSPEL HALL, OR YOU'LL DIE A HORRIBLE DEATH. Shuddering, I folded the nasty thing up and shoved it back into my handbag.

By that time it was nearly five o'clock, and I doubted Ernie would have returned to the office, but I had the cabbie take me there anyway.

When I entered the lobby, Lulu had stopped filing her nails for the day and was just picking up her handbag. "Hey, Mercy. Ernie was looking for you."

"He's here?" My heart did one of those little dancey things it occasionally did when things went right for me.

"Yeah. Looked real bad, too. I guess they grilled him down at the station. Darned coppers. They're all on the take, you know. Every last one of them."

Although Lulu's opinion of the L.A.P.D. was rather extreme, it was also, unfortunately, pretty accurate. I knew that dismal fact from the things Ernie had told me. "Oh, dear. I hope they didn't give him too hard a time." He'd gone with Phil. If Phil had manhandled Ernie, I'd have something to say to him the next time I saw him.

Shrugging, Lulu said, "Dunno. All's I know is that Ernie

looked beat."

"They *beat* him?" I cried, shocked.

"No, no, no. I don't mean that. I mean he looked whipped. Tired. You know. Worn out. Beat."

"Oh. Yes, I see." Every now and then the language differences between Lulu and me got in the way of clear communication, although I was learning Los Angeles street cant quite quickly, if I do say so myself.

"Well, I gotta go now. See ya tomorrow."

"Have a good evening."

"You, too."

With our conversation over, I went up the stairs to Ernie's office, happy that I had something pertinent to tell him but sorry he'd had a bad day.

I opened the outer office door. Every time I saw the office, I felt a sense of accomplishment. When I'd first been hired by Ernie, the office had been dull, dusty, and ugly. Now it was quite perky, and I dusted it every day. It looked ever so much better than it had when I'd first entered it. I'd mentioned to Ernie that I'd like to spiff up his office, too, but he'd adopted a horrified expression and told me to keep my hands off his stuff. Men.

Anyhow, I called, "Ernie? Are you still here?"

"What are you doing here?" came a disgruntled voice from Ernie's office.

"I found out something!"

He grunted.

I walked to his office and entered, only to find Ernie with his arms folded on his desk and his head resting on his arms. My heart did a flip-flop, and I darted over to him.

"Oh, Ernie! Did they hurt you? They *did*, didn't they? I'm going to kill Phil Bigelow!"

Ernie lifted his head and scowled at me. "For God's sake,

Mercy, take it easy, will you? Nobody hurt anybody. I'm just tired. It was a rough day, and I don't like being a murder suspect." He hesitated for a moment and added, "And O'Reilly is a real ass. He's just aching to pin the murder on me."

"Oh." I guessed having to endure such a frightful day might exhaust a man.

"Yeah."

"But I found out who'd been sending Mrs. Chalmers those nasty letters, by gum!"

"You did?" He perked up slightly

"I did." I was feeling quite proud of myself by that time.

"Well?" he demanded. "Who the hell was it?"

Some of my exultation slipped a bit. "Honestly, Ernie Templeton. You can be the most aggravating—"

"Dammit, Mercy, will you just tell me who sent the damned letters?"

I huffed, but gave in. "Mr. Gaylord Pinkney."

"I'll be damned."

"Of that I have no doubt," I said bitterly.

"Huh."

"Well, you're going to tell Phil, aren't you?"

"Of course, I am."

"And then they'll investigate him?"

"Sure they will."

We were both silent for a moment. Then Ernie said, "I don't suppose you managed to get your hands on one of those letters, did you?"

My pride kicked in again. "As a matter of fact, I did."

Ernie actually smiled at me. "Good work, Mercy. Can I see it?"

Without overtly correcting his grammar, I said, "Yes, you may. Mrs. Pinkney gave me the one she found in his desk drawer. I guess he didn't send it because he killed her before he

Fallen Angels

got around to it."

He lifted an eyebrow. "You've pegged him as the killer, eh?"

"It makes sense." I fished in my handbag and withdrew the letter. "Here." I held it out to him.

Ernie read it and wrinkled his nose. "Ugly. He really hated her, didn't he?"

"Looks like it to me."

"Yeah, well, you never know. Maybe he was just peeved. Anyhow, I'll give this to Phil, and the police will check on his location at the time of the murder."

"You don't sound very encouraged by this new discovery," I said, feeling slightly miffed.

With a shrug, Ernie rose from his chair and took his hat from the rack beside his desk. "Come on, kiddo, let's beat this joint. You gotta get home for dinner or anything?"

"Well, I generally dine with Chloe and Harvey, but I don't have to. What did you have in mind?"

"Call your sister and tell her you're *dining* in Chinatown with me this evening."

So I did, thrilled with the possibility that Ernie was actually going to discuss the case with me and ask for my input.

CHAPTER THIRTEEN

I ought to have known better.

"Mercy, I don't want to talk about the damned case," he told me flatly as we drove the few blocks to Chinatown in his battered Studebaker. And all I'd done is ask if he considered Mr. Pinkney a viable suspect. "All I want to do is get some Chinese grub at Hop Luey's, then go home and go to sleep. I'm bushed."

Hmph. So much for that. Feeling put out, I said, "Very well."

After Ernie parked his car on Hill Street, we walked to Hop Luey's, climbed upstairs to the restaurant, and were seated by a dignified Chinese waiter. Hop Luey's interior was dim and lovely, with Chinese hangings on the walls and little Chinese candle holders on the tables. Holding candles, I'm sure I need not add. Although I just did. Oh, never mind.

"I'm sure I can help you with this case if you'll only let me," I pressed him after we'd been handed menus and the waiter had gone off to get our tea. "In fact, I already *have* helped you with it. You have to admit that's so, Ernie."

"I don't want to talk about the damned case." Ernie's words were measured, as if he were deliberately putting large spaces in between them so I'd get the message.

Irked, I said, "Well, we have to talk about something, don't we?"

Lowering his menu so he could squint at me from across the table, Ernie said, "Yeah. How's your mother?"

"Darn you, Ernest Templeton. I don't want to talk about my

176

overbearing mother! And you certainly don't need *me* to eat Chinese food with you if you don't want to talk about anything pertinent."

He carefully set his menu on the table, and I took a good look at him. He appeared exhausted and defeated, and I felt a little guilty.

"Can't we just have a nice little dinner and chat like friends?" he said at last. "I'm sick and tired of the case, crime, the L.A.P.D. and everything else that's happened lately. Give me a break, can't you?"

Chastened, I said, "I'm sorry, Ernie. I know you've had a hard time these past few days."

He heaved a big sigh and picked up his menu. "I think I'll have number two, with the egg-flower soup. What about you?"

"That sounds good to me." In truth, it was too much food, but I supposed I could always take the leftovers home and bring them with me for luncheon on the morrow. That's what other working girls did. At least, I think that's what they did.

I tried to think of something to talk about that wasn't connected with the case. My mind floundered. Then I thought about Chloe and Harvey selling their house and moving, so I told Ernie about that. "It's because the studio's going to move to Culver City," I said.

He tilted his head to one side. "They're moving to Beverly Hills? That's where all the flicker folks are moving to these days."

"So I hear. Harvey wants to build a house there. He might get started on the building part, but they aren't going to move into the new house until after the baby's born."

Was it indiscrete for a single lady to discuss people having babies with a single gentleman? There was *so* much I still didn't know about real life! It got downright discouraging sometimes.

"Are you going to move with them?" Ernie asked, surprising

me out of dismal thoughts about my inadequacies.

Aiming for a lightness I didn't feel, I said, "No. I want to stay around here and keep my job. You can't get rid of me that easily, Ernest Templeton."

He chuckled. "I don't want to get rid of you, Mercy. Most of the time."

The waiter returned and took our menus and our orders.

"I'm so hungry, I could eat a horse and follow it up with a moose," Ernie said.

"Didn't they feed you at the police station? Gee, they came and took you away right about lunchtime, didn't they?" I was counting up grudges against the L.A.P.D., and the stack was getting awfully high.

"Phil had them bring me a sandwich and coffee, but they were both so bad, I didn't eat much. Besides, I didn't feel like eating at the time. I was too busy being grilled."

There was that word again. Grilled. The waiter placed soup before the two of us, and I fiddled with my bone spoon. Ernie dipped his spoon into his soup and dug right in. He glanced at me. "What's the matter? Don't like your soup?"

I took a sip. "It's delicious." Then, because I couldn't seem to help myself, I said, "Ernie, I know you don't want to talk about the case, but I really want to know what they did to you at the station. I don't want you to be hurt."

Another sigh rippled the soup in Ernie's bowl. "They didn't hurt me. They asked me questions for hours and hours. It seemed like the same questions over and over. Phil was there, so nothing got out of hand. I think they're frustrated because they can't find any other likely suspects, so they've fixed their attention on me."

"Well, now they've got Mr. Gaylord Pinkney. Even his wife wants it to be him."

Ernie's eyebrows lifted and he grinned at me. "Yeah?"

"That's what it sounded like to me. He's dead set against her involvement in the Angelica Gospel Hall, and that's about the only thing she's interested in now that her best friend is deceased."

"Sounds like a pathetic life to me." Ernie grimaced into his soup.

"Well . . ." I let out a smallish sigh. "It does to me, too."

"Can't she join the library guild or a garden club or something?"

"I guess she has a religious bent."

"Huh." Ernie sipped more soup.

"What about the son?" I asked, feeling a trifle frustrated.

"Clean as a whistle."

"You're sure?"

"Phil's sure. And I trust Phil."

"I'm not so sure I do anymore," I said, thinking black thoughts about Phil Bigelow, even if he was Ernie's best friend. Glumly, I sipped more of my own soup. It really was good. "Well, I don't think her husband did her in, either," I said, laying my spoon on the plate, surprised that I'd managed to finish all the soup that had been in it. Maybe I was hungrier than I'd thought I was.

"Phil's opinion, too. And mine," said Ernie, leaning back so the waiter could pick up our soup plates. "Poor man's been a total blubbering mess ever since you found the body."

He would have to bring my discovering the body into the conversation, the mere remembrance of which made me shudder, wouldn't he? "Of course, he could be faking his grief," I said, not believing it.

"I suppose so, but I don't think so. Neither does Phil."

Well, that was just great. We were eliminating suspects right and left. I decided to lead the conversation in another direction on my own, even without Ernie's prodding.

"Lulu's coming with me to the Angelica Gospel Hall this coming Sunday."

Ernie's eyes bulged. "Lulu? She's doing what?"

"She's coming with me to the Angelica Gospel Hall."

Darned if he didn't lean back and laugh. For the first time in a long time, his laugh sounded as though he were truly amused.

I couldn't help but grin myself. "It's true. In fact, she came over to Chloe's house with me last night, and we picked out a dull gray suit for her to wear on Sunday. I don't think the Angelica Gospel Hall folks would appreciate her usual attire."

"Lordy." Ernie actually had to wipe tears of amusement from his eyes. "I'd love to see that."

I shrugged. "You can come, too, if you want to."

"No thanks. I don't like going to church. Had too much of that when I was a kid."

Now there was an excellent topic of conversation, and one that was totally unrelated to the case: Ernie's childhood. I didn't know a thing about Ernie as a child. As a matter of fact, it was difficult for me to imagine him as a little boy in knee britches. He seemed to me as if he'd always been . . . well, Ernie.

Before I could pry, however, the waiter was back, carrying lots of dishes full of wonderful, delicious-smelling things, which he placed on a rotating lazy-Susan-type of device on our table. Ernie twirled the gadget and said, "Dig in."

So I took a little bit of everything. Actually, I took two spare ribs and three shrimp. I love Chinese spare ribs and fried shrimp. Not that my taste in food matters to the story. I just mention it.

"I suppose you're going to poke around some more at the church. That's why you're going, right?" I noticed that Ernie had taken several ribs and lots of shrimp, so I didn't feel quite so piggish.

"Right." At least we'd been provided with silverware. Since

I'd worked for Ernie, I'd been with him to Chinatown a time or two. He favored a little noodle place on the other side of Hill, where the only eating implements were bowls and chopsticks. I wasn't a chopstick expert at that point in my life, although using chopsticks was another skill I aimed to master with more practice.

"I can't quite feature Lulu in that joint." He shook his head and grinned.

"I can't, either, but she'll be one more person to talk to the people there about Mrs. Chalmers. I figured it can't hurt to revisit the church and pry a bit."

Shaking his head, Ernie said, "I don't know, Mercy. I think you're wrong about the church angle. We already know that Pinkney guy wrote the letters, but he didn't have anything to do with the church. It's his wife who's the church person. It's a long way from being against a church and sending poison-pen letters to killing the dame."

The dame? I stared at Ernie over the food piled in the middle of the table. "I thought you liked Mrs. Chalmers. Now she's a dame?" My voice was cold even to my own ears. But really!

"Sorry. Actually, I didn't like her much. She was pretty, but she was . . . loopy."

"Well, I suspect you're right about that, but I still don't think you should call her a dame. That's not a nice thing to call anyone, Ernie, especially one who's no longer with us. Didn't anyone ever teach you not to speak ill of the dead?"

"Yes, Mother," he said.

I could feel myself blush. "Well, it isn't a very nice thing to call anybody."

"I know. I'm tired and out of sorts. Anyhow, you know I use bad language all the time, so you ought to be used to it by this time. Let's forget the dame thing, okay?"

"Very well."

"In fact, let's forget the case. Just for a little while? Can you at least do me that favor? Please?"

His voice had an honestly pleading quality to it that surprised me. Gazing at him in the dim light, I once again noticed how tired and wan he appeared. He looked nowhere near as awful as he had on that ghastly Thursday when I'd found him tied up and drugged, but he was clearly worn to a frazzle. And worried. My boss, the ever-nonchalant Ernie Templeton, was definitely worried.

"Yes, Ernie. I can do you that favor." Unfortunately, I couldn't think of anything else to talk about. I sensed his childhood would have to wait.

Fortunately, Ernie took care of the problem for me. "So what are you going to do when Chloe and Harvey move?"

Aha! A new topic, and one that interested me almost as much as the case.

"I'm thinking of buying their house and having Lulu and maybe another working girl or two live there with me. You know, as tenants. There are suites of rooms there that would make great apartments."

Ernie had speared a shrimp and dipped it into the wonderful sauce Hop Luey's provided for same, but his fork stopped in midair, and the shrimp dangled there, dripping red sauce like blood. "You and Lulu are going to be *roommates?*"

He sounded so incredulous, I took umbrage. "Yes. Lulu thinks it's a wonderful idea, and I've also thought about hiring Mr. and Mrs. Buck. Mr. Buck can still work at the Figueroa Building, and Mrs. Buck can be cook and housekeeper.

The shrimp made it the rest of its way to Ernie's mouth, and he chewed thoughtfully. Then he grinned. I wasn't sure I liked that grin. I felt a sarcasm coming my way and braced myself.

"You and Lulu. Roommates. With a cook and a housekeeper. Exactly how much are you going to charge Lulu for this change in her status? Will she be able to afford it on the wages she gets as receptionist at the Figueroa Building? I know *you* can afford it, but can she?"

I struggled to find a hot retort but couldn't. Instead, I nibbled on a sparerib and thought. It had always galled me that Ernie teased me about "coming from money," as he'd put it. But, darn it, money meant a whole lot, especially to people who didn't have any, and Lulu didn't. I'd be darned if I'd gouge my tenants, provided I could find any besides Lulu to rent an apartment from me.

After I swallowed, I said, "I haven't looked into the money angle yet. I'm sure I can peruse the *Times* classified ads and see how much people pay for nice apartments."

"Yeah. It's the *nice* part that might put it out of Lulu's range."

"Darn you, Ernie, Lulu and I are friends! Do you honestly think I'd make her pay more than she can afford for an apartment in my own house?"

He shook his head, looking weary and almost overwhelmed. "No, I don't. See? That's the thing. You don't have a clue about how real people live. You'd probably end up letting her stay there for free. Then she'd feel guilty, and eventually you'd end up feeling used and abused. And that situation wouldn't be Lulu's fault."

My heart squished, and I felt my face heat up again. "Do you really think I'd do that?"

"Not on purpose." He waved an empty chopstick in the air—the restaurant had provided chopsticks for adventurous diners, and Ernie was an expert with the implements—and said, "But you might end up doing it anyway." He paused for a minute while I fumed and felt humiliated. "Tell you what," he said eventually. "Let me help you with this new enterprise of yours."

I blinked at him. "I beg your pardon?"

"I can help you. I've been on my own a hell of a lot longer

than you have. I've rented places for a long, long time. I assume Lulu has, too. She's probably rented some dump of an apartment somewhere ever since she got here from Oklahoma, or wherever she's from. I'm sure if we work on this together, we'll figure out something that's fair for you and Lulu both. And any other girls you can find to rent apartments to."

Humbled, I said, "You do?"

"Yes. I do. Your heart's in the right place, kiddo. I know that. So does Lulu. But you need a few lessons in life before you charge into things. I'll be happy to help you."

"Thanks, Ernie."

"Any time, kid."

We ate in silence for quite a while. I wasn't certain I liked being called *kid* by Ernie, although I know he didn't mean anything bad by it. I only wished he'd think of me as . . . well, his equal, I guess. *Kid* didn't sound equal to me. It sounded as though he considered me a child in need of a big brother.

But the word did remind me of something else. "Say, Ernie, did you have any brothers or sisters?"

"Three sisters and a brother."

"My goodness. That's a nice-sized family."

He gazed at me squinty-eyed. "You think so, do you?"

"Let me guess," I continued, only faintly daunted. "You're the oldest?"

"Yup."

"You're . . . from back east, aren't you?"

"Sort of. Illinois."

"Don't they call that the Midwest?"

"Yeah, although I don't know why. It's more east than west, if you ask me."

"I think so, too."

He eyed me again, looking far from pleased. "Why are you asking me all these questions? You trying to dig up my past for some reason? You can't blackmail me, because I don't have any money."

I ignored the last part of his comment. "Well . . . yes, I'd like to know about your childhood, but not for any sinister purpose. I'm just interested. That's why I'm asking you these questions. Do you mind that? You don't want to talk about the case, after all, and we have to talk about something."

He shrugged. "I guess I don't mind. My father worked in a shoe plant in Chicago, and I grew up there. In Chicago, not the shoe plant. My mother still lives there. My sisters are all married, and so's my brother."

"What about your father?"

"He died a couple of years ago."

"I'm sorry."

"Don't be. He was a pig."

Oh, my. I decided not to pursue the father issue.

"Do you stay in close touch with your family?"

"Not close touch, no. I send 'em Christmas cards."

"Boy, I wish I could get away with that with my parents and my brother," I blurted out before remembering I shouldn't say things like that.

Ernie only grinned again, so I guess he didn't mind. "My folks were just too . . . I don't know. Stiff and religious. You know the type?"

"I think so." I thought about Mrs. Pinkney and Mrs. Chalmers, whom I guess were both religious, although Mrs. Pinkney didn't seem awfully stiff, and Mrs. Chalmers definitely wasn't. Actually, come to think of it, in street parlance she was definitely a stiff, although that's not what Ernie meant.

Ernie interrupted those fruitless thoughts. "My father read the Bible to us kids every day and used his belt on us when we did anything he didn't like, which was most of the time. My mother just stayed in the background. I think she was afraid of him. God knows the rest of us were."

"That doesn't sound like very religious behavior to me," I said, indignant that the childish Ernie had been so badly treated.

"It's religious, all right. Whether it's Christian or not is another matter entirely."

Interesting way to put it. I pondered for a second before I said, "Good point."

"How about you? Your parents have a religious streak?"

"Hmm." I thought about it as I munched some fried rice. "Not really. We all went to church on Sundays, but I'm sure that's only because doing so was expected of us. My mother always made sure she fit into what she deemed society would expect of her. She was involved in all the church women's activities, joined the best social clubs. That sort of thing."

"I can see that," said Ernie with a nod as he sprinkled soy sauce on his chow mein noodles.

"It seems to me that the only thing my mother cares about is what society thinks of her and, therefore, her children. That's why she's so irked with me."

"I'd call it more furious than irked. She considers you a rebel and a disgrace to the family, I'll warrant."

I'd have sighed if I didn't have a mouth full of shrimp. As soon as I swallowed, I asked, "Did Chloe tell you that?"

"Tell me what? Your sister and I don't chat on a regular basis."

"Tell you that Mother called me a disgrace to the family."

"Ha!" Ernie fairly hooted. "No. I just figured your mother would use an expression like that. She sure hates me for hiring you."

"Well, she'd be happy to know you offered to fire me."

"Would firing you put me in her good graces?" Ernie eyed me cynically.

I caught his meaning. This time I did sigh. "Of course it wouldn't. She'd merely continue to pretend people farther down the social ladder than she is don't exist. She hates that I've brought *lowness* into her limited vision."

"You have had dealings with some pretty low types since you came to work for me," said Ernie, grinning like the fiend he sometimes was.

"Yes, that's true. But I've also met Lulu and you and Phil Bigelow—although I'm truly annoyed with Phil at the moment—and Mr. Emerald Buck, who is a very nice man and ever so much more competent than Ned ever was."

"Ned was nuts," said Ernie succinctly.

"True." But I didn't like to think about Ned.

"Your mother got kind of interested in the spiritualists, though," he said, mentioning another case of ours in which spiritualists had been involved.

"She did, indeed. She also nearly fainted when John Gilbert and Rene Adoree came to dinner at Chloe and Harvey's house the other night."

"John Gilbert and Renee Adoree? My, my, you *do* move in exalted circles, don't you?"

I didn't like the tone that had crept into Ernie's voice. It was the tone he used when he thought I was being hoity-toity, which I'm not, curse him. "No, I don't," I said firmly. "Chloe and Harvey do. I was there because I live with them, and our mother had demanded to meet some stars of the silver screen. God knows why. She doesn't approve of them any more than she does me."

"Well, at least they're famous," Ernie suggested, and I was pleased to hear his voice return to normal.

"In her eyes, being famous is vulgar," I told him.

"Good God."

"Exactly. So don't you dare tease me about my background, because it's not my fault. And, as you can tell, my mother is definitely a hypocrite. My life in Boston was stifling, and I'm ever so much happier living in what I consider the real world and what mother considers the squalid side of life."

"You're an interesting girl, kiddo," said Ernie.

I lifted my chin. "Thank you."

"I'm not sure that's a good thing," he said then, spoiling the moment. "Charlie Wu once told me there's a Chinese curse that says, 'May you live in interesting times.' Meaning that interesting times are generally pretty rough."

"Well, I'm not rough," I said with some asperity.

"Definitely not," agreed Ernie.

I'm not sure he meant it as a compliment.

Chapter Fourteen

Taken all in all, our meal was enjoyable. And I thought it quite kind of Ernie to offer his assistance in setting up suitable rental schedules in the event I actually did buy the Nash home on Bunker Hill and let out apartments. The lovely home could eventually be kind of like a boardinghouse, only not run-down, like the ones Ernie had told me about. It made me feel sad to think that Lulu might be living in such a dismal place as Ernie described. If I did buy the Nash home, I'd be sure to keep the interior light and airy and serve good food.

Another good thing about that evening was that Chloe didn't tease me after Ernie drove me home. In fact, she invited him in for a glass of sherry.

He agreed and was soon sorry he'd done so, because all Chloe and Harvey wanted to know about was the Chalmers case. I finally understood the term "grill." Both Chloe and Harvey grilled poor Ernie like a fish over hot coals. No matter how many questions they asked, however, Ernie buffaloed them by saying he was prohibited from talking about official business.

"But I thought you weren't a policeman anymore!" Chloe cried in dismay.

"I'm not, but as a private investigator, I'm unable to talk about my clients' cases with others."

"Even though your client is . . . deceased?" Chloe, too, was occasionally hampered by her upbringing. The Allcutt daughters weren't supposed to say "dead" in front of others. We were supposed to use euphemisms like "passed away" or "gone to a better place." Heck, "deceased" was a relatively bold word for her to use.

"The client's expectation of privacy doesn't die with him or her, I'm afraid. After the case is all cleared up, I'll be able to talk more about it," Ernie said gently, understanding Chloe's frustration.

"Oh." Disappointed, Chloe lapsed into silence.

"I guess that makes sense," said Harvey, sounding doubtful. "Sort of like a client's privilege of privacy when he consults with an attorney."

"Exactly," said Ernie. "Only I'm not trying to cheat anybody."

Which goes to prove that nothing's changed since Shakespeare's time. To this day, nobody seems to trust lawyers. A month before, I'd been envious of the secretary of a lawyer who'd moved into the Figueroa Building. No longer. I'd stick with Ernie. His clients might sometimes be less than impeccable citizens, but at least they didn't pretend to be otherwise.

Chloe didn't take sherry, since she didn't believe alcohol and pregnancy belonged together. I agreed with her, although I'm not sure why. Probably our mother had told us so once upon a time. See how difficult it can be to overcome one's upbringing?

"Well, I'm sure you'll catch the crook in no time," said Harvey heartily. He liked Ernie, too.

"I sure hope so. Otherwise, it looks as if I'll end up in the slammer."

"Oh, surely that won't happen," said Chloe, appalled. "Mercy says she's not going to rest until she discovers who really killed that woman."

Ernie, blast him, rolled his eyes.

Chloe tutted. "Mercy's been quite upset about how the police have been treating you, Ernie. She's only trying to help. I should think you'd welcome her assistance."

"That will be the day," I grumbled, irritated by Ernie's dismissal of my usefulness.

"It's not that I don't appreciate her help, Chloe," Ernie explained patiently. He was seldom so patient with me. "It's that she's my *secretary*. I hired her as a secretary, not as an assistant P.I. And," he said with emphasis, "as her employer, I feel responsible for her welfare. I don't want her to get hurt again."

"I haven't been hurt!" I cried, stung.

"No? What about when that maniac tried to kill you? And what about the time when that other maniac tried to kill you? You might not have been killed, but I remember those scrapes and bruises pretty darned well."

So did I. Nevertheless, I lifted my chin. He would have to bring up those incidents, wouldn't he? "I haven't been badly hurt," I said primly. "And I *did* help catch the criminals. You can't deny that, Ernest Templeton."

He downed the last of his sherry. "I won't deny it." With a sigh, he stood. "But I have to get going now. It's late, and I've had a bad day."

"Oh?" Chloe's eyes brightened. "What happened?"

"Chloe, the poor man's exhausted," said Harvey in as close to a chiding tone as he ever used, at least with Chloe.

"I'm sure Mercy can tell you all about it." Ernie gave me what I could only consider an evil grin. "She'll probably even embellish the tale to make it more dramatic."

"I will not!"

He laughed and took his exit while I continued to fume.

However, fuming didn't accomplish anything, and I thought that perhaps if I talked the matter over with Chloe and Harvey, I might come up with an idea I hadn't thought of yet as to whom I should next interrogate.

Even after I'd carefully explained what I'd done that day, and how the wicked policemen had treated Ernie, neither one of

191

them had much to offer.

"Well," said Harvey at one point, "it sounds as if you've covered all the suspects, and so have the police. Doesn't anyone look good to you? That Pinkney guy, maybe?"

I puzzled over that question for a moment before I realized that *good* in this instance meant *appropriate,* as in an appropriate suspect.

"I've pinned my hopes on Mr. Pinkney," I told him. "After all, he's the one who wrote those terrible threatening letters. Unless he turns out to have a rock-solid alibi, he's the man I think probably did it."

"In the pictures, the ones with the solid alibis are always the ones who turn out to be the real killers," said Chloe.

"I know," I said, wishing for once that real life was more like the flickers.

The rest of that week passed uneventfully. Phil came to the office daily to chat with Ernie, but he didn't take him down to the station to grill him again, and fortunately, O'Reilly stayed away. Phil attempted to be friendly with me, as he'd been in the good old days, before the L.A.P.D. began trying to pin a murder on my boss, but I remained chilly toward him.

After his visit on the day after our dinner at Chinatown, I went into Ernie's office to find him slumped in his chair, looking discouraged.

"What's the matter, Ernie? Did that man O'Reilly—"

"O'Reilly didn't do anything to me. But Pinkney didn't commit the murder."

"But he must have!" I cried. "He's such a logical suspect!"

"I thought so, too. But he didn't do it."

I plopped myself in one of the chairs in front of Ernie's desk, determined to have the whole story. If what Ernie said was true . . . My heart creaked painfully. This was awful. "How do you know that?"

"He has an alibi."

Huh. As Chloe had mentioned about the pictures, in all the books I read, people with alibis are always the ones who did the deed. I sensed I'd be better off not telling Ernie that. "What's his alibi?"

"He was in San Bernardino on the day Mrs. Chalmers was killed."

"How do the police know he's telling the truth?"

"The L.A.P.D. got in touch with his employer, and his employer told them he was in San Bernardino, dealing with an account."

"Do they know this for certain? How do they know he's telling the truth? What does he do, anyhow?"

"He works for a shipping company. On Thursday last, he was visiting an orange-processing plant in San Bernardino. He's got the paperwork to prove it."

"There's no way he could have forged the paperwork? He seems to be pretty handy with pen and ink," I said dryly.

"Phil's convinced Pinkney's telling the truth. Pinkney's boss corroborates his actions that day, and when the L.A.P.D. put a trunk call through to the San Bernardino orange-processing plant, they confirmed his visit."

I heaved a big sigh. "What a shame. He'd be a perfect suspect, and his wife would dearly love to be rid of him."

Although I could scarcely believe I'd actually said that out loud, Ernie laughed, so I guess it was okay.

Still and all, I was sorely disappointed. I was so hoping Mr. Pinkney would turn out to be the killer. I was almost positive that Phil didn't consider Ernie a truly viable suspect, but he didn't seem to be relenting on his persistent questioning of him. The way I saw it, when I tried to do so from the perspective of the L.A.P.D.—which wasn't easy for me, as you can well imagine—was that if they ruled out Ernie, nobody else was left to fit the frame. That's another piece of L.A. argot I picked up from Ernie. *Frame,* I mean.

"That stinks, Ernie," I said.

"I agree," he said, running his hands through his hair.

At lunch that day, which we took at a diner across the street from the Figueroa Building, Lulu and I made arrangements to meet at the Angelica Gospel Hall for services on Sunday. I aimed to take a cab. I didn't ask how Lulu planned to get there. I have to admit to having some slight trepidation about how Lulu would present herself, but when, on the following Sunday, the cabbie dropped me off in front of the church, darned if Lulu wasn't there waiting for me, sans red lipstick and nail polish, and with her bottle-blond hair covered demurely under a black hat. I almost didn't recognize her. In fact, I was about to walk right past her and on into the Hall when she spoke.

"Well?"

I whirled around and gasped when I recognized her. "Lulu! You're perfect!"

She looked quite pleased with herself. "Told you I was a good actress."

Actually, she hadn't told me that. She'd told me many times that she wanted to get into the pictures and be a star, but she hadn't mentioned anything about acting. Not that it matters. "You certainly are."

Lulu looked up at the huge cross on top of the Hall. "I've heard a lot about this place, but I never seen it before."

"Whereabouts do you live, Lulu?"

"In a boardinghouse on Clay. It's not fancy, and there are a lot of Chinese around, but I don't mind that."

"Oh, my. Angels Flight goes right over Clay Street. Do you live near the railroad? It must be quite noisy."

"It's noisy everywhere around there," she said. "But it's cheap. I can't afford anything better."

She gave me kind of a slanty-eyed look, as though she were warning me about her financial circumstances for my future reference. I got the point. "Well, Ernie said that if I do decide to buy Chloe and Harvey's house, he'll help me establish fair rentals for tenants."

"Yeah? Ernie's a good guy. I just hope 'fair' will include me. I'd sure love to live in a joint like that. It's like a . . . a palace or something."

"I suppose it must seem like that," I said, thinking that Lulu hadn't seen very many palaces in her life if she thought the Nash home anything close to resembling a palace. On the other hand, my own personal education had included a trip to Europe during my sixteenth summer, so I'd actually been inside a palace or two. Yet another indication, if one were needed, that the United States of America did indeed have a class system, even if it wasn't as overt as those of some other countries. Shoot, Chloe and I had even dined with the daughter of some duke or other in Great Britain during that trip. I decided not to tell Lulu that. She'd think dining with a duke's daughter was something special, and it had only been lunch, really, and the duke's daughter was a pallid, insipid creature with no conversation. In other words, she was the sort of girl our mother wanted Chloe and me to be, which really didn't bear thinking of, so I stopped thinking of it.

We climbed the stairs leading into the Hall, and I saw Brother Everett handing out bulletins at the door. We smiled at each other, and I said, "Good morning, Brother Everett."

"Good morning, sister."

He'd forgotten my name, I have no doubt.

"I brought my friend Miss LaBelle with me today."

"Good for you, sister!" He spoke with the enthusiasm of a

true believer. "We're so happy to have you join us, Sister La-Belle."

After a moment of hesitation while she absorbed Brother Everett's zest for his church, Lulu said, "Um . . . likewise, I'm sure."

I hustled Lulu into the sanctuary before she could say anything else. Not that I didn't trust her, but I didn't want Brother Everett to know we were, in effect, there as spies. I don't suppose it would have mattered if he knew the truth, but I felt better having him think I was there out of ardor for Sister Emmanuel's message rather than in an investigatory capacity.

We sat in the pew I'd sat in the Sunday before. My choice was made on purpose, because I hoped this was Mrs. Pinkney's regular pew.

"What's this 'brother' and 'sister' stuff?" Lulu whispered in my ear when we were seated.

"Well, according to Sister Emmanuel," I whispered back, "they believe that titles like 'mister' and 'missus' are designations of this earth and, as such, are not intended by God. Therefore, they eschew those types of social titles . . . and 'doctor,' too, I suppose."

Lulu said, "Huh?"

I could understand her confusion, since the "brother" and "sister" stuff puzzled me a bit, too. Therefore, I shrugged. "I honestly don't know, Lulu. I think they prefer to think of themselves as siblings in this new religious endeavor, so they use the words 'brother' and 'sister.' Like they're all brothers and sisters in God's eyes or something."

Because Lulu still looked at me blankly, I don't think I'd explained the matter any better. She said, "I guess." Then she said, "Do I have to call you Sister Allcutt?"

"Good Lord, no. Just call me Mercy. Please. And I'll call you

Lulu. We'll let the others call us Sister LaBelle and Sister Allcutt."

"If you say so."

"Sister Allcutt!"

Aha! I'd been correct about this being Mrs. Pinkney's usual
pew, because when I glanced up to see who'd spoken, there she
was, beaming as if I were the one person on earth whom she
wanted to see this bright, hot Sunday morning. I thought that
was sweet, so I smiled back at her and introduced her to Lulu
LaBelle, leaving out the sister part.

"I'm so very happy to see you here today, Sister Allcutt, and
so very, *very* happy to meet your friend." Her smile for Lulu
expressed so much rapture, I felt guilty. I'd been doing that a
lot lately. "The more people who get the message, the more sin-
ners will come to God."

From the furrow in Lulu's brow, I got the impression she
didn't much like being called a sinner, but I grimaced at her to
beg her not to react, and her forehead smoothed out. "Mercy's
told me so much about this place, and I'm *so* happy to be here,"
said Lulu, trying on a simper that didn't quite fit the Lulu I
knew, but that went well with her boring gray outfit. *My* boring
gray outfit.

Hmm. Perhaps my sister was right about my wardrobe. But
this wasn't the time or place to worry about that.

"That's wonderful," said Mrs. Pinkney. "I do so miss
Persephone." She hauled a hankie out of her handbag and
dabbed at a corner of her eye. "It's nice to have new people to
speak to now that she's gone."

Oh, dear. I hoped the poor woman wouldn't be too disappointed when Lulu and I vanished as soon as we discovered
who'd murdered her best friend.

"Do you think the police are any closer to finding who the
murderer of poor Mrs. Chalmers was?" Mrs. Pinkney asked in a

whisper, looking around the sanctuary as if she didn't want to be overheard.

"I'm not sure." I decided not to tell her the police had cleared her husband, for fear the disappointment would make her faint. "But they're working hard on the case, and so is my employer."

"Well, I'm glad to hear that, but I hope they find the fiend who killed her soon." She shook her head and frowned. "You wouldn't think it would be so difficult to find a murderer, would you? I mean, just look at . . ."

I think she was going to say, "Just look at my husband," but wasn't sure. Anyhow, I got the impression she was also hoping the fiend would turn out to be Mr. Gaylord Pinkney. What an odd thought.

"How do you do, Sister Allcutt?" a female voice said. I turned to discover Sister Everett smiling at me. Although it sounds odd, she had a severe, somewhat strained smile. I'd noticed that quirk of hers that before. It was still difficult for me to picture her as the wife of the insubstantial Mr. Everett.

"Very well, thank you, Sister Everett."

"I must say I'm rather surprised to see you here today," she said.

I lifted my eyebrows. "Oh? Why is that?" I didn't know whether or not to be offended, but I leaned toward the pro side.

Now her smile seemed a trifle too sugary to me, as if she had to force it. "Oh, I don't know. Perhaps I didn't sense great spiritual awakening in you when you attended services here last week."

"I'm sure it's up to God to decide a person's worth, Sister Everett." My tone was frigid, and I guess it made her back off from making any more judgmental statements about me.

She only said, "Of course."

"Besides, there were other things going on that rather interfered with my total absorption with Sister Emmanuel's message," I reminded her. I didn't want to outright blame Mrs. Pinkney for having made a scene and distracting my attention from the church's message, even though she had.

"Yes, of course there were. I meant nothing by my comment."

"I see," I said, my tone still chilly. "May I introduce my friend, Miss LaBelle? Lulu, this is Sister Everett."

Sister Everett looked Lulu up and down in what I didn't consider a very Christian way, but her smile didn't fade. It didn't look too awfully sincere, either, and I was beginning to think maybe she couldn't help herself. Perhaps she was simply a cold woman with a cold demeanor. For all I knew, she wanted to be warm and friendly, but had been stifled in her childhood. I understood such things better than most people. "How do you do, Sister LaBelle?" she said, and held out her hand for Lulu to shake.

Taking the proffered hand, Lulu said, "Swell, thanks."

Was there the hint of a wrinkle on Sister Everett's nose? I couldn't tell, but I suspected her of not being quite as zealous about this Angelica Gospel Hall thing as her husband. Not that I knew a single, solitary thing about the woman except that she'd brought tea to Sister Emmanuel when requested to do so after last week's faint on Sister Pinkney's part. She and I shook hands next, and then Sister Everett moseyed along the aisle, looking for other prey.

Lulu leaned over and whispered, "I don't think she likes me much."

I whispered back, "I don't think she likes anyone much."

"Please don't take offense at Sister Everett," Mrs. Pinkney told us. I don't know if she overheard us or only suspected what we'd been talking about. "She does so much for the church. It's . . . unfortunate that she doesn't . . . um, project the warmth and so forth one might expect from a follower of Sister Emmanuel. Her husband . . . well, he's another story. He's most enthusiastic about Sister Emmanuel's message. And he absolutely adores his wife." She spoke the latter sentence in something akin to awe.

Lulu and I exchanged a glance that was undoubtedly similarly awe-inspired. So the weedy Mr. Everett adored the Herculean Mrs. Everett, did he? Well, nobody ever said life made sense.

After that, I thought for a moment and decided to say something that might be considered detectival. After all, that's why I was here, wasn't it? "I didn't realize Sister Everett works so hard for the church. What does she do?"

"Oh, she comes in every single day to tidy up the pews, set the hymnals to rights, and arrange flowers and so forth. She's most conscientious about keeping the Angelica Gospel Hall looking tip-top."

"Every day?" I said, amazed.

"Oh, my goodness, yes. Sister Emmanuel broadcasts sermons daily, you know, and holds a service every single evening."

"My word, I didn't realize that. Is Brother Everett as involved in the church as his wife?"

"Gracious sakes, yes. To tell the truth, I think he's . . . it's not my place to judge, mind you, but I sense he's more attached to the church and its message than his wife is, even though," Mrs. Pinkney hastened to add, "he does most of the driving and that sort of thing. Picks up supplies when they're needed. Things like that. He drives Sister Emmanuel to interviews and appearances, too. He retired not very long ago from his former job, I believe."

"Oh? What sort of work did he do?"

"I'm not sure. Something involving clerking at a store, I believe." Mrs. Pinkney lowered her voice when she added, "I don't think he made a lot of money, but he's a good man for all that."

"I'm sure he is," I said. "I firmly believe that the amount of money one has doesn't have a thing to do with one's moral fiber."

"Absolutely," said Mrs. Pinkney, smiling upon me as if I'd said something profound.

I heard Lulu sniff, but didn't pursue her notions on the money issue, mainly because I already knew what they were and didn't consider them appropriate for this present conversation.

Then the organist began playing, and we all sat down, shut up, and listened. The music was quite lovely, and very loud. Whoever their organist was, he or she had a real gift.

Lulu gasped audibly when Adelaide Burkhard Emmanuel took the stage. I mean the chancel. But she sure used it like a stage. She possessed all the warmth and love Sister Everett lacked and then some. Her message was the same as it had been the week before, although she used different words to make it. You know: God's love was everywhere, and His people here on earth needed to spread the message with joy and enthusiasm and stuff like that. She was quite a motivated and motivational speaker, Sister Emmanuel. I'd never heard so vibrant a religious speaker before her, and I haven't heard one since. Not even Billy Sunday, although I did manage to catch a broadcast of his once. My mother would die if she knew.

Lulu and I each made a contribution when the plate was passed, and when we stood to sing the hymns, I realized Lulu had quite a lovely soprano voice. I envied her that, having always had trouble reaching the high notes myself. It occurred to me that she might do better trying out for radio positions than for a position on the silver screen. Not that she wasn't pretty or anything like that, but after meeting a few screen stars, I thought Lulu fell a teeny bit short of the . . . what word am I searching for? The *aura* required for the picture business? The magical essence? I don't know, but I don't think Lulu had it. She could sure sing, though.

The last hymn of the day was "Bringing in the Sheaves," I guess because it was September and harvesttime in some parts of the country. The hymn had probably also been selected because Sister Emmanuel was attempting to sow the seeds of her brand of religion and seemed to be reaping enormous results, to judge from the size of the congregation and the size of the Angelica Gospel Hall itself. The enormous place was packed from the floor to the rafters with, literally, hundreds of worshipers.

After the rites were over, the general hugging, kissing, blessings, and greetings commenced. Lulu hugged me and then she hugged Mrs. Pinkney, and I saw there were tears in her eyes. Oh, dear. I wasn't sure what those tears portended, but I wasn't awfully happy to see them.

"I'm so very happy you came, Sister LaBelle," said Mrs. Pinkney.

"I'm blessed that Sister Allcutt invited me," said Lulu in a quavery voice.

Oh, boy, I *really* didn't like the sound of that!

"You certainly are," said Mrs. Pinkney. Sister Pinkney. Whatever her name was.

Then Lulu turned on me again and wrapped me in a hug the likes of which I don't believe I'd ever experienced before, my family being rather cold and stand-offish and not having anyone else given to hugging me around on a regular basis.

"That was *wonderful*, Mercy! I *loved* it! I think Sister Emmanuel is wonderful!"

"I'm . . . so glad," I gasped when she finally let me go.

"I'm going to come here again next week," she declared. "I've never had so much fun in a church before in my life!"

Mrs. Pinkney grinned from ear to ear. "Don't you just love Sister Emmanuel's message, Sister LaBelle? She's so open and loving and . . . and . . . Oh, I don't know, but she's a gift from

God. She's joyful and happy. None of that hellfire-and-brimstone stuff here, even though we all know Satan is lurking right around the corner."

We did, did we? Hmm. I wasn't so sure about that.

"I wonder if I can volunteer to do something for the church," Lulu then said, further astounding me.

"Well, we have a ladies' circle," said Mrs. Pinkney. "We meet every Wednesday morning at ten and do good works of various sorts. You know, like collecting clothes for the needy and collecting food for the poor and starving and other things like that."

"I couldn't do that," said a clearly disappointed Lulu. "I have to work during the day."

"Oh, dear. Yes, I suppose so many young women do have to hold jobs these days, don't they? I don't suppose there's a young man on the horizon?" Mrs. Pinkney's face took on a bright and inquiring look, as if she were hoping Lulu had a beau. And this from a woman who was hoping her own husband would be arrested for murder. Shoot. Romance never dies, I reckon.

"No," said Lulu, sounding a little discouraged. "No young man yet."

Mrs. Pinkney heaved a largish sigh. "That's too bad."

"Yeah. Well, if you can think of anything else I can do to help the church, like maybe at night, will you let me know? I work at the Figueroa Building with Mercy here."

"Of course. May I have your telephone exchange?"

"Sure." So Lulu gave Mrs. Pinkney the Figueroa Building's telephone number, and we joined the throng filing out of the church. Lulu darned near knelt before Sister Emmanuel and kissed her feet when we finally got to where she stood at the back of the sanctuary, bestowing blessings and farewells upon her many hundreds of parishioners. I introduced Lulu to Sister Emmanuel.

"I just loved your sermon," Lulu said in an awed voice.

"Thank you. I'm so glad you came today, Sister LaBelle," said Sister Emmanuel. Then she turned at me. "And Sister Allcutt. I'm so pleased to see you again this week. I pray you will become a regular member of our congregation."

She remembered me! No wonder the woman was so popular. She had charm and a half, that one. "Thank you very much, Sister Emmanuel."

"Mercy's the one who invited me to come today," Lulu said quickly, as if reluctant to have Sister Emmanuel's attention diverted from her. I didn't blame her. Sister Emmanuel was quite a compelling woman.

Seeming to sense Lulu's need for attention, Sister Emmanuel grasped her hand in both of her own, and said, "How lovely to have our message spreading among friends. I pray you'll join us again, too, Sister LaBelle."

"Th-thank you," whispered Lulu.

I had to lend my support to Lulu as we left the church, since she was so overwhelmed she wobbled on her pins. "How about I take us both to lunch somewhere, Lulu? We can talk about our observations."

It didn't seem to me that Lulu was in any condition to add much to any sensible conversation about the case, which was the reason we'd attended church this morning, but I figured it was the least I could do for her, as I sort of blamed myself for her present condition. Said condition seemed to be one of vicarious ecstasy or something akin to that. I'd had no idea Sister Emmanuel would affect her so.

"Sure. That sounds nice." Lulu's voice was almost back to normal.

"Want to go to Chinatown, or would you prefer somewhere else?"

"Chinatown's fine, and it's close to home."

"It is for me, too. Good. Let's have Chinese for lunch." I'd never eaten so much Chinese food in my life until I moved to L.A. I loved it. Still do.

We dined at a restaurant in Chinatown I'd never been to before, but which Lulu said was tasty, and she was right.

When we were about halfway through our delicious meal, and hoping Lulu's state of exaltation had deflated some, I asked, "So what did you think about Mrs. Pinkney and Mrs. Everett?"

"I liked Mrs. Pinkney. She seems kind of lost, though."

The description captured my attention. "Lost? What do you mean, lost?"

"I dunno. Like she wasn't sure what to do with herself in the world or something. Like she doesn't have any goals or ambitions or anything like that."

"Interesting." The most amazing things came out of Lulu's mouth sometimes. I was becoming increasingly clear to me that Lulu wasn't one bit stupid. She'd been born into a family of farmers in reduced circumstances, but that didn't mean she didn't have a keen brain or know how to use it. "I see what you mean. That would explain her . . . I don't know. Vagueness?"

Lulu shrugged. "Vagueness works, too. I bet she doesn't like her husband much."

Astounded, I gasped out, "How did you figure that out?"

"I've met women like her before. They're stuck in lousy marriages and don't think they have any alternatives to 'em, yet she hopes other women will find good husbands. You saw the way she asked if I had any men in my life, didn't you?"

"Yes. I noticed that."

"That's what I mean. She's in a stinking marriage, yet she thinks other girls can only find happiness with a man. If I ever found myself with a lousy guy, I'd divorce him."

It grieves me to say I was shocked by those callous words, but I was. "You believe in divorce?" I did my very best not to sound judgmental.

"I believe in not being married to a lousy man," Lulu said, looking up from her plate of chop suey. "Do you think a woman ought to stay with a fellow who knocks her around?"

"Well . . . I don't know that Mr. Pinkney, uh, knocks Mrs. Pinkney around, Lulu."

Another shrug. "Well, she's sure not happy. That's probably why she goes to that church. She's hoping she'll find something to take the place of a crummy marriage."

I stared at her for a moment before saying in an awed voice, "You're a woman of amazing insight, Lulu LaBelle."

"Yeah? Y'think so?" She seemed quite pleased by my assessment.

"I do indeed. What did you make of Mr. and Mrs. Everett?"

Lulu thought for a moment. "He seems like a nice guy. Loves that church. Bet he hated his job and is glad he's finally able to do something he likes doing."

Another astounding insight from Lulu LaBelle. "Yes, I got the same impression."

"Didn't like Mrs. Everett. She seemed like a real snob. Like she's judging everyone and finding them beneath her. Not like Sister Emmanuel at all. Or her husband, either, for that matter."

"No, she isn't, is she?" I said, then chewed thoughtfully for a moment. "It's difficult to imagine Mr. and Mrs. Everett as a couple, isn't it? Yet Mrs. Pinkney says he adores her."

"Bet she doesn't adore him so much," opined Lulu.

"Hmm. Maybe so. Maybe that's why she seems so sour."

"Wouldn't surprise me." Lulu dipped an egg roll in soy sauce and bit off a chunk.

"I wonder why she's so involved in the church. She certainly doesn't seem to have embraced the same joy and love in the message Sister Emmanuel preaches that her husband has."

Lulu shrugged. "Some folks are just like that. They do what they think's their duty. Won't even admit to themselves they hate doing it."

I considered my mother for a moment. "I think you're right. For example, I don't think my mother ever does anything she doesn't want to do, but she makes sure she doesn't enjoy it, so that makes it all right." I narrowed my eyes at Lulu, who was forking up some rice. "Did that make any sense?"

"Yeah. I have an aunt like that. Devil of a woman, although she devotes all her spare time to that little Baptist church in Enid."

"Enid, Oklahoma?"

"Yeah. Me and Rupert used to have to go to church three or four times a week 'cause of Aunt Ruth. You'd have thought she hated the both of us from the way she treated us, but she claimed to be doing the Lord's work."

"Sounds awful," I murmured. Aunt Ruth also sounded a good deal like my own mother and Ernie's father, although I didn't say so to Lulu.

"It was. I like Sister Emmanuel's God a whole lot better than Aunt Ruthless's. That's what me and Rupert used to call her, Aunt Ruthless."

I smiled at the name. "It certainly is interesting to learn about people's early lives, isn't it? Ernie told me his family was religious like that. Like your aunt Ruthless, I mean."

"Oh, shoot. Really? Poor Ernie."

We both burst out laughing. Poor Ernie, indeed.

CHAPTER FIFTEEN

"I'm telling you, Mercy, that damned church doesn't have anything to do with anything," Ernie growled at me the next morning when I told him about my foray with Lulu to the Angelica Gospel Hall the prior morning.

"Blast you, Ernie Templeton! Why do you have to throw cold water over every idea I have? For heaven's sake, you and the police have already ruled out everybody else in the case. Do you *want* to be convicted of a murder you didn't commit? That's what it sounds like to me." To say I was indignant would be an extreme understatement. I stood before his desk now, my fists on my hips, glaring at him, glad I was dressed in one of my suitable-but-not-flashy working outfits. It was easier to be on one's dignity when one was soberly clad.

Ernie'd come ambling into the office around nine o'clock, flung his hat at the rack in his office, and didn't even bother to pick it up when it hit the floor. He'd taken his suit coat off and it hung at an ungainly angle on the rack. It was beginning to look to me as if my boss was losing hope and spirit, and his attitude irked the dickens out of me.

Ernie sighed and began running his hands through his hair, a habit he'd adopted since the murder of that pesky Chalmers woman, and which seemed to be almost perpetual with him by this time. "Ah, shit," he grumbled.

"And don't use foul language in front of me, either! In fact, the more I think about it, the more I believe that the answer *has* to be connected with that church. Everything else has turned out to be a big, fat blank, including the two Misters Chalmers and that ratty Mr. Pinkney. Have Phil or O'Reilly even bothered to talk to Sister Emmanuel?"

Looking up at me with one of his more cynical grins, Ernie said, "Yeah. Phil himself talked to the lady of God. Says she's crazy as a loon, but not murderous, so I think you're all wet about the church angle."

"Oh! The two of you ought to . . . to go soak your heads!" I said, and then I turned and marched out of the office, furious.

By gum, if the police and Ernie had given up on discovering the real killer, Mercy Allcutt was on the job. The more I thought about it, the more it made sense that, given the alibis proven for the two Misters Chalmers and the horrible Mr. Pinkney, the only logical place to look was that wretched church. That's where Mrs. Chalmers had been spending all her time and money. Shoot, she'd even sold jewelry and then claimed it had been stolen, just to slip the loss by her husband. And he claimed not even to care if she was involved in the Hall. What's more, after talking to him twice, I believed him.

I also believed his son hadn't cared enough about his father's money to take the life of his father's wife. He was fond of his father, and his affection showed. Besides, he was living on money of his own through his trust fund, something with which I could identify. Which might be considered unfortunate, since I was attempting to make my own living. Abysmal job I was doing of it, too. However, the younger Mr. Chalmers clearly didn't share my sentiments, and I believed him when he said he didn't covet his father's money.

Susan the maid and Mrs. Hanratty the housekeeper clearly weren't guilty parties. They'd been horrified, terrified, and downright shocked when they'd come home to discover the body of their mistress at the foot of the staircase. Occasionally my ears still rang from the decibel level of their discovery, in fact, and I didn't believe either woman had strength of character or wit enough to do that good an acting job.

There was always Mrs. Pinkney, but I couldn't believe her to be guilty of such a ghastly crime. Heck, she was still in a tattered emotional state about Mrs. Chalmers' death. In fact, as I've already mentioned, I got the distinct impression she rather wished her husband would be discovered to be the perpetrator because she was so annoyed at his shenanigans and his opposition to her church attendance. I thought about Lulu's assessment of the woman. *Lost* was a good word to describe her. Small wonder she clung to the church as if it were a lifeline.

That church . . .

Something was odd about that church, and it wasn't Sister Emmanuel. She had converts by the thousands, but I got the impression—not that I'm always right about people—that she honestly believed the message she preached so eloquently. Her church was all about uninhibited joyfulness combined with religious fervor and a total rejection of evil, as personified by scarlet women, gamblers, thieves, and so forth. It was the uninhibited part that made my Boston soul withdraw with something of a sneer from the Angelica Gospel Hall, but it was that same part of her message that drew people like Lulu and Mrs. Pinkney and Mrs. Chalmers to her.

"Bother." The whole mess was making me feel crazy.

At that moment the front door opened, and who should walk in but Detective Phil Bigelow. I didn't even try to smile at him. I was too angry.

"Phil," I said in a stony voice that reminded me of my mother.

He took off his hat and walked over to stand in front of my desk, placing one of his hands on one of the chairs I'd placed there so that clients wouldn't get too close. "Listen, Mercy, we're doing everything we can to find out the murderer of that woman."

"So Ernie thinks. I don't share his opinion. Or yours. And you know as well as I do that O'Reilly is just longing to pin the murder on Ernie."

Phil winced. I suppose my statement had been bald and merciless—unlike my name—but I didn't care. I was still furious, darn it.

"Mercy." Phil sounded almost desperate. "Ernie's my best friend. Do you think I *want* him to go to prison for such a heinous crime? I'm not going to allow O'Reilly to railroad him, either."

"I don't know what you want, Detective Bigelow, but *I* aim to clear my boss's name. And I don't trust your precious Detective O'Reilly any farther than I could toss a . . . a grand piano!"

Ernie appeared, looking disheveled, at his office door. "Don't even bother talking with her, Phil. She's sure that damned church is involved in the case somehow, and once Mercy's mind is set on something, it takes a crowbar and a blowtorch to get it unstuck."

I rose regally from my office chair. "Fine. If that's what you think, that's just fine. I'll just go out and do some snooping on my own then."

"Hey, Mercy, don't you have to work until lunchtime?"

I guess Ernie thought he was being cute.

Turning to glare at him, I said, "So fire me."

Then I grabbed my hat and handbag and barged past Phil and out into the hallway. I heard a faint "Mercy!" as I headed down the hall to the staircase, but I didn't stop in my progress. I didn't know which man had said my name, either.

When I got to the lobby, Lulu asked, "Where you going, Mercy? You look steamed."

"I am steamed," I declared. "Ernie and Phil Bigelow are

such . . . such *men!*"

I saw Lulu's eyes widen. "Uh-oh. Sounds like you guys had a little disagreement."

"A *little* one? I swear to heaven, Lulu, if I don't take charge of this case, Ernie will swing. Or go to prison for the rest of his life. Neither Phil nor he seem to have the slightest interest in the most important aspect of the death of Mrs. Chalmers! And that man who's supposed to be in charge of the case, that Detective O'Reilly, hates Ernie's guts!"

"Golly. I thought Bigelow was in charge of the case."

"No. Unfortunately, one of Ernie's bitterest enemies has that privilege. And I'm darned sure he doesn't care any more than Ernie or Phil do about what seems to me to be the most glaring aspect of the case!"

"They don't?" Lulu paused in the act of filing her nails and glanced up at me, standing rigid before her, my handbag under my arm and my fists clenched. "Well, that Bigelow character did try to pin a murder on Rupert, so I believe it about him. And I don't know O'Reilly, but I'd believe anything about an L.A. copper. But Ernie? Shoot, Mercy, it's his life that's at risk here. Don't you think he wants to find out who the real killer is?"

I sagged a trifle. "I'm sure he does, but he seems to have lost heart, Lulu, and that worries me. A whole lot."

Lulu shook her head. "It's hard to imagine Ernie losing heart. He's so . . . I dunno. So . . ."

She couldn't come up with the right word, so I supplied a few of my own. "Nonchalant? Insouciant? Casual?"

"Um . . . I'm not sure what those two first words mean, but you're right about the casual part. I can't imagine Ernie caring a whole lot about anything."

Her words gave me pause, and I sank into the chair in front of her desk. "He doesn't care that his life might be in danger?" I thought about the unsettling notion.

"Well. I don't mean that, exactly. It's just that . . . I dunno."

"I think I know what you mean," I said. "Ernie gives the impression that he's a devil-may-care man of the world. He wants everyone to think he's jaded and cynical. What I think is that he cares too much. He puts on that casual air, but you do know he quit the police department because he couldn't stand the corruption there, don't you?"

With a sniff, Lulu said, "I can believe that. About the corruption, I mean."

"And if he truly didn't care about anything, the corruption wouldn't bother him, would it?"

"I suppose not."

"And he considers Phil Bigelow about the only honest copper in Los Angeles."

"I *don't* believe that," Lulu said, still in stout defense of her innocent brother whom Phil had locked up the prior month.

"Well . . . I don't know. I think he's as honest as he can be. Whatever that means." The idea of Phil Bigelow manfully attempting to maintain his integrity in the face of monumental police corruption gave me pause.

Was Phil truly an honest man in a dishonest profession? How could he stand it? I don't believe I could. On the other hand, while I didn't know a single thing about Phil's background, I know mine was grounded in the fundamentals of Bostonian propriety and, therefore, not particularly tolerant of any digressions therefrom. But did Phil really tolerate the misdemeanors—perhaps even the felonies—of his fellow policemen without objecting or trying to make such behavior cease? How could he?

Then again, what else could he do? Maybe being a copper was the only thing he knew how to do. Maybe he had a family to support. I didn't know much about Phil personally. I suppose he could quit and take up the profession of private investigator.

If he had a family, he probably wouldn't dare do that. Knowing how little income Ernie's private investigation business produced, it was difficult for me to imagine competition from dozens of honest coppers who quit the force because of corruption in the L.A.P.D. Heck, there weren't enough straying husbands and wives or fraudulent insurance claims in the entire city of Los Angeles to keep a whole army of private eyes in work.

I sat in the chair, slouched in a position of which my mother would never approve, and thought dismal thoughts.

"Where were you going in such a hurry, Mercy?" Lulu asked at last.

"Hmm?" I looked from my handbag in my lap to Lulu's face, which was plastered again this morning with makeup. Well, why not? Nothing Sister Emmanuel had harangued us with yesterday mentioned anything about makeup or the use thereof, although I knew from articles I'd read that she greatly disapproved of what she considered "wicked women." I wondered what she thought about the "wicked men" who used them. But that was a whole 'nother kettle of fish. Anyhow, Lulu wasn't wicked, but she did wear a lot of makeup, which was a trademark of the "wicked" group, or so I'd been led to understand.

"You came down those stairs like a man on a mission. Or a girl on a mission, I guess."

"Yeah," I said, borrowing a word from Lulu's vocabulary. "I'm definitely on a mission. I'm going back to the Angelica Gospel Hall, and I'm going to get a handle on exactly what Mrs. Chalmers did there."

"You really think the church is involved somehow in her murder?" Lulu appeared as skeptical as she sounded.

"Not the church itself, but somebody connected with it. Yes, I do."

"Yeah?"

I lifted my hands and spread them in a gesture of despair. "Everyone else has been ruled out, Lulu! *Somebody* committed that murder, and it wasn't Ernie! I'm the one who found him drugged and tied up, remember?" I added bitterly, "Even though the police don't believe me."

"Rotten bananas, all of them," she muttered.

"Besides, while I can see Ernie killing if he had to . . . say, if someone he loved was in danger or something, I can't feature him brutally bashing a client on the head and pushing her down the stairs. Especially if the client was a woman. For one thing, we don't have enough clients that we can afford to be killing them off."

Although I hadn't meant the comment to be funny, Lulu laughed. Eventually, even I saw the humor in my boss's too-few clients. With a sigh, I rose, feeling a little more chipper after my chat with Lulu. "Don't forget, we've got a date for lunch at the Ambassador this coming Wednesday, Lulu."

Her eyes brightened up. "That's right. I can hardly wait. I'll wear my very best dress."

Oh, boy. I couldn't wait to see that. "I'll be back in a bit. If Ernie or Phil ask after me, tell them I've gone to do their jobs for them."

"At the Angelica Gospel Hall?"

"That's where I aim to begin, yes."

"I dunno, Mercy. That lead seems kind of slim to me."

"Yes. It seems slim to Ernie and Phil and Detective O'Reilly, too, curse them."

"Hey, don't curse me."

"I won't. I'm just angry with those three men at the moment."

"See ya later." Lulu went back to filing her nails.

Were they all right? Ernie, Phil, O'Reilly, and Lulu? Was there no connection between that wretched church and the death of

Mrs. Persephone Chalmers? And, of all nonsensical things, I still wanted to know why she didn't call herself Mrs. Franchot Chalmers. Was that something to do with the church, too? I understood that Sister Emmanuel didn't care for earthly titles, but why wouldn't Mrs. Chalmers use her husband's first name in correspondence and stuff like that? When she first called Ernie in that stupid, breathy voice of hers, she'd called herself Mrs. Persephone Chalmers.

Nuts.

Thanks to the generous legacy of my late great-aunt Agatha, I took a cab from the Figueroa Building to the Angelica Gospel Hall. Only when we were almost there did I wonder if the church might not be open on Mondays. But churches were always open, weren't they, so that people could go in and pray? Or was it only Catholic churches that were open all the time? Shoot. I didn't know. Still, at least the administrative staff should be there, I thought.

Did churches have administrative staffs?

Nuts again. The things I didn't know about the Angelica Gospel Hall could fill a library. Actually, they probably would, if you cut out and pasted into books all the articles written about the Hall and Adelaide Burkhard Emmanuel. My mind boggled at such a library, and I wondered if religious libraries really existed. They must, mustn't they? Heck, before King Henry VIII, didn't the monks in all the monasteries write those illuminated manuscripts? They must have been kept in libraries. I think.

The cab pulling to a stop in front of the Hall stopped my mind from wandering down fruitless paths, which was a good thing since I was already confused enough. I paid the cabbie, got out, and stared at the immense edifice before me for a few moments. Two huge radio towers had been installed a few years before, so that people all over the United States could hear

Sister Emmanuel's message. From what I read in the papers, thousands of people believed that message and sent her money to prove it.

Was Sister Emmanuel only in this religious thing for the money? After meeting her, I couldn't believe it.

That didn't leave out all the people who worked with her, though. What if Mrs. Chalmers had uncovered some dire plot to divert some of the money that people sent in, supposedly to help with the church, so the money was lining non-church pockets? That would be a good motive to kill her, wouldn't it?

It was difficult for me to imagine the fluttery Persephone Chalmers uncovering much of anything, but that was because I held her in what I'm sure was irrational dislike. And she was dead. Shame on me.

With a sigh, I started walking up the wide, white stairs to the big doors of the church. If I were to guess, I'd guess, Sister Emmanuel had designed those stairs—or she'd had someone else design them—so that people would believe themselves to be on a stairway leading to heaven as they climbed them. Was that a cynical thought? Was I turning into an Ernie-type female?

Ghastly thought. Almost as ghastly as the notion of turning into a Mother-type female.

On the way up those stairs, I worried that the huge double doors might be locked. Then what would I do? Was there a back entrance to the place? Well, of course, there was. And a couple of side ones, too, but they wouldn't help me gain entry if they were all locked, would they?

I needn't have worried. The front door to the sanctuary opened with nary a whisper, thanks to whoever oiled the hinges on a regular basis; perhaps that, too, was one of Brother Everett's many tasks. The church was very well maintained. Well, it should be, given that it had such a huge congregation, all of whom, I presumed, donated money, or time and effort, or some of all of these to its upkeep. Imagine that. One smallish woman had created her own gigantic empire in the name of God. While I was still of two minds about Sister Emmanuel's message, I admired her sincerity and plain, good old marketing ability. That she'd also, according to some published articles I read, trampled the Bible under her feet to come up with her own version of Jesus Christ's message wasn't anything new. People had done that since the year aught, I suppose. Otherwise, we wouldn't have huge churches of all denominations, would we? And probably before the year aught, as well. If not, we'd all be united under one idea about God and how His church should be run.

My philosophical mood dissipated as I walked through the gigantic lobby and into the sanctuary. By gum, people were there! There weren't many of them, but still, it was kind of nice to know the Hall welcomed folks all day long. One woman knelt at the altar, and a couple of other folks seemed to be praying in pews.

Looking around, I didn't see hide nor hair of Sister Emmanuel, however. Drat. I'd really wanted to speak to her. For all her religious fervor, she'd seemed a sensible woman when I'd met her, and I was pretty sure she wouldn't pooh-pooh my ideas as Ernie had. In fact, she was probably eager to discover who had murdered one of her flock. It didn't look good to have congregants butchered, after all. Mrs. Chalmers' affiliation with the Angelica Gospel Hall had been written about in many a local newspaper, and Sister Emmanuel would undoubtedly welcome the arrest and conviction of her murderer.

That's what I told myself as I walked toward the chancel, trying to recollect how one got to Sister Emmanuel's office. There had been a door and a hall and . . . Oh, bother.

"Sister Allcutt?"

Startled, I spun around to see a familiar face. Thank goodness! "Sister Everett, I'm so glad to see you."

"I must say I'm rather surprised to see you," she responded in what didn't sound to me like a very welcoming voice. Nevertheless, she walked toward me, a very, very large, robust woman in a white gown. I got the impression most of the insiders who worked within these hallowed walls wore white regularly.

"If I could, I'd like to speak with Sister Emmanuel for a minute or two. I won't take up much of her time."

Sister Everett reached me. She towered over me, and I had to bend my head back to look into her eyes, which seemed cold and distant, although that might just be my prejudice showing. "Sister Emmanuel and Brother Everett left some time ago to go to an interview at a radio station downtown."

"Oh." Darn it. "Do you know how long they'll be gone?"

"No, I don't." She pasted on a smile. "Is there anything I can do for you?"

Was there? Shoot, I didn't know. What the heck. I suppose it was the duty of a good private investigator to use the materials at hand. "Well . . . I'm here to do some more investigation into the Chalmers murder," I said, rather weakly I'm afraid.

Sister Everett heaved a deep sigh. "I don't know what you expect to find out here, but if you'll assist me in straightening out the hymnals in the pews, perhaps I can answer questions for you while we wait the return of Sister Emmanuel."

"Happy to help," I said, meaning it. At least the woman was willing to answer my questions, providing I could think of any.

"What we need to do," she said as she walked to the front of the sanctuary, "is make sure all the pews contain two hymnals and one Bible in each holder. People are always stuffing Sunday bulletins into the holders, and we must be sure to remove them and any other trash they leave behind." She sniffed. "You'd expect people would treat the house of God with some respect, wouldn't you?"

"Indeed, yes." We sure did back in Boston, anyway. If Chloe or I had even thought about leaving behind a hankie or a church bulletin, we'd hear about it for weeks.

She carried a big white cloth bag kind of like a pillow case, into which we stuffed all left-over bulletins, irrelevant pieces of paper, and so forth. "So, what did you want to ask?" Her voice sounded crisp and efficient.

"Well, let me see." Sheesh. I'd already asked everybody all the questions I could think of. "Um, how long was Mrs. Chalmers a member of the church?"

Another sniff. "I recall seeing her for the first time about a year ago."

"I see. And did she ever attend church with another person?"

"She and Sister Pinkney were very close, I believe. I don't know if they ever traveled here together."

"I see." Now what? Well, what the heck. "What about Mr. Chalmers? Did he ever attend church with her?"

"Not that I know of. I don't even know what the man looks like, but I don't recall seeing her enter the sanctuary with a man."

"I see."

"The only person I recall seeing Sister Chalmers with regularly was Sister Pinkney."

"I see. Did you know that Mrs. Pinkney's husband was— probably still is—against Mrs. Pinkney attending the Angelica Gospel Hall?"

"Yes, indeed. Sinful man. I pray daily for Sister Pinkney and for Mr. Pinkney, too, that he'll see the light and stop persecuting the poor woman for doing God's work."

"Did you know that he wrote threatening letters to Mrs.—I mean Sister Chalmers?"

Sister Everett's eyes widened, and she turned her head to

look at me. "Goodness gracious, no! Did he really? Is the man insane?"

"I don't know. Writing threatening letters certainly isn't a very nice thing to do."

"Do you believe he might be guilty of the woman's death?" Sister Everett went back to tidying the sanctuary.

"I thought so, but he seems to have a solid alibi. The police have looked into his whereabouts at the time of the crime thoroughly."

Frowning, Sister Everett said, "Hmm. That's too bad."

Her words surprised me a little bit, even though I agreed with them. Mr. Pinkney would have made a great villain. "Yes, it is, but now we have to find out who else might have had a motive for her murder."

"I shouldn't think there would be a paucity of suspects," Sister Everett said dryly.

"Oh? Why is that?"

We'd worked ourselves to the middle of the sanctuary, Sister Everett tossing bulletins away and tidying up hymnals and Bibles like a mechanical wind-up doll, and I following meekly in her wake, straightening hymnals and Bibles and picking up extraneous trash.

Still frowning, she said, "Sister Chalmers was an odd woman."

She could say that again! "She was? In what way?"

"I don't mean to speak harshly of the dead, but she did some very strange things from time to time. She was forever fainting during the sermon—from an excess of heavenly zeal, she said." From the tone of her voice, I gathered Sister Everett believed the fainter had other motives. "She certainly garnered unto herself a lot of attention when she did that. From lots of men. As well as women." She added that last comment almost grudgingly.

My goodness! Could we have been wrong about Mr. Chalmers? Had he been jealous of his wife's attending church here for personal reasons? I struggled to find a tactful way to find out.

"Um . . . do you think Mrs. Chalmers was . . . ah, trying to attract the attention of men? Or of one man in particular?" I hate to admit it, since it points out my own naivety, but I was shocked. Intellectually, I knew that men and women had affairs with other people's spouses all the time, but . . . well, I was still shocked. And I worked for a private investigator who pursued straying spouses all the time. Maybe there was no hope for me. Dismal thought.

Lifting her chin a bit, Sister Everett said, "I couldn't say. All I'm saying is that she got a good deal more than her fair share of attention with her antics."

"What kinds of antics? Besides fainting, I mean." For that matter, Mrs. Pinkney did her fair share of fainting, although I believed she could be acquitted of doing so in order to grab attention. The poor woman was, as Lulu had so astutely judged, merely lost.

"Oh, those silly clothes she wore, and the flighty way she had about her. And she'd fall into what she called 'ecstasies' during the sermons. Ecstasies, my foot."

Without meaning to, I glanced at Sister Everett's feet. They were big. Really big. They went well with the rest of her. Feet aside, once again I gathered the impression that Sister Everett hadn't cared for Sister Chalmers. At all. Could it be that Brother Everett . . . ? Thinking about the short, slightly bald man who was this woman's husband and who, from all accounts, adored her, I decided that was a no-go, as Ernie might have said. Not that Brother Everett couldn't have been taken with Sister Chalmers, but that Sister Chalmers had returned his favor? No. In fact, the thought was vaguely revolting. Because I couldn't think of anything else to say, I said, "I see" again.

By that time we'd reached the back of the sanctuary, and

Sister Everett led me to the stairs to the upper gallery, which had been packed both of the Sundays I'd gone to the Hall, as had the lower sanctuary, where Mrs. Pinkney, Lulu, and I had sat. "We'll tidy up the gallery last. Sister Emmanuel holds services most evenings, you know, so this is a never-ending job for me."

"You do it very well," I said, hoping to make her warm to me. She sniffed, so I guess my ploy didn't work. Therefore, I decided to probe a bit more on the Chalmers' theme. "What else did Sister Chalmers do? I mean, I always thought she was kind of . . . overly dramatic, I guess. When I saw her, I mean. When she came to Mr. Templeton's office about her stolen jewelry."

I nearly jumped out of my skin when Sister Everett turned on me, her face red with fury. She was kind of scary when she got mad, probably because she was so big. She looked kind of like a lady wrestler, actually.

"Stolen jewelry! She donated that jewelry to the church, and then she lied about it!"

"Oh, you knew about that?" I said, not really surprised but a trifle stunned by her anger over the matter. By that time, we'd entered the gallery and started tidying the first row of pews.

"Everyone knows about that. She donated the jewelry to the church and then lied and said it had been stolen. Brazen, lying, sinner!"

My goodness.

Her eyes narrowing, Sister Everett maneuvered so that she was behind me. "Why are you asking me all these questions, anyway? I don't believe you came here to speak with Sister Emmanuel at all. I think you're here to talk to *me*. Why is that, *Sister* Allcutt?"

It was then I began to get the sickening feeling in the pit of my stomach that I might just be in the presence of a mad-woman.

CHAPTER SIXTEEN

Feeling slightly panicky, I looked out over the balcony to the sanctuary, which seemed an awfully long way down from up there in the gallery. Rats. Everyone seemed to have deserted the Hall. Just when I might need one of them.

Or maybe not. After all, I didn't *know* this woman was crazy. Not for a fact. Although she appeared pretty darned nuts to me at that moment. But even if she was as crazy as a loon, she wasn't a threat to me. Was she? I sure hoped not. She was so big, she could probably squash me like a bug if she took it into her head to do so.

"Um . . . I really want to speak with Sister Emmanuel, Sister Everett. That's why I came here today. Don't you remember? I asked for her when I first arrived. I was hoping she might give me some insight into Mrs. Chalmers' character. I think it's important to ascertain the character of a person who was murdered in order to gain insight into who might have murdered her." Very well, so I was babbling. You try interrogating someone you suspect of being a madwoman someday and see how well you do it.

"Character? Bah. The woman had no character."

"Oh." So much for that. "But I did ask to see Sister Emmanuel, if you'll recall."

Sister Everett seemed to creep toward me, so I backed up a little. Not that I was scared. Well, all right, I was scared, although I wasn't yet sure why.

225

"I remember you asked, but I didn't believe you then, and I don't believe you now."

I decided to put on my Boston clothes and see how they fitted. Straightening and looking Sister Everett right in the eyes, which was a stretch—literally—I demanded, "Do you routinely accuse people who attend the Angelica Gospel Hall of lying, Sister Everett? Perhaps Sister Emmanuel might have something to say about that."

"Ha. Sister Emmanuel is as gullible as anyone else with a clean conscience. She believed that Chalmers fiend's fancy airs and her lies, and I'm sure she'll believe you. If you ever get the chance to speak with her."

Oh, my. This situation was becoming quite disconcerting. I tried lifting an eyebrow in the imperious gesture my mother used to such good effect. "I'm sure Sister Emmanuel is as good and clean of conscience as you believe her to be. But *you* must be hiding some pretty ghastly sins if you can imagine things about people that she can't. I meant exactly what I said when I came here today. I wanted to speak with Sister Emmanuel, yet you persist on believing I lied. Why is that, *Sister* Everett?"

She started snarling at me, and I decided Boston wasn't going to work in this case. "You know why. Yes, I have sins on my conscience. But I also saved Sister Emmanuel from the clutches of an evil, deceitful woman! I saved the church! It was *I* who did that! *I!*"

Goodness gracious. I swallowed and said in a small voice, Boston completely forgotten, "You mean *you* . . ." For some reason, the end of the sentence got stuck in my throat.

"I am a good and loyal daughter of the Lord," she said, still snarling.

"Are you? Do good and loyal daughters of the Lord routinely accuse other church attendees of being wicked and sinful?"

"Don't you talk to me like that, you wretched sinner!"

"You don't even know me! How do you know I'm a sinner?"

"I know. I can tell."

"I thought it was up to God to judge." I'd been backing up steadily, but she'd been stalking me. Unfortunately she had a bigger stride than I, and she was gaining on me. It occurred to me that perhaps I shouldn't be baiting the woman. On the other hand, I could probably run faster than she, being younger and, with luck, more agile.

"God uses his minions here on earth to carry out His will."

"And you think it was God's will that somebody murder Mrs. Chalmers?" Good grief. The woman truly was a nut case, as Ernie might have said.

"I know it was His will," she said firmly.

"How do you know that?" I thought it was a good question. Did God speak to this woman on a daily basis? If He did, He was a lot more kindhearted than I was. All I wanted was to get away from her.

"I know. God told me so."

Very well. That answered my last question. "Um . . . He did?"

"Yes. He did."

"He said she needed killing?" I'd heard people say that some people needed killing, but I'd never heard them say God wanted them to do the deed.

"Yes."

"Um . . . and what did you say when God told you that?" I wasn't sure I really wanted to know. Or maybe I was only nervous because I thought I knew the answer already.

I was right about that.

"I killed her," Sister Everett said baldly. "And I saved the church by doing it."

"Oh."

This would never do. That squeaky "oh" shamed me. Squaring my shoulders yet one more time, I said, "And you drugged

Mrs. Chalmers and my boss, Ernest Templeton? And you tied my boss up and gagged him and dragged him upstairs?"

She sneered. "Yes. Yes, I did those things. Your *boss!* What's a young lady like you doing with a *boss?* You should be home with your family until you marry some poor man who'll watch out for you and take care of you. You have no business with a *boss.*"

"He must have been really heavy."

Her smile was truly ghastly. "I'm a very strong woman, *Sister* Allcutt."

Oh, dear. I hope she hadn't received any messages from God regarding me. "Um . . . is that so?"

"Yes. That's so. And he's told me what to do about you, too."

Golly, she sounded like my mother. Only more sinister.

"Well, you won't get away with it. I won't see my bo—Mr. Templeton framed for a murder he didn't commit."

She started coming at me again. Since I was standing at the middle of the first pew, I decided to try for some kind of escape. The stairs down from the gallery seemed a long way off, but not as far down as the path straight through the air to the pews in the sanctuary. Therefore, although I felt cowardly about it, I ran up the stairs in the center aisle. Naturally, this didn't daunt Sister Everett, who was a good deal better acquainted with the Hall than was I.

"Did you drag Mrs. Chalmers up the stairs, too?" I asked, trying to keep her talking in the hope that she'd stop and consider her answers. Didn't work.

"Yes. They were both asleep. Drugged. I saw to that." She giggled. Coming from such a huge woman, a giggle sounded truly insane. "She was light compared to him. I just carried her. Then I hit her on the head with a poker and threw her down the stairs."

Oh, my goodness gracious sakes alive. "You . . . Sister Everett, that makes you a murderer. Murder is a sin. You must know that."

"It wasn't murder. You don't accuse men who rid houses of rats of murder, do you? You don't call doctors murderers when they kill the germs infecting sick people, do you? You don't call bug exterminators murderers, do you? That's what I did for Sister Emmanuel. I rid her of a rat. A germ. A cockroach. That woman was evil, and she was bringing evil to the Hall, and I stopped her."

Okay, the jury was in, and the verdict was that Sister Everett was stark, staring out of her mind. Not that the verdict helped me any. I picked up a hymnal. "Don't come any closer, Sister Everett!"

"Or what? You'll throw a hymnal at me? Go ahead. I'll get you, and I'll stop your lying tongue, too!"

"I haven't lied about anything!" I protested.

"You're lying right now!" she screeched. She started to run after me, and I skedaddled as fast as I could. Up. I tried to go up. But once I was up as far as the gallery went, I didn't know where to go next. I ran toward the stairs we'd come up, but the madwoman was quick, and she got there first. So I ran in the other direction. Surely there was another stairway on the other side. There was. Sister Everett got there first, too, and she loomed there like the wrath of God—an image I wished I hadn't thought of at that moment. Oh, boy. We seemed to be kind of stuck, and it didn't look good for yours truly.

Then Sister Everett started up the gallery's center aisle. Every time I darted one direction, she did the same thing, but somehow or other, she seemed to be catching up with me, climbing higher and higher, while I was as high up as I could get, and there didn't seem to be any way down, except in a way I didn't want to go. Maybe she was quicker than I because she wasn't burdened with a hymnal. I heaved it at her, hoping to hit her in the head. Missed by a mile. Drat!

She shrieked with laughter. "God is on my side, young woman. You're as evil and wicked as *she* was! You can't escape from God!"

"I don't want to escape from God!" I panted. "I want to get away from you. You're not God! You're crazy! You're mad! God would hate that you killed an innocent woman!"

"That Chalmers witch wasn't an innocent woman!"

"But *I* am!" I said desperately.

"Huh. You're just another silly *flapper*, pretending to be as good as a man and forsaking your upbringing. You and your *boss*. You're as evil as she was. Maybe more."

"I am not!" Now I was indignant as well as frightened.

She didn't bother to answer. She didn't have to. She was coming ever closer. So I picked up another hymnal. This time my aim was better. The book actually connected with her head, staggering her.

Leaping to take advantage of the situation, I raced for the side aisle, hoping to run down those stairs and get help, wishing for a banister I could slide down.

Unfortunately, Sister Everett regained her footing before I got to the door. Just as I had almost reached the staircase, I felt a grip like iron go round my arm. I spun around, my fist clenched, and whacked the side of Sister Everett's head. She didn't seem to be noticeably weakened thereby.

"You fool!" she shrieked. "You evil bitch!"

The foul word shocked me, even in that precarious situation. "Don't you call me names!" I said, doing some screeching of my own.

It was a good thing I'd had my hair bobbed. I could grab Sister Emmanuel's long locks, which she'd wound into a knot at the back of her head, but all she could do was flail helplessly at my shorn head. She hollered in pain when I yanked at her knot. It came undone in my hand, scattering hairpins hither and yon, and I pulled harder. She yelled again.

But she was sure strong. Probably from all that cleaning up of sanctuaries and galleries and so forth. We wrestled for what seemed like forever, always getting closer and closer to the railing separating us from a fall onto the empty pews below. I finally managed to get a hold on her with my two arms around her waist while she hammered at me with her fists, connecting with my face and head and ears time and again. Then we hit the rail. For a second, I thought the entire railing would break away from its moorings, it shook so hard. Then Sister Everett seemed to recover, put her hands over my arms, and slowly but surely managed to loosen my grip.

"Stop it!" I cried desperately. "You don't have to kill me, too! I'm sure the police will go easy on you when they realize you're insane!"

That didn't seem to be the right thing to say to her. She bellowed, "Insane, am I? I killed that Chalmers bitch because she was evil! That's not insane! That's doing the Lord's work! And now I'm going to get rid of you, too, because you're a cheating, lying cow! You came here under false pretences, and you're as guilty as she was!"

Try as I might, I couldn't maintain my hold on her. Anyhow, I was getting lightheaded from all the blows she was connecting with my face and head. I was going to be black and blue all over come morning. Providing I survived until morning.

But my efforts proved to be of no use. She was too strong and I was too tired, and my arms eventually slipped from her waist.

I couldn't think of anything else to do, so as my arms came free from around her, I gave a mighty shove. My heart shot to my stomach as she flailed helplessly for a second and then, with a terrible scream, fell over the railing. Her scream was cut brutally short by a tremendous crash.

By that time, I was on my hands and knees, panting from exertion and horror. Had I really pushed a woman to her death over the balcony of a church gallery? Being such a large woman, she'd hit hard—I'd heard her land—and I doubted she'd survived. My heart scrunched up and ached almost as much as the rest of me.

Knowing I'd have to find out for myself sooner or later, I crawled to the railing, grabbed it, and somehow managed to stagger, breathless, to my feet. Wishing I could cover my eyes and knowing I couldn't, I took a quick peek over the gallery railing.

And darned if I didn't see Ernie Templeton, Phil Bigelow, Detective O'Reilly, Sister Emmanuel, and Brother Everett all standing there, gaping up at me, mouths open, as if I were some sort of act on a vaudeville stage!

"It's okay, kiddo. We heard everything. You didn't do anything wrong."

I was still shaking like a leaf in a high wind, although somehow or other Ernie had managed to get me to the refuge of Sister Emmanuel's office. I sat huddled in a chair. Ernie had pulled up another chair and sat facing me, holding my hands in both of his. Someone had thrown an afghan over my shoulders, but I still shook from head to toe like the proverbial aspen in autumn. Sister Emmanuel herself, Phil Bigelow, Detective O'Reilly, and Brother Everett were in the sanctuary, presumably investigating and/or cleaning up the damage I'd wrought.

"I-I-I d-d-didn't mean to k-k-kill her," I stuttered, sounding pathetic to my own ears.

"I know that. We all know it. You only did what you had to do in your own defense. Self-defense is not a crime. It's a sensible act. She's the one who was in the wrong. You were right about that, too. The murder did involve the church."

"Not the church. Just a crazy member of it. You can't blame any of this on Sister Emmanuel or the Angelica Gospel Hall."

"Hey, you're not becoming a convert, are you?"

I heard the grin in his voice, and it irritated me. Lifting my head and regaining perhaps a half-ounce of my former vigor, I frowned at him. "No, I am not. But you can't blame that insane woman's deeds on Sister Emmanuel, Ernest Templeton."

He squeezed my hands. "Just funnin' you, kiddo. I know you're right. Sister Emmanuel didn't have anything to do with the murder. I know. So do Phil and that rat O'Reilly now."

I forgave him, although I didn't tell him that. However, sparring with him, even gently, was reviving me a trifle. "I wonder, though, if religious zealotry isn't perhaps a sign of an unstable personality. I guess Sister Everett was here virtually night and day. She was terribly jealous of Mrs. Chalmers. I think she thought Mrs. Chalmers was taking Sister Emmanuel's attention away from her or something." I stopped talking and gazed earnestly at Ernie. "Does that make any sense?"

"Well . . . no, but I understand what you mean. If it made sense, none of this would have happened."

"How come you and Phil and that horrid O'Reilly person happened to be here when . . . you know." I shivered again, and again Ernie squeezed my hands.

"After you stormed out of the office, we started talking about the possibility that somebody from the church might be involved in the crime. Hell, we'd eliminated everyone else. We tossed around all sorts of scenarios and didn't come up with anything, but I was getting a nervous feeling about you coming out here alone. Then O'Reilly showed up and started throwing his weight around. Phil told him to shut up and sit down, and I told them I aimed to go after you, and they came with me."

"Why didn't somebody try to rescue me?" I thought it a

reasonable question. I also really wanted to know. Why had they all just been standing there? Why hadn't one of them raced to the stairs to help me out? Yet when I'd taken that one tentative look over the balcony railing—before ignominiously falling senselessly to the floor, something of which I'd never have believed myself capable—they'd just been standing there in the sanctuary, frozen, like a bunch of statues, staring up at me.

"We would have, but there wasn't time."

"Oh?"

"Yeah. We heard hollering when we arrived at the church, and we all ran to get in. First there was a logjam at the door. The Emmanuel woman and that other guy arrived just when Phil, O'Reilly, and I did. When we got inside, we heard a lot more yelling and screaming, but couldn't hear what it was about. When we began to discern words in all the hollering, we all started to run toward the stairs to the gallery. We heard the lunatic say she'd killed Mrs. Chalmers and that she was going to kill you, and then . . . well, you know what happened next."

Pulling my hands free from Ernie's, I buried my face in them. "Oh, Lord, Ernie. It was so awful. She was . . . crazy."

"I know. We heard."

Spreading my fingers, I peered at him through them. "What . . . what did she look like? After she hit the pews, I mean."

His nose wrinkled. "She didn't look like much of anything. I mean she didn't look all that bad. Just dead. If you know what I mean. Glassy eyes and all that. She landed on her back, so I guess it's the back of her head and the rest of her back that took the brunt of the fall. Phil called in the medical examiner and some more of his colleagues, and they're out there now, questioning the woman's husband and your Sister Emmanuel."

"She's not *my* Sister Emmanuel, curse you, Ernie Templeton! If anyone had bothered to listen to me, this horrid thing wouldn't have happened!"

"I know. Sorry, kid."

"And stop calling me kid!"

Ernie looked surprised and his mouth opened, I imagine so that he could make some sort of a retort, but a soft knock came at the door, and we both looked at it. It slowly opened, and another minion of the church—I could tell, because she was clad in white—one I hadn't met yet, came in carrying a tray laden with tea things.

Before I could help myself, the words slipped out. "God bless you, sister." But, darn it, I *really* wanted some of that tea. With lots of sugar and milk.

"Of course, sister," she said.

I cast a quick glance at Ernie but, although his lips twitched, he didn't say anything. He'd better not, what with a pot of boiling hot water to hand.

How long we remained in Sister Emmanuel's office, I don't know. It seemed like hours. Phil sent in a doctor to check me over, and he said I'd be all right barring some bangs, bruises, and bumps.

"Looks like you'll have one hell of a shiner for a while," said Ernie, looking on impassively as the doctor palpated my head and face in several areas. I tried not to cry out in pain, but I'm sure both men noticed my winces.

I didn't move when I asked, "What's a shiner?"

"A mouse. A black eye."

"A black *eye?*" I must have said the words rather loudly, because the doctor sat back abruptly. "Sorry," I muttered.

"It's all right," he said. "I understand why a young lady might not want to walk around with a black eye." He smiled at me, and I decided I liked him. "But I suspect you will have one for several days. Your left eye will probably be swollen and black and blue by this time tomorrow. You might not be able to see out of it until the swelling subsides."

"Oh, great," I said.

"You can probably hide the bruising with powder," Ernie said, sounding doubtful.

"Right," I said, beginning to feel depressed as well as sore and tired. I could have a powdered, swollen-shut eye. That would look lovely, wouldn't it?

"When they release us to go, I'll drive you home, kiddo. I mean Mercy."

I lifted an arm, intending to give him an insouciant wave, but my muscles were starting to hurt, and all I managed was to say, "Mph." Oh, boy, the next few days were going to be rough. And . . .

"Oh, no!"

"What's the matter?" Ernie and the doctor sang the words in a duet.

"I promised to take Lulu to lunch at the Ambassador on Wednesday! How can I go to the Ambassador looking like this?"

Tilting his head, Ernie, said, "You don't look so bad."

I didn't believe him. Talk about a tone lacking conviction.

With a judicious frown, the doctor said, "I don't think you ought to be going out and about for a few days yet. You need to rest and heal first."

Once again, I buried my head in my hands. I groaned.

The door opened once more, and I decided I might as well face the music. So I lifted my head, dropped my hands, and turned to see Phil and Sister Emmanuel enter the office. The office was large for an office, but it wasn't all that big, and it was getting mighty crowded. Sister Emmanuel appeared pale and distressed, which made perfect sense to me.

"I hate to ask this, Mercy, but would you mind coming to the station? We can have a steno take your report and Ernie's and mine and Sister Emmanuel's. I'm afraid Mr. Everett's will have to wait. He collapsed when he realized that it was his wife squashed on the pews, and—"

"Phil!" I said, scandalized.

"Well, you know what I mean." He had the grace to look abashed.

I looked from him to Ernie, and noticed they both appeared as tired and drawn as I felt—although probably not as sore and definitely not as bruised. I resented them in that moment. If they'd only listened to me, none of these past horrible hours would have been necessary.

"Yes," I said. "I know what you mean. And yes. Let's go to the police station and get this over with. You may be certain I won't gloss over your neglect of my suggestions in the matter, too."

Phil heaved a gigantic sigh. "I'm sure you won't."

Sister Emmanuel still stood in the open doorway. When I glanced at her again, she looked awfully pale and . . . I don't know. Diminished, somehow, if you know what I mean.

"I'm so terribly sorry about all this, Sister Allcutt. If I'd had any indication . . ."

"It's all right," I said wearily. "Nobody had any indication." Except me. Curse them all.

CHAPTER SEVENTEEN

I called Chloe from the police station to give her a brief run-down on what had happened. "I'll probably be late getting home, but don't worry. Everything's all right, and Ernie's going to drive me."

"Oh, Lord, Mercy." Chloe sounded upset.

"Really, Chloe, everything's all right now." Very well, so I'd just lied again.

"You only wish it were."

"What do you mean?" Terrible things rushed through my mind. In a panic, I said, "Oh, Chloe, it's not the baby, is it? Or Harvey? Or—"

"No, no. It's nothing bad. Well, not that bad. It's only . . ." Chloe hesitated for a moment and then whispered, "*Mother's* coming to dinner."

It needed only this. I hung up, wishing I lived in Wisconsin or somewhere else far, far away from Los Angeles. Or at least from my mother.

I don't know how long we spent at the police station, but it wasn't long enough. By the time Ernie, Sister Emmanuel, and I were allowed to go, we'd all given statements, read them, and signed them. Even Phil had testified to his shorthand-taking cohort—not Officer Bloom this time—that he'd heard Sister Everett, whose first name, I learned, had been Gwendolyn, confess to murder. He also said that he'd seen her trying to murder me, what's more. That pretty much cleared Ernie of any lingering suspicion of having done Mrs. Chalmers to death. I don't know where Detective O'Reilly was, but I suspected he was so disgusted that Ernie wasn't guilty that he'd taken himself off somewhere.

Brother Everett, whose given name turned out to be Richard, was led into the station some time after we arrived there, looking haggard, miserable, and embarrassed. Poor fellow. I knew in my heart that he'd had nothing to do with his demented wife's ugly deeds.

When a policeman escorted him to Phil's desk in the crowded room, he looked pleadingly at me. "I'm so very sorry, Sister Allcutt. These fellows tell me my wife confessed to murdering Sister Chalmers. I . . . I can't quite take it all in."

I nodded, feeling sorry for him.

"I knew she wasn't happy," continued Brother Everett. "But she was never happy." He shook his head sadly, as if he blamed himself for his wife's unhappiness.

"I understand," I said. "It's not your fault."

"She tried to kill Miss Allcutt, too," said Ernie, who evidently didn't share my forgiving nature. His voice was hard as granite. "Didn't you know your wife was a lunatic, man?"

"Ernie," I mumbled, too tired to take him to task.

Richard Everett hung his head. "No," he said simply. "I knew she was unhappy, but I had no idea . . ." His words trailed off, and tears filled his eyes.

Ignoring the policemen all around us, Sister Emmanuel rose from her metal folding chair and went to her minion. "Brother Everett, take heart. The Lord is still with us, and He is still good. He and I will help you through this terrible time. No one could have known that Sister Everett had let Satan into her heart. The poor woman must have gone mad."

"Christ," muttered Ernie. I kicked him, but not awfully hard, my limbs being miserably stiff by that time.

I don't think Ernie's blasphemy mattered, since neither Sister Emmanuel nor Brother Everett seemed to hear him. The gaze Richard Everett cast upon Sister Emmanuel was all but worshipful. "God bless you, sister," he said, hiccupping slightly, but I think that was from his tearful state.

"With God's help, the terrible burden on your soul will be lifted, brother," Sister Emmanuel promised.

"God bless you. God bless you. I thank God for you every day, sister."

Ernie said, "Huh."

I didn't bother to kick him again. I was getting a little tired of the maudlin sentimentality flowing between the church folk myself by that time.

Phil, looking tired and distracted, said, "Please, everyone, take a seat. Mr. Everett, I know this is difficult for you, but you'll have to save the prayers until later. We need to get this police business finished first."

"Of course, Detective. Matters of this world need to be accomplished. Then we can remove ourselves to a higher plane." Sister Emmanuel answered for the poor, beleaguered Brother Everett. I guess she sensed he didn't possess her strength of character, at least not at that moment in time.

And she was right. Brother Everett pretty much collapsed into another uncomfortable chair, crying quietly, while she, looking out of place but regal in her white robe, reclaimed her own seat. I was impressed yet again by the way she'd totally given herself to her role. Or to God. At that point, I neither knew nor cared if she was a fraud or a genuine minister of the Gospel who believed the message she spouted.

And so the questioning recommenced, only this time to the accompaniment of little gasps and moans from Brother Everett, who'd been completely oblivious to his wife's nuttiness. And that shocked me. I mean, it became apparent that the couple had been married for more than thirty years. He'd noticed nothing odd about her in all that time? But as often as Phil asked the question, and in as many varied ways, Brother Everett's answer was always the same: he hadn't noticed a single, solitary odd thing about his wife except that she was unhappy, but she'd always been unhappy so he hadn't thought much about it.

Good Lord, was this what marriage was? Completely losing track of one's spouse's behavior? I wondered if the Everetts had ceased all forms of communication with each other, or if they'd just stopped listening to each other. Chloe and Harvey didn't ignore each other's changes of mood or behavior. In fact, Harvey was very solicitous of every nuance of Chloe's comfort or discomfort. Would they end up like the Everetts in time? What an abysmal thought.

Finally, at long last, Phil said we were free to leave. Although I didn't much want to, I asked to use the ladies' facilities at the station to assess the damage to my person before going home. I had some thought that I might somehow cover up most of the worst of it before having to face my mother.

Ernie said, "Um . . . are you sure, Mercy? You don't look so great."

I glared at him through eyes that were beginning to swell. Oh, boy. Shiners? Is that what he'd called them? I wanted to see them for myself. "My mother is waiting for me at Chloe's, Ernie, and I'd better assess how not great I look before I have to enter into her presence."

"Oh, boy," said Ernie. "I'm sorry, kid. But you're probably right. Got any powder in that handbag of yours?"

Rising painfully to my feet, I sighed heavily. "Yes. Whatever good powder will do."

"You never know."

I think he was trying to be encouraging.

Unfortunately, once I got to the ladies' room, the direction of which I knew from a previous visit to the police station, I realized that no encouraging words were going to help me. Neither was powder. I was a total mess. Big red spots on my cheeks, chin, forehead, and arms would surely turn black and blue before morning, and my swollen eyelids, which now looked merely red, would be purple in the morning, too.

Mother would have a fit. And she was waiting for me at Chloe's, like a lioness ready to pounce on her prey. Only lionesses pounced in defense of their children, didn't they? They didn't pounce *on* their children. Did they?

Well, it didn't matter what lionesses did. I knew very well what my mother would do. I washed my face with soap and water, dried it on the rather unsanitary towel resting on a rack for the purpose, and did my best with my powder puff. My best wasn't too good.

As I climbed painfully into Ernie's Studebaker, Ernie asked, "Are you sure you want to go to your sister's house tonight?"

I turned and stared at him. Staring was gradually becoming more difficult as my eyelids continued to swell. "I don't have much of a choice, do I?"

"Well, what about Lulu? Can you stay at her place?"

"She doesn't have room enough for me." I knew that, because I'd seen her apartment when my cab dropped her there on our way home from lunch after visiting the Angelica Gospel Hall the prior Sunday.

Thinking of Lulu made me think of our promised luncheon at the Ambassador, which was but one day hence. Two, if you counted this one, but you might as well not since it was nearly over. Oh, Lord.

"Too bad," said Ernie. He sounded genuinely concerned.

"I agree. Too bad I don't know more people in L.A. I guess maybe Mr. Easthope would take me in, but I hate to ask him out of the blue and all."

"You'd stay with Easthope?"

As I've mentioned before, for some reason Ernie didn't like Francis Easthope. I still didn't know why that was, but I sure didn't want to discuss the matter that evening.

"I would if I'd already made arrangements," I said mildly. "But I'm not going to pop in on him tonight, looking like this. I'd probably frighten the poor man."

"You probably would." Ernie's voice was snide.

Again, I felt no desire to pursue his attitude, so I just sighed and remained silent.

"I suppose your mother would die of some kind of attack if you came to my place," Ernie said, sounding ruminative, as if he were thinking hard about alternatives to my going to Chloe's.

My head swiveled, and I squinted at him. Squinting was easier than staring, but still no fun. "I couldn't stay at your place," I said. "You know as well as I do that it wouldn't be proper."

"Proper. Huh." I could tell he was rolling his eyes, even though it was too dark by then for me to see his face clearly. "Yeah, I know. It would be terribly improper."

I only sighed once more.

"But I hate the thought of you walking into that lion's den. It would be all right if it were just your sister and brother-in-law. They're swell folks. But that mother of yours . . ."

I tried to grin at the realization that Ernie and I were thinking of my mother in the same terms. It was then I remembered that I had a split lip, so I stopped grinning. "She's a dragon," I said, mixing my metaphors, although Ernie couldn't know that.

"How about a hotel? You've got money. You could stay at the Ambassador, where they'd pamper you until you healed up, and then you'd be okay."

"It's kind of you to be concerned, Ernie, but I've braved my mother before now. I can do it again."

"I guess. I just hate to think of her beating up on you. You're already beat up."

"Too true. I never would have believed Sister Everett could be so strong."

"She was nuts. I think when people go crazy, it gives them strength."

"I've heard that theory, too. Maybe it's true. She darned near threw me over that railing. I know she wanted to."

I shuddered, and was surprised when Ernie laid a hand on my arm. "You'll be all right, kiddo. It'll take a few days, but you'll heal up and be right as rain. And eventually the memories of that final fatal push will fade, too. Remember that it was her or you. I'm glad you chose yourself. I just wish you didn't have to."

How very kind of him. Before I could succumb to emotion, I sucked in a deep breath and said, "Thank you, Ernie. I wish I didn't have to, too."

"Well, I'll stick with you through the worst of it, kiddo."

"Thanks, Ernie." I meant it sincerely. Somehow, the thought of facing my mother with Ernie and Chloe at my side didn't sound half as difficult as the notion of dealing with her all by my battered self.

We got to Bunker Hill at last which, unfortunately, wasn't very far away from the police station, and Ernie pulled his disreputable-looking Studebaker to a stop in front of the iron gates of the Nash residence. I gazed out my side of the machine at the house, my heart residing somewhere around my kneecaps, knowing the peril awaiting me within those elaborately decorated walls.

But Ernie played the gentleman that night. He got out of the automobile on his side and came around to open the door for me. It was a good thing he did so, because I wasn't sure I had strength enough to shove the door open on my own.

"Chin up, kid. I mean Mercy."

"Don't worry about it, Ernie." I was too dispirited to fuss with him about calling me kid. In truth, the notion of being this man's kid sister didn't seem at all distasteful to me at the moment. I'd rather have a big brother like Ernie than the one I had, who was a big poop.

He helped me out of the car and up the walkway to the big front door of the Nash home. I was so tired, I didn't even look around to see how nice it would be to own the place myself.

"You have a key?"

"Yes, but please ring the bell. I don't feel like getting the key out of my bag."

"Sure."

So Ernie rang the doorbell, and Mrs. Biddle opened the door after a very few minutes. She gasped when she saw me.

"It's not as bad as it looks," I assured her, although I was lying. I'd been lying a whole lot lately.

"I certainly hope not," said Mrs. Biddle, staggering back slightly. She hadn't known what to make of me ever since I invaded her territory—the kitchen, I mean—seeking cleaning stuffs in order to spiff up my office when Ernie first hired me. She stepped aside, and Ernie tenderly guided me into the foyer.

Out of the corner of his mouth, he said, "Where to? Want to go to your room before you face the monster, or would you rather get it over with?"

I considered for only a couple of seconds. The notion of hiding away in my room and locking my mother out held a certain charm, but it would have been cowardly. "Let's get it over with," I muttered. Besides, I wanted to see Buttercup, and I was pretty sure she was in the living room with Chloe.

So, holding my arm in a way that didn't touch any of the bruises, Ernie led me through the archway and to the living room, where we both stopped to look around.

They were all there: my mother, Chloe, Harvey, Buttercup,

Francis Easthope, and—oh, my God—John Gilbert. Of all the nights in the world for Chloe to be holding a casual get-together at her house . . .

Buttercup scampered over to me, and Ernie, bless his heart, bent and picked her up so she could lick my wounds without my having to bend my battered body.

"Mercedes Louise Allcutt, what *have* you been doing this time?"

My mother's autocratic tones cut through the air like a sword through a churl's throat.

Chloe leapt to her feet. "Mother, poor Mercy has been through—"

Mother turned on Chloe. "Don't you 'poor Mercy' me!"

Chloe swallowed and subsided.

"Your daughter performed an heroic feat today, Mrs. Allcutt. You should be proud of her."

I'd have blinked if my eyelids were capable of it. But I did turn to gape at Ernie.

"And *you*—" Mother began.

But Ernie cut her off.

"Yes, sirree, she foiled a crook in her lair. Almost got herself done in for it. I wouldn't be surprised if the police don't pin a medal on her for this day's work."

Oh, dear. He was laying it on really thickly.

"My dear Miss Allcutt!" Francis Easthope, who had been appalled by my appearance—I could tell by the look of horror and distaste on his face—rushed over to me. "Whatever in the world happened to you?"

"It's that so-called *job* of hers," my mother said. "If she—"

But again she was interrupted, this time by none other than John Gilbert himself. He hurried up to me, too. "Good God, Miss Allcutt, whatever in the world has happened to you?"

"Mercy took on the crooks and won," said Ernie, who didn't

246

seem at all awed to be in the presence of one of Hollywood's most celebrated stars.

"How . . . how intrepid of you, Miss Allcutt," Mr. Gilbert said. He held out a hand, as if he wanted to help me but didn't quite know how.

I didn't know how he could help, either, but I appreciated the gesture. "Thanks," I said.

But Mother didn't like it that the conversation had got away from her.

"Stuff and nonsense! If you were at home with your mother and father, where you belong, and not pretending to be some kind of working-class—"

It was Ernie who cut her off this time. "Hey, that's my secretary you're talking about. Best secretary I've ever had, and I'll thank you not to speak unkindly to her."

God bless Ernie Templeton.

"And *you*," Mother went on. "How dare you speak to me—"

"Hey, Mercy," said Ernie, running roughshod over my mother's words once more. "Are you really up to this nonsense? How's about we take a powder to Chinatown and have a little grub there?"

"I will *not*—"

"Thanks, Ernie. Help me upstairs, so I can put some ointment on the worst of my scratches, and I'll be happy to go to Chinatown with you. Carry Buttercup up, won't you?"

"Mind if I go along?" asked John Gilbert.

"Not at all," said Ernie.

The two men smiled companionably at each other. Mr. Gilbert turned to Chloe. "Do you mind, Chloe? I've just got to hear what happened."

"I will *not*—" Mother tried again.

"Please," said Chloe. "Be my guest. Poor Mercy needs some tender, loving care."

Our mother turned upon her elder daughter. "I will *not*—"

"And," continued Chloe, anger swelling her voice for one of the first times I could remember, "she sure won't get it from her mother."

"Why, I never!"

Both Ernie and John Gilbert lolled on the sofa in my sitting room, playing with Buttercup, while I took a change of clothes and retired to my bathroom. I'm sure my mother thought such behavior on all our parts shocking, but by that time I didn't give a care. The two men and the dog on my sofa were kind to me. My mother wasn't.

My hair was more easily tamed than the rest of me, but I managed to daub some pancake makeup on the worst of my bruises, smear ointment on my cuts and bandage them, and lay a cold washcloth across my eyes for several minutes.

"Need any help?" Ernie hollered at one point.

"No, thanks," I hollered back. For some reason, I was feeling much more chipper now that I knew I'd be able to escape from Mother's clutches, at least for the evening. God alone knew what she'd do to me when she got me alone again, but tonight I would be free of her.

"Hope I didn't keep you too long," I said as I hobbled back into the sitting room where Ernie and Mr. Gilbert seemed to be getting along like a house on fire. Both men jumped to their feet when I entered. Poor Buttercup tumbled to the floor, but she didn't seem to mind. Dogs are so forgiving.

"You look much, much better, Miss Allcutt," said Mr. Gilbert approvingly.

"Thank you." I looked at Ernie, whose opinion I valued more than Mr. Gilbert's. Not that I didn't care what Mr. Gilbert thought of me, but I trusted Ernie to be honest.

He tilted his head and stared at me for a few seconds. Then

he said, "You still look as if you've been in a barroom brawl, but you'll do okay in Chinatown."

"Thank you ever so much," I said dryly.

"Any time." He grinned broadly at me.

Then, flanked by two handsome men and leaving poor Buttercup in the sitting room, I tottered down the staircase and out into the night. When we reached the curb, we got into Mr. Gilbert's Stutz Bearcat, which was a most remarkable automobile, and tootled on down the hill to Chinatown. All things considered, the evening was quite enjoyable. What was even better was that, by the time Mr. Gilbert drove us back to Chloe's house, Mother had gone to bed with a sick headache.

"Golly, Mercy, Ernie told me what happened."

As soon as Lulu saw me limp into the lobby of the Figueroa Building the day after my adventures at the Angelica Gospel Hall, she jumped up from her chair, darted around her desk—leaving an open bottle of nail varnish sitting there, drying out—and hurried to me. I guess she aimed to help me if I needed help.

She went on, "But he said he told you to take a few days off. Said you were pretty beat up. I can see he was right. What are you doing here? You ought to be home resting!"

"My mother's at Chloe's house," I said.

"Oh, my God."

Nothing else needed to be said. Lulu understood completely.

"But I've got some exciting news for you, Lulu."

"Yeah? What's that?"

"You know the luncheon we were going to have at the Ambassador tomorrow?"

We'd been slowly making our way to Lulu's desk. When I got to the "we were going to have" part of my speech, Lulu stopped dead. "You mean we're not going?"

249

I thought for a minute she was going to cry.

"Not tomorrow, because I'm too battered, but there's good news," I hurried to assure her.

"Oh?" She walked around her desk and resumed her chair, looking up at me dubiously.

"We're all going to dine at the Ambassador. On the Tuesday after next."

Her mouth fell open.

"And it's not just you and me, either, Lulu. Ernie's invited, and Chloe and Harvey will be there, and you'll never guess who else will be joining us."

"That handsome Easthope fellow?" she asked hopefully.

"Him, too, but you'll never guess who else."

She thought for a minute, but I was pretty sure she'd never come up with the right name. Eventually, she shook her head and said, "Who?"

"John Gilbert."

Shoot. I'd expected my news would shock her, but darned if Lulu didn't join in with the rest of the women I'd met recently and faint dead away.

The worst part of this whole story, however, was that I never did learn why Mrs. Chalmers persisted in calling herself Mrs. Persephone Chalmers. I suppose some mysteries are too deep for even the best detectives, darn it.

ABOUT THE AUTHOR

Award-winning author **Alice Duncan** lives with a herd of wild dachshunds (enriched from time to time with fosterees from New Mexico Dachshund Rescue) in Roswell, New Mexico. She's not a UFO enthusiast; she's in Roswell because her mother's family settled there fifty years before the aliens crashed. Since her two daughters live in California, where Alice was born, she'd like to return there but can't afford it. Alice would love to hear from you at alice@aliceduncan.net. And be sure to visit her website at http//www.aliceduncan.net